ALSO BY ERIC BOGOSIAN

Mall

subUrbia

Notes from Underground

Sex, Drugs, Rock & Roll

*The Essential Bogosian: Talk Radio,
Drinking in America, Fun House & Men Inside*

Pounding Nails in the Floor with My Forehead

Talk Radio

Drinking in America

WASTED
Beauty

A NOVEL

Eric Bogosian

Simon & Schuster
NEW YORK   LONDON   TORONTO   SYDNEY

SIMON & SCHUSTER
Rockefeller Center
1230 Avenue of the Americas
New York, NY 10020

For information about special discounts for bulk purchases,
please contact Simon & Schuster Special Sales at
1-800-456-6798 or business@simonandschuster.com.

DESIGNED BY PAUL DIPPOLITO

Manufactured in the United States of America

1   3   5   7   9   10   8   6   4   2

Library of Congress Cataloging-in-Publication Data
Bogosian, Eric.
Wasted beauty : a novel / Eric Bogosian.
p. cm.
1. Drug abuse—Fiction. 2. Young Women—Fiction.
3. Models (Persons)—Fiction. 4. Narcotic addicts—Fiction.
5. New York (N.Y.)—Fiction. I. Title.

PS3552.O46W37 2005
813'.6—dc22   2004062571

ISBN 0-7432-3588-6

Is it so small a thing
To have enjoy'd the sun,
To have lived light in the spring,
To have loved, to have thought, to have done . . . ?

—MATTHEW ARNOLD,
"EMPEDOCLES ON ETNA"

WASTED
Beauty

SHE PERCHES on the rim of the monstrous porcelain bathtub and slaps the crook of her Auschwitz-thin arm, trying to raise one pastel green subcutaneous thoroughfare. Stick it in, stick it in, stick it in. Find the blood. The shouts and screams of alley kids vibrate the rank fizzy air. A fat fly swoops through the brick-propped window, exits disappointed. All you have to do is hump one tiny blood vessel with this tiny but extra-sharp metal dick. Like a heron hunting fish she sticks the syringe in over and over, smearing blood all over the place, impossible to see what's what. Fucking skinny veins. Almost as fine as the needle itself. There are other places, but not sure how to do that. Under the tongue, along the belly, back of the hand, in the neck. Focus, fucking focus! Time is running out. Stomach's growling, brain's aching. Gonna shit my panties in a sec.

He pops his head in and says, "You want help with that?" snatching the soot-blackened bottlecap. "LEAVE ME ALONE! FUCKING LET ME HAVE TWO MINUTES PEACE FOR GOD'S SAKE!" The creep withdraws, slamming the door.

Beads of sweat, or are they tears, drop a million miles to the floor while an amazingly busy cockroach scuttles out from under the tub and licks unaware, of course, of how rare this stuff is, packed with molecules of private stock Issey Miyake perfume and this morning's wake-up dose of diacetylmorphine not to mention the hormones and pheromones of one of the most beautiful girls in the world. And does the bug give a shit? No. Probably all tastes the same.

The most beautiful girl in the world mashes the bad cockroach under her Manolo and spies the promised land. A vein running just south of her sculpted ankle. Could do that. She grabs her own calf, leaning way forward, and slides in the stainless, careful not to go too far and puncture the opposing vein wall. Yeah, that works, that works.

I

Set the trigger, cock it, the little red bomb of blood blooms up into the clear barrelful of puro. Satisfied with all the intravenous arrangements, she thumbs the plunger, gives the universe a hard shove and it all comes down like a tsunami crushing a beach. In three seconds the heroin runs from ankle to heart and back out to the reticular formation, the hypothalamus, the thalamus, the cerebral hemispheres, showering the cerebral cortex with an ecstatic saturation of opiates and she thinks, OK, gotta get organized. The relief of knowing the dope will arrive is almost as big a high as the dope itself. Then bam, the tidal wave hits and she's rolling in the drug surf, upside down, all around, lost in the biggest washing machine of ecstasy and perfection known. No thought. No nothin'. She forgets to sit up straight and tilts toward the dingy, dust ball, hair ball, cockroach carcassed, shit floor. Now if everyone will please look out the right side of the cockpit you'll see the underside of the toilet passing by. Notice how junkie urine has oozed down through the bowl-sweat like streaks of yellow paint, dripping down and then drying away, forming a small brown puddle beneath the sweating stinking pissoir. Please fasten your seatbelts, we'll be landing soon.

She attains Superwoman eyes and Superwoman knowledge for exactly five seconds. Almost has the foresight to pull the spike out of her ankle before crossing the tipping point and falling onto her photogenically flawless face, though she does avoid the disgusting floor by cracking her most perfect skull on the porcelain with an act of great acrobatic skill, spinning and landing on her back.

She lifts her head and pukes onto her brand-new A/X tank top. She feels really great. Before she passes out, she thinks, I wanna go home.

REBA COOK (THAT WAS HER NAME BEFORE ALL THIS), and her brother, Billy Cook, watch the car coming up at them like destiny itself. One month to the day after the funeral, Frank Decker is finally showing his grim face, finally making good on his promise to visit the old farm and conduct a proper appraisal. A pall of ignorance and confusion has hung over the sibling orphans. Mom's probate has finally ended, and Dad's just begun. Expectations have shrunk. Taxes are due. Winter's 'round the corner. The future has withered into a little black nut. But Frank has arrived and Frank will know what to do.

Crouching under the cold wet spittle of the late rain, Frank the banker hurries across the lawn, slips on a wasp-eaten apple, kicks it away and mutters, "OK, show me, I don't have all day."

Billy nods and the three make their way toward the orchard. Eighteen of the original apple trees, toughened by cruel upstate winters, still stand. Old and diseased, they insist on bearing fruit. Their wood is hunched and gnarled, lopsided where the rotten limbs have dropped off. But their buds still set, eager for another year of honeybees and sunshine, another season of crisp produce whether or not anyone's around to gather it.

The brother, the sister and the banker tramp through the defeated acreage, as if immersion among the old trees will help them make sense of it all. Reba, unlike red-haired Billy, is as tall as her dead dad and as blond as her dead mom. What a year. First Mom, her delicate nodes devoured by malignancy, took sick and died. Daddy chucked a handful of dirt onto the coffin, waited exactly six months and then started coughing blood into a wrinkled handkerchief. It only took Daddy eight months to follow Mom into the ground.

Reba, Billy and Frank survey the property while the rain thrums into the surrounding brush and grass. The orchard is soft and dead like a corpse, the soil congested with glacial till and ancient arrowheads. Staghorn sumac has invaded the chinks in the lichen-covered stone walls. Red cedar and swamp maple saplings have sprung up where a hundred years ago the adjacent fields lay flat and perfect. A corroded Ford LTD is parked permanently by the empty corncrib.

Amid the rain-hiss, something snorts and a spooked three-point buck crashes through the scrub, showing them his tail. This time of year the big boys make themselves scarce, but the scent of the rotting apples, even the sweet twigs, are too tempting for the deer to stay away.

Frank picks his way through the wet weeds, aimless. Reba whispers to Billy, "Walks like he's got something shoved up his crack, like an old man. He's not even forty! And why doesn't he smile ever? Looks like an old troll." Billy shushes her as Frank turns his black eyes their way.

Rain falls straight down now. Birds either gone south or silent. No sound of anything except the rain. Frank squints into the wetness. Reba sneaks another glance at Billy, who furrows his brow in warning. Finally Frank wipes his face with a pocket handkerchief and shouts, "OK. I seen it. And I'm getting cold." He heads back toward the house, carefully negotiating the clinging whips of wild rose.

The men push into the kitchen and Reba follows, chagrined to find a bean tin of bacon grease sitting on the countertop, a spray of damp coffee grounds staining the sink. The air smells of unwashed ashtrays and stale beer. A curling strip of wallpaper marks the spot where Billy plans to install paneling. A fluorescent fixture flickers overhead. The place has all the tidiness of a cat box.

Frank draws a glass of water from the tap, studies it before bringing it to his mouth. The wet clings to his lip like the slobber of a senile idiot. He runs a palm over the countertop. Reba wants to say, "Feeling for toast crumbs, Frank? Appraising the woodwork?"

Frank says, "I have an opening." His flat eyes turn to Reba, not Billy, for a response.

Billy says, "But what about the apples?"

"Apples?" Frank spits out the word. "What are you bullshitting about, 'apples'? Billy, you're not going to tell me you get apples off those old trees."

Billy checks his shoes. "We go to the city once a week and sell 'em in the farmer's market."

Frank sips, scowls, empties the glass into the sink and places it on top of the spilled grounds. "Billy, you got an empty thousand-gallon tank in the basement and the price of heating oil just went up. Not to mention you got a property tax bill due since June, you got a mortgage and a second mortgage which I told your daddy was ill advised. There's insurance for the van. You're not going to cover that with no apples. And don't plan on living on the life insurance for too long, either. Ten thousand doesn't go that far and you've already spent half of it." Frank addresses Reba for the first time since he's come up the drive, "Reba, how old are you now?"

"I'm twenty. Almost twenty-one." You know exactly how old I am.

"Ever since your mom passed, I haven't been able to find anyone as dependable. You need a job."

Reba tries to smile and she feels herself grimace. "I don't have the qualifications for banking, Mr. Decker."

Billy blurts, "She works with me on Saturdays. That's when we go down to the market. I need her there."

Frank says, "OK. No Saturdays, I'll give you that. That make you happy? It's not a problem. Reba, be there at eight on Monday. Wear something nice."

Frank moves toward the door and Reba calls to him. "Mr. Decker? What about the farm? What do you think it's worth? Approximately?"

Frank sucks a tooth, checks his watch. "Approximately? This

place? Well, a rough estimate would be approximately: zero. People are trying to escape the damned county, not move in. Take my advice, don't even put it on the market, or you'll regret it." Turning away, he says, "I'll see you on Monday. And better make it seven forty-five." Frank slips out the screen door, letting it slam behind him.

Billy picks a beer from the fridge and follows Frank. Deserted, Reba overhears the rumbling of the solemn voices on the porch. Like the way people talked at the funerals. Heads close, looking at the ground. There's not going to be any money. With my share, I could have gone anywhere. Now I'm going nowhere.

In the wet orange dusk, torn ribbons of cloud garland the sun. Through the kitchen window, the awesome hairy witches of the orchard stand in silhouette. Beyond the apple trees, the poplars are straight and tall, festooned with ropes of fox grape. The leafy wild vines shimmer with a sure promise of slow death. If not this year, then next.

Reba digs out an icy brick from the freezer and runs hot water over the pink and yellow slab of frozen flesh, letting it soften under her thumb. Above her head the rolly-eyed Felix-the-Cat clock swishes his stiff tail, marking time, second by second. The fridge growls just as Frank's car starts up outside. So that's that. I will swab the green and dirty-white linoleum tiles, thaw and fry the food, sponge Billy's pubic hairs off the toilet, iron his work shirts. And I will stand behind a counter at the bank all day, just like Mom did. I'll take my cigarette breaks, a half hour for lunch and all the peppermints I can eat. Maybe someday I'll grow a few tumors of my own.

Reba scratches a matchstick on the wall, jabs it into the hissing gas. The tiny blue imps puff and she slips the chunk into the skillet's puddle of oil. The old skillet, the cabinets, the stove—they've all been here as long as I have. What if I forget how to remember what day it is? How would I know if it was today or yesterday or ever?

Felix's tummy reads seven forty-five. With the cooking fork her mom held a thousand times, Reba maneuvers the seared lumps of chicken through the sizzling fat. Her heart races. I own a piece of nothing. I am part of something that is nothing. Nothing plus nothing is nothing.

The door bangs and Billy is beside her. "Well, that's that." He eyes the skillet. "I'll puke if you fry chicken legs again."

Reba offers no options. "With baked beans. And I got those nice frozen artichoke hearts you like."

"Who says I like artichoke hearts? I don't even know what the fuck an artichoke heart is. I hate artichoke hearts. Artichoke hearts make me puke."

"Everything makes you puke." Bits of flying oil sting Reba's arm.

"That's right, it does. Fuck." Billy's face flushes pink.

"You want hot dogs, then? Just tell me what you want, Billy." You're not going to blame this on me.

"You gonna take Frank's job?"

"As far as I can tell, you two made up my mind for me. And besides, I don't have a choice, do I? Unless you're planning to lose the cable TV and our phone and our heat. And like the all-knowing Decker said, it's gonna get pretty cold in February."

"I've got a lot riding on that apple business and it's a good business. I've built it up. People come by looking for my product."

"It's a gold mine, we all heard you."

Billy digs another beer from the fridge, slams it. Jars and bottles tinkle within. "Fuck the chicken legs, I'm going out."

"Where?"

"Hey, I work hard all fucking week, I have a right. In case you missed it, I'm at that damn gas station every day. That's how the bills get paid. I'm not gonna stay cooped up in this slum. This shithole."

"So you don't want chicken?" If he hits me, at least it'll kill the boredom.

"You going deaf now, too?"

"Too?" Hit me. Come on. Please.

"Laughing at me behind my back. Too good for everybody. Too good for a job with Frank . . ."

"I thought you don't want me working for Frank!"

"I can't carry you forever, you know." Billy's bulk looms, his eyes wet with anger. "You're useless. You don't clean. You don't fucking work. You just lay around and read your stupid female magazines. Guys don't even like you 'cause you're so fucking stuck up and anorexic."

"I'm not anorexic! Don't say that."

"You're skinny enough to be. You're just a skinny, lazy, good-for-nothing cunt."

Reba feels the heat in her face. "If Daddy heard you talking to me like that, he'd skin your ass." I know what I am, I don't need you reminding me.

Billy whips his empty at the trash can, misses, a slash of beer foam tattoos the wall. For a moment, he stares at the can on the floor as at some kind of enemy, then scoops it up, furiously shoves it into the bin, and finds a third in the fridge. "OK, bitch. She-cat. Whatever you are. But no one wants you. And I'm stuck with you. And Daddy isn't here, is he? So you're stuck, too."

Reba sponges the beer off the wall. "When should I expect you home?"

"I'll be home when I'm home. You just be ready to hit the road first thing 'cause I'm not waking your bony carcass."

"Don't you be telling me to be ready. You be ready. You're the one with hangovers."

"You've never seen me drunk." Billy snatches up the van keys and thumps out. The whack of the slamming screen door is followed by the whinny of the loose fan belt and the crunch of tires easing down the gravel drive. Reba flips the hunk of white-edged flesh into the sink and snaps off the gas.

LIKE A GLISTENING GREASED PISTON, RICK DRIVES IN and out of his assistant's body. Staving off orgasm, he focuses on the bob of her thick red blond hair, letting the rhythm lull him into a deeper place. He lifts his eyes and tries to focus on the art poster on the wall. Modigliani, the weirdly sexy-unsexy chick with black hair and great hips. Now I'm thinking about it too much. Why do I have to think so much when I'm fucking? Why can't I just fuck like a man?

Through clenched teeth, Zoe moans, rubbing herself down there. Even if he can't see her face, Rick can imagine it. Her brow barely furrowed with concentration, lips parted. Her hair hangs down, swaying, obscuring her further. I can touch her hair all I want now, but somehow it's different here, wherever we are. Maybe I should try tugging it? Her moaning grows, he thinks, oh she likes that.

Zoe groans louder, reaches around behind herself and urges his buttocks toward her. Rick's train of thought misses a cog. His hand slips over her slick skin, finds a breast, then sees the Modigliani again. She's coming. Screaming. Can't stay focused. I've been trying to get into her pants for months, maybe years, and now all I want to do is come. Please. Please let me come. Please!

Rick wakes, his wife asleep beside him.

Until I brush my teeth, no way is Laura going to kiss me, let alone have sex with me. It's not my fault. She's the one who put red onions in the salad. Plus the Burgundy. Plus the coffee and the surreptitious cigarette. Probably stink like a homeless wino. But look, you wake up with a hard dick, you should put it somewhere. It's a health issue. The prostate gets clogged.

Rick creeps into the bathroom and scrubs at the plaque, gargles, rinses. In the mirror, his eyes are puffy and dim, his cheeks slack. His hair forms a matted, asymmetrical sculpture. This is what I will look like when I'm old. No, friend, this is what you look like now.

Freshened and inoffensive, Rick slips between the air-conditioned sheets and burrows into the warmth of Laura's large slack body. She wiggles her ass into him and yawns. He lifts her nightgown, presses himself against the back of her thigh. Bumping. Someone's bumping up the stairs. Pause.

"Daddy, I'm hungry." Rick can sense the little girl standing by the bed, her face inches from his. Don't move. Don't breathe. But children are hard to fool because they are survivors. "Daddy!!!"

With a violent flourish, Laura whips back the eiderdown. "Daddy's sleeping, honey. I'll get you something. Did you go wee yet?"

"Yes."

"Are you sure? Show me." Laura and Trina head for the bathroom the four-year-old shares with her older brother, Henry. Rick shifts onto his belly and mime-fucks the mattress. He can hear Laura's muted approval of bladder evacuation, doors opening and closing, more footsteps, all of which draws Rick along the escarpment of sleep. He can almost see them in the sunny kitchen as Laura fills bowls with Honey Nut Cheerios and skim milk.

Rick floats in his bed, unready, resistant to the new day. Bladder full, he meditates on the excretions collected from children, the excretions he will soon be collecting from his patients.

This is how you know someone, by changing their diaper, by taking their blood. By looking inside, getting inside. Urine. Blood. Fecal smears. Semen? Only the week before, Rick had examined a young stockbroker. As the patient shimmied his pants up and Rick washed his hands he saw a droplet of cum on the tip of the guy's prick. I made him cum. Like a five-buck hooker. That's me, nothing but an old whore. Prostates. Bladders. Urethras. My prick. In Laura. Maybe. Rarely. Not that rarely. What is the urge to spritz sperm at a womb? Only the greatest force in the universe. Kingdoms won and lost. Let's face it, Macbeth just wanted to get laid. And look what happened to him.

Rick tries to make a mental list of everyone he's ever fucked. Blow jobs don't count. Comes up with twenty-two first names. Twenty-three if he includes Laura, which is kind of perverse. Wife on the fuck-list. Too weird. So, twenty-two. Can't remember all the last names. There was that time in med school when sex was just a part of getting drunk. You got drunk, ended up with someone. That's all. Intercourse happened in there somewhere. Usually not memorable. Unless you caught crabs. Or worse. And then there was that other period as an intern and too exhausted to fuck. If I had started my medical practice when I was a bachelor, I'd have had a much longer list of women. Cheated two times. Those count. Definitely count.

Maybe the list is more like thirty. If I had any balls, the number would be over one hundred. I'm a doctor, for god's sake! Doctors are supposed to get laid! Over a hundred would be something to be proud of. I could walk with my head high, even if my own wife is bored by me. Pride can be a good thing. Pride fixes things. Dad was proud. Used to swagger around town, and everybody knew. "Now there's a guy who knows how to use his schlong!" A fucker who was a real fucker. Admit it, I want to be a fucker, too. But I have no balls. Wanted the easy road. Afraid of being alone. Still wanted the action, though. Is that why I became a doctor? For the pussy?

In the shower, Rick weighs the pros and cons of masturbation. Decides it's not a good way to start the day, too much like defeat. He shaves and dresses and lets the missed moment fold into the nothingness that is this particular morning. He trots downstairs, joins his family, reads the paper and drinks coffee. The headlines eclipse his horniness. Clearly, Laura's mind is elsewhere, too. Where are you in your life when you forget your own sex drive? Near the end, probably. Maybe if I flossed before going to bed Laura would have sex with me. Floss gets into those crevices of putrefaction. Removes the essential grossness. If she fucked me, the morning would go so much better. And if I arrived at work satiated, I wouldn't find Zoe so interesting. I'd be able to focus, do my work.

A horn cheeps outside and Laura ushers the kids to the door. Out on the street, an undersized SUV lingers and a fellow carpool parent waves. Can't remember her name. After a while all the parents look the same. Slightly anxious. Sexless. The kids run to the car. The smell of fall enters the house. First days of the school year, everything is potential. Rick watches Laura cross the lawn.

As she reenters the house, the cool air clings to her robe. Rick says, "Uh, what are you doing, say, for the next fifteen minutes?"

"I have the gym." Her eyes are warm, but her mouth is set.

"Skip the gym." Rick follows Laura back into the kitchen and as she refills her coffee, he embraces her from behind and cups a breast. "You go to the gym to look good, right? What's the point of having that if you don't put it to use pleasing your horny husband?"

"Maybe I'm not doing it to please my horny husband. Maybe I want to preserve my health, Doctor."

"Sex is the best thing for your health."

"And debating it like this really turns me on." She flashes her bathrobe open. "Look at me. Do you want me to get fatter?"

"Uh, yes. I want you to get fatter." He wants to say, "Laura, you are overweight. You will always be overweight. Who cares? My libido doesn't know the difference." She treats her leisure time like a job. Reading, exercising, meditating.

Laura fits a plate into the dishwasher and gives Rick a maternal kiss. "Tonight, when the kids are in bed. Not now."

"I have my shift at the ER tonight. I'll be home after midnight."

"I have a lot of reading to do. I'll wait."

When Rick gets to the clinic, Zoe smiles at him. Zoe with the peach-colored skin, miniature breasts, and frizzy red hair. Today she's wearing slacks that offer her butt like a gift. The top two buttons of her blouse are undone. She's wearing extra-moist lipstick. She has the barest hint of sunburn.

The waiting room is full and this cheers Rick up. He's proud of his waiting room. Cool and sparsely decorated, featuring exposed cement walls and muted lighting, it's Laura's finest hour. She selected every element, from the chrome fittings to the handmade Uzbeki kilims scattered artistically over the industrial carpeting. The hi-tech lighting and the eight-foot-tall potted ming arelia in the corner give the place the feel of a Malaysian hotel lobby designed by Germans. It says "new age," it says "cutting-edge medicine," it says, "no HMOs."

The day has begun like most days and continues that way. Rick takes blood pressure, dispenses Lipitor and discusses omega-3 fatty acids. His patients like the new-age nutritional talk, then want the same pharmaceuticals everyone else takes. For this, Rick charges double and accepts only the highest grade of insurance.

Zoe brings Rick's lunch to him in his office and he dreams of her naked body collapsed over the front desk while he has his way with her sweet bottom. Passersby on the street stop and watch through the plate glass window. She says, "Fuck me, Rick."

After work, Rick eats a slice of pizza off a paper plate and wanders up to the hospital. Ten hours a week at the ER balances out his exclusive practice. He checks in at the nurses' station, dresses and scrubs. Tonight unfolds like most of the others, fraught with an edge of drama but in the end, forgettable. During the shift he stitches up five lacerations, bandages a burn, writes three ampicillin scrips and orders seven X-rays. No gunshot wounds. No massive bleeding. No deaths.

The time passes quickly, and soon he's on his way back to the suburbs, feeling as he does every Thursday night, how lucky he is not to be stuck in an urban wasteland in which the hospital is the only oasis.

On the ferry Rick considers the hour, considers imminent union with his wife and swallows a Viagra washed down with half a can of Sprite. Better safe than sorry. The ferry docks. It's late. Rick and his fellow ghosts wander off the ship and find their respective vehicles, no one acknowledges the other. In the almost empty parking lot, each commuter is anonymous. Soon we'll all be home, safe and sound and reconstituted.

Rick motors up the hill toward his quiet town and the press of his foot on the accelerator reminds him of his horniness. Or maybe it's the pill he's popped. The libido is a nasty little pet that has to be fed and taken for walks. He neither likes nor dislikes the sensation. It's just something that's part of him. Rick thinks, someday I won't feel this way and I probably won't miss it.

Laura has left the kitchen light on and the house is still. Rick tiptoes up the stairs, past the night-light glow of the children's rooms. He finds Laura sprawled against pillows, eyes closed. Her book has fallen off her lap and the bedside lamp bathes her in sweet light. Gotta give her an A for effort. When Rick switches off the lamp, Laura begins to snore. Fifteen years ago, she slept like a fairy princess. Now she snores because she's carrying the extra forty pounds she kept after Trina was born.

Rick returns to the kitchen, pries open a tub of Häagen-Dazs and roams the quiescent house ladling frozen cream into his mouth. He likes the place when it's calm like this. It feels like a home, the polished floors cast with moonlight, the aroma of food and children. A very clean house. The woman from Nicaragua comes twice a week and injects her simple energy into their congested life, fixing it briefly.

Rick surveys the detritus of the time they spend here—the dead screen of the TV, kids' tattered books, unidentifiable electronic junk trailing a confusion of wires, forgotten bits of clothes, shoes. Could I live here alone without them? Without the relentless clamor of domesticity? Without their clatter and babble and warm respiration? No. I'd be lonely and sad. But aren't I lonely and sad anyway, living with them? No, that's not true. I like my life. I'm proud of my life. I brag about it to my patients. Even to Zoe. Everyone thinks I'm lucky, and I am. I like my life, it's just living my life that makes me unhappy.

In the den, Rick sprawls on the couch, scraping the dregs, stoned on sugar and fat. He tosses the spoon into the damp carton and leaves the whole mess on the coffee table. Laura will find it in the morning. So what? Rick's foot nudges a camcorder lying under the coffee table.

Propping the machine on his slightly distended belly, Rick inserts a tape from another time. Trina not born yet, Henry just turned four. Laura gorgeous and in a good mood. A young family, as frisky and carefree as puppies.

He doesn't recognize himself. Tan and thin. Laura laughs out loud. Who's holding the camera? It must have been someone we saw every day, someone important to our lives then. A parent from Henry's preschool? A blur of a face, a name, lost. Yes, wait a minute, there he is. Old what's-his-face—Charlie. Whatever happened to Charlie? Didn't they get divorced? Or the kid had ADD? Whatever.

I used to talk to this guy. Told him about that one-nighter with the Dutch hematologist at the convention. All chewed up about it and Charlie had said, "Shit happens." I guess so. That must have been why you got divorced, Charlie. You didn't take it seriously enough. I should never have told him. This guy doesn't know me, doesn't know why I do what I do. What was I confiding in him for? Because I was bragging, that's why. He probably told his wife. Wonder if she told Laura?

The camera is passed back and again Charlie holds Rick's family in the palm of his hand. A long time ago. Cut to: Rick telling a joke. He makes a face. The camera angle drops, Laura has the giggles. Henry is wheeling and screaming.

On the couch, in the present, Rick wonders. Was I there? Do I recall living any of this? Do those memories exist in me somewhere? No. It's on the tape but I could never come up with this on my own. That guy on the tape isn't me.

I don't remember being happy then. I remember being tired. The clinic was overwhelming and that was when Henry was wetting the bed and we had no money and Laura and I never had time for sex. Then when we got past all that, she got pregnant again. What's changed? Nothing, except I am five years older.

A closeup of Rick and Laura smooching. She touches his face as she kisses him. Look at her! My god, she's so beautiful! On the couch Rick is suddenly bawling. Oh shit. This is so fucked up. It's like we died or something! He stops the tape. Sits, heart aching, damp-eyed, alarmed by his own emotion. Rick slips the camera back in the carrying case.

The Viagra is calling. Fuckit.

Once the computer boots up, Rick logs onto the Internet. What choice do I have? Should I wait and see if Laura will be in the mood tomorrow morning? And what, roll around all night with a hard-on? Nah, her mind is elsewhere. Face it, you don't turn her on anymore.

Rick begins the free porn site odyssey. Not that I'm cheap, just don't want Laura questioning credit card billings from the Netherlands or the French Antilles. Wouldn't take her long to figure it out. Not that she'd be shocked. She thinks my sexuality is about as interesting as my bowel movements. If she ever figured out I was checking out cyber porn, she'd just wrinkle her nose and yawn.

After half a dozen pop-ups promise "Latin Bondage Babes" and "Co-Eds Who Thrive on Cum" and "Refinance your Mortgage Now!" Rick uncovers a site featuring a smorgasbord of downloadable digital "thumbnails." He begins the arduous process of sorting through the various categories and dead ends.

There is a repetitiveness. Lots of dick-sucking and silicone-inflated jugs. A girl with cum dripping off her nose. Another girl holding on to a swollen ropy-veined cock, smiling a toothy smile for the camera. More cheerful girls getting fucked in the butt while spreading their labia with their fingers. Girls lip-locked onto even more enormous cocks, bigger than possible, wincing with the task at hand. Girls getting fucked by two guys at once, by three guys at once, four guys. Everyone is hung like a Shetland. Are there that many big-dicked guys in the world? Someone once told Rick that the guys actually aren't that big, it's the girls who are small. Right.

Rick is bored and moves on.

Girls in bobby socks. Girls wearing leather masks. Girls in pigtails. Girls in frilly panties. Girls being tied up. Girls pulling strings of giant beads out of their ass. Girls lifting their T-shirts, pulling their underwear down. Girls getting pissed on. Girls spreading their thighs on couches, on desks, on floors, on beds. Girls kissing each other, licking each other, sticking dildoes into one another, into themselves. Girls grabbing two cocks at the same time, beaming at the camera.

Most of them have shaved their pubes. Many have tattoos on their backsides. Some have pierced belly buttons or pierced tongues. Their eyes are eager and flat at the same time. The girls look as if they are playacting with their own flimsy lives. In sum, the girls are all attractive, but none really first class.

Rick imagines a story behind each picture. These are lonely people, looking for attention, right? Maybe a plain-Jane discovers that men pay attention to her if she'll do these things? Or maybe it starts out gradually, the girl poses for soft porn, then harder and harder stuff, next thing you know she's doing anal. Then she's selling herself. Or maybe they're all prostitutes in the first place. From Eastern Europe? Vegas? Ottawa?

It's a mystery. What are they? Who are they? Where are they? Is there a suburb of L.A. where hundreds of people screw 'round the clock surrounded by film crews and photographers? (And if prostitution is illegal, how come it's legal to film people who are paid to fuck each other?) What do they get paid, anyway? A thousand bucks? Two thousand? A hundred?

Maybe these photos are months old. Years old? Maybe the girl posed for one session five years ago, she's got three kids and a teaching certificate and now the picture is being endlessly recycled in a vast sea of j-pegs? Maybe these women have renounced sex and become nuns? Or no longer alive. But digital photos never die. They are like characters in novels or history, even. We're out here fantasizing about them, and they don't even exist.

Rick likes the girls who smile at the camera. Why is that? More nurturing, maybe? In the sixties, stroke mags always featured doe-eyed women with huge breasts. When did tastes change? And why do some men need to see women getting fucked three ways? And what is it about ass-fucking that is so compelling? Maybe pictures of ass-fucking stimulate a specific part of the brain? But I don't give a hoot about ass-fucking. I do care about naked spread-eagled girls. Is that perverse? Am I, in some way, pathological? No. Not possible. They're not making these sites for me. Or are they?

The depressing fact is that hundreds of thousands of men, if not millions, are simultaneously jerking off, fiery eyeballs glued to the same collection of megapixilated flesh. It's one thing to secretly groove on some anonymous babe's derriere, but it's sickening to think some other slob has his BVDs around his ankles, beating to the same rhythm. The human soul has melded with silicon technology. We're automata, this proves it. The machine knows what we want before we want it.

Once in a while Rick sees the same girl on more than one site. But apparently there are an unlimited number of women in the world who want to be ravaged before the camera. Is the world that big? And if it is, how small am I?

Rick gets it. He's seen all these girls before. These are the poor white girls who walk the fairway at the county fair or pick through the cheap cosmetics the street vendors sell. These are the girls who show up on the confessional talk shows, the ones whose lives are such messes. These are the girls who have nothing, come from nothing, and go nowhere.

Of course, there must be lots of men like me who are either single or divorced or can't find the time to have sex with their wives. On the other hand, how sad is that? It's really sad. It's pathetic and disturbing. Rick's gone soft. So he logs off.

Pants back up, Rick makes the rounds of the house one more time, pausing in each of the children's rooms to observe the slack-jawed slumber. What are you dreaming about, guys? Something fun, I hope. I love you so much, I am so lucky. And I am so alone.

When he was eleven, Rick caught his dad cheating on his mom in their own home. Actually found the woman in a closet in his parents' bedroom. Heard a noise, went to investigate and there she was sandwiched between his father's herringbone and seersucker suits. Her luminous face frightened him. What's worse, she was pretending to be invisible. She put a finger to her lips and said, "Shhhh! Honey, I'm working for your daddy. It's a secret. Make sure you don't tell Mommy." And Rick let it go. What else could he do?

Years later when he went into therapy and was urged to relive the experience, Rick realized she must have been drunk. In those days, if Dad wasn't working, he was drinking. And anybody hanging out with him was drinking. Hard stuff: highballs, Manhattans, even boilermakers. But the ridiculousness of her explanation worked. Not because Rick believed her, but because he knew if he told his mother, his parents would fight. Maybe split up. Something bad. It made his stomach hurt and he spent hours locked in his bedroom alternately fantasizing revenge against his father and jacking off to bondage fantasies starring the closet lady. He planned to wait the fifty or so years until his mom passed away and then he would confront his father with the facts to be followed by a spectacular act of patri-suicide.

Rick never got the chance. Dad divorced Mom, married the woman in the closet and moved to another suburb only a few miles away. There, he established another family and was too busy with the new babies to bother with Rick. The less Rick saw of his dad the more he obsessed about him. In his mind's eye, his father grew into a massive, bullnecked tyrant. Around that time, he had seen his father almost completely naked at the beach. The sight of his father's broad hairy back as he trotted down to the roaring surf was indelible. Somehow everything connected. Dad was a real man who could never be matched. He drank, he fucked, he had a hairy back and he abandoned his family.

Rick never became a tough guy like his dad. Maybe it was the difference in diet. Dad grew up on matzo, fatty soups, corned beef and smoked fish. Rick's dad was a true Jew, a "schtarker," a bad-ass. Rick's dad lost uncles and aunts in the Holocaust. Dad had been that much closer to the death and destruction of war. Gave him some kind of license to do whatever the fuck he wanted.

Rick has always just been Rick. A vaguely Semitic-looking guy with brown eyes and no feeling for his roots. Never bar mitzvahed because Dad and Mom were too busy getting divorced. Hadn't entered temple in years. Always forgot to observe the holidays. Couldn't stomach gefilte fish. People from the Midwest (Laura?) thought he was Italian. Uncle Morrie used to call it "passing." Like "passing as a non-Jew." Passing over. Passover, right? Two different things, or is it the same? Trying to be invisible. Being invisible.

My kids have inherited my lack of self. They're not Jewish, not Christian either. Just suburban Disney-worshipping, electronics consumers. Like most of their little friends, they're mutts, little olive-skinned blond kids whose hair will turn brown and wavy when they hit puberty. Kids with no roots other than an address where two parents live. Or maybe two addresses?

Rick figured his father was happy to be absolved of any kind of deep responsibility. The guy was more interested in a deck of cards than the Torah. Any sense of roots he might have had had been left behind a generation ago in Europe, burned to ash in the Nazi ovens. I'm getting to be more like him all the time. No sense of tradition, no sense of anything. Him and me, all we have is our physical selves, our bodies, our dicks. How can I blame him for being nothing more or less than what he is, a man?

Rick shuts himself into the downstairs bathroom. Laura has decided that a clutch of periodicals in a large handwoven basket is a nice touch. All fashion and homemaking mags. Rick picks out a copy of *Elle*. Does Laura subscribe to this dreck? He finds a swimsuit ad. The babe in the ad has something. She's looking right at me, slim and pretty. What is that look? What does it mean? Is it just an accident of the moment? Is it real? Is there someone in her life who gets this attention? Could anyone be this deeply passionate? Doubtful. When you meet them, models and famous people never look like their pictures. Always shorter. Grayer. Homelier.

But this one girl. It's as if she's looking right into my heart. Like she wants to penetrate me with her eyes. I guess that's why they pay her the big bucks. To look like that. Rick squirts a dab of Laura's hand lotion onto his palm.

If Laura ever caught me at this, what would she think? How insanely embarrassing would it be to have your own wife catch you choking the chicken while checking out a swimsuit ad in *Elle*?

Dad never felt guilty. Just lived his life. He was married to Mom and then didn't want to be married anymore, so he fucked around, left her and married his second wife. He'd had kids with Mom and then more kids with his second wife. He earned a living, watched TV, played golf, drank with his buddies and as far as anyone can tell, never had a second thought about anything.

And here I am at two AM, with my putz in my hand, in the

guest bathroom surrounded by embroidered towels and scented soap cakes. Something Dad never would have done. If he wanted some tail, he went out and got it. Probably masturbated two times in his whole life. Doesn't matter. A man's got to do what a man's got to do. Rick hunches over and with hollow fury focuses on the swimsuit girl from *Elle*. Those eyes. Sad like mine. I know you, baby. I know you. Finally it comes, the energy building. The wrecking ball of orgasm. Rick comes so marvelously and terrifically he moans out loud. Everything disappears for a moment.

"Daddy?" The bathroom door opens a crack. Rick lets his robe drop closed, draping his erection. He turns, red-faced from the exertion, reading glasses still hanging off his fat, aging nose. "Daddy, I can't sleep."

Kids know when something's up. They're attracted by any disturbance, curious, sometimes fatally. Henry stands in the doorway, sleepy eyes adjusting to the fluorescence.

The canned response pops out of Rick. "What are you doing up?"

"I was having a nightmare. Why were you shouting?"

"I wasn't shouting. Must have been part of your nightmare. Well, maybe you have to pee." Welcome to the club, kid. The wonderful world of excretion. It rules your life. "Pee. Have a drink of water and I'll tuck you in."

Henry eyes him suspiciously. A picture's worth a thousand words. "What were you doing, Daddy?"

"I was reading. I didn't want to wake your mother."

"Oh." Henry shuffles over to the toilet and turning his back on his father, tugs out his tiny white wiener and blasts a surprisingly strong jet into the limpid pool.

"OK. All set? Back to bed. I'll be right there."

Henry leaves and Rick snatches an extrasoft facial tissue, collects the coagulating gob and tosses it into the pastel water. Ah yes. Father and son. The passing of the phallic torch. He flushes.

REBA HAS INHERITED THE BUSIEST WINDOW, THE MIDDLE window. Everyone comes to her first. A red-faced elder in pressed overalls hobbles up and passes her a check. His fingers are callused and the backs of his hands speckled with liver spots. She gives him her best smile. "Hello, Mr. Van Pelt, and how are we today?"

Mr. Van Pelt fondles a beet red boil under his right ear. "Alive." The parchment skin on his rosy cheeks flakes off like dandruff.

Reba tries not to stare. "Well, it is a lovely day, that's for sure."

"What's that got to do with the price of fish?" Van Pelt runs his tongue over his brown teeth.

"When it's a nice day out I always think I'm happy to be alive."

Van Pelt stares at her with pinhead pupils. "Don't gimme any fifties. I can't use the fifties. I don't even know why they make 'em. Ulysses S. Grant was a lousy president and a drunk."

"Yessir." Reba glances at the clock over the drive-through window. Five more hours.

"Just gimme my money. Did you put the ten dollars in the Christmas Club?"

"Would you like me to do that, sir?"

"You do it every week, don't you?" Van Pelt turns and bellows at Frank in his cubicle. "Cheese Louise, Frank, where do you get these girls?"

From behind the plate glass, Frank glances up and waves to Van Pelt. Frank wants none of this. A clear drop of pus has appeared on the boil. Anne, Reba's teller-mate, arrives, crowding into her just as Van Pelt lets out a loud fart.

"Good morning, Mr. Van Pelt. Is everything OK? Reba?" Anne's warm, reassuring breast brushes Reba's arm. Anne, like almost every young mother in town, is overweight and her hair is snipped into a frizzy poodle curl. Reba imagines dropping to her knees, lifting Anne's sweater and hiding away in those pillowy breasts until the old jerk goes away. Until they all go away. Until everything goes away.

"Is everyone here a retarded moron?" Van Pelt squeezes the pearl of fluid onto his grimy fingertips and wipes it onto his shirtfront.

Anne, unaware of his grossness, keeps things moving. "Reba, why don't you go refill the ATM cartridges?" Anne has it covered. Anne is good at this. I'm lucky this time.

As Reba stacks piles of tens and twenties, Maureen, the third bankerette, joins her. "See any good-looking guys down in the city Saturday?" Maureen's breath is shallow and rapid, her fingers gray from pouring the filthy nickels and pennies into the sorting machine.

"Why don't you grab the bus one day and take a look for yourself?" Maureen looks more and more dried out with each passing day, like those miniature bouquets of yellow roses they sell at the crafts fair. On Fridays Reba sees Maureen steering her cart at the Shop-Rite, her mom tottering at her side. Maureen's mom wears the pinched look of a martyr exhausted by life with an unmarried daughter.

"Go to the city? No thanks. I went down there once with mother and we saw things you wouldn't believe. A Negro man was standing on a street corner just clapping his hands! Can you imagine? Wearing three overcoats, clapping his hands like a lunatic. I bet he hadn't taken a bath in a week. I just don't feel comfortable around those kind of people, especially the blacks, Negroes, whatever you call 'em."

Reba loses her count and begins again.

Having disposed of Van Pelt, Anne sidles up to Reba and Maureen. "He hasn't been the same since his wife had that stroke. Now she's blind. I dropped by there once to bring a cake from the church? The place smelled like pee-pee, newspapers stacked all over the place. His daughter told me she won't even go in there anymore. And he's not the only one. All the farmers are getting older and older. Sometimes we don't know they're there until they die. No one knows they're there."

Across from the bank, the woods are deep. The cars pass on the two-lane and Reba thinks, in those deep woods are the farmhouses and in the farmhouses are the old people. The living dead.

Maureen chirps, "Reba wants me to go to New York with her and pick up guys."

Anne, an eye on Frank in his cell, whispers. "I knew a fella who used to go down there all the time. And you know what he did? Rented stretch limos and picked up whores. Had sex with them in the back while he drove around." Anne assumes her wisest expression, "I wouldn't go down there if you paid me a million dollars."

Frank emerges clutching a sheaf of paperwork, steps behind the three women and types entries into the computer terminal. Under his breath he says, "Maureen, could you run next door and get me a Diet Coke, please?" In the two months since she's been there, Reba has learned that this is Frank's way of warning them to get back to work. Frank alternates between gruff verging on rude and exceeding politeness, as if he isn't sure how he should act. Reba sees that Frank is more complex than she first thought. And he isn't all that old. Not even forty.

Frank has developed minty breath. And despite his apparent testiness, he's always full of pep. Reba is drawn to this energy. Frank seems to be a person who has taken control of his life. She watches him more carefully, noticing the way he dresses, the way he chews his food.

Frank gives Reba lots of room, never bosses her around. He respects her. One day he visits her window and asks for her advice about the correct way to change the paper in his adding machine. That's when she notices his breath. And his cleanliness. He's a bachelor and yet he's always spic and span.

The afternoon of Van Pelt's visit, Frank asks Reba to stay and help him sort out some old files he wants moved to the main office in Albany. He'll pay her overtime. While they work, he neither speaks to nor looks at her. Reba likes spending time like this, side by side, in unspoken companionship. In the fading light outside, the cicadas begin to whir.

Frank gives Reba money for dinner from the Italian place four doors down the mini-mall. While waiting for the take-out meal, she contemplates the framed photos of the Colosseum and the Forum on the walls of the restaurant. Reba wonders what it would be like to go to Italy. She's pretty sure no one who works in the pizza place has ever been there. Does Frank wonder about things like that? It's hard to tell what he thinks. Obviously he thinks about something.

When she returns with the food, Frank tells her it's his treat. She figures that's fair. The food comes in round aluminum pans. Pried open, some of the rust-colored sauce sticks to the underside of the circular lid. The garlic bread steams when the foil is unwrapped. They eat in silence until Reba asks him, "Worried about work?"

As if roused from a catnap, Frank blinks and knits his thick eyebrows. "No. Not work."

"You're thinking about something."

Frank swabs sauce with a piece of bread, looks up at Reba with his flat eyes. "I was thinking about you." He places the piece of bread in his mouth and swallows it whole.

"Me?"

"I was thinking that you're a good person. In your heart, you're kind. You're loving. More than most people. Your eyes are kind, your smile, your hands."

"My hands?"

"You're very gentle. Like your mother was. Your mother was very beautiful. And gentle. Like you."

"I never think about myself that way. I'm just me." Reba examines her hands. They're just hands. If anything they're too long and skinny.

Frank pushes on. "Maybe you can't tell because it's just the way you are. Me, I have a hard time being a nice person. Inside, I feel like a nice person, but I don't think people see me that way. It's not easy for me. Being a boss and all. It's . . . it's a struggle."

"But I can see that. In you. I think."

"People don't like me. I know it." Frank picks a crumb of garlic bread off his pants and hurls it into the now empty bank lobby.

"That's not true."

As if thwarted by an insurmountable roadblock, Frank hunches over his food and resumes eating. Reba collects her rubbish and shoves it into a large clear plastic sack of shredded documents.

It's almost nine o'clock by the time they've sorted out the heaps of slips and receipts. As Frank locks up and sets the alarms, he mentions he's going to drive out by the old canal to scout the height of the water, since he was hoping to go fishing this weekend. Reba asks, "Mind if I go with you?"

When they get to the banks of the canal, Frank switches off the engine. He says nothing more about how gentle Reba is or how people don't like him. He hooks an arm around her shoulders, pulls her toward him and presses his mouth against hers.

For almost five minutes, Reba is in love. For almost five minutes Frank is affectionate and handsome and sexy. She gazes into his black eyes and sees that his good side has been there all along—kindness and passion and intelligence and even empathy. He's a man, complete and fine in many ways. His dark eyes are masculine, his anger is masculine. His arms are firm. With this man, I could make a life. Frank just has difficulty showing his love. But with me, it would be different. He opens up with me. I could work at the bank and we could make a life. Affection between us would be our secret. People will talk, of course, but so what?

Frank kisses Reba again and her heart lifts. When they stop for breath, Reba thinks, I could nurse him when he's sick, I could have his babies. I could love him.

And when Frank nudges her head down into his lap, she isn't surprised. He is a man, after all. It doesn't seem like the most natural thing in the world, but she once read a piece in *Cosmo* which explained that men need this and really appreciate it when women who love them do this kind of thing. Frank helps her by opening his pants and tilting the seat back so she can get her face down past the steering wheel.

His touch is gentle as he caresses her hair. Reba can barely see the thing in the gloom, but it's there, waiting. Reba smiles to herself. This isn't so bad. It's almost fun. She opens her mouth and a shiver runs over her shoulders.

With surprising urgency, the knobbed stem springs upward. She bends over the insistent thing and treats it like the little baby it is. She caresses it and fondles it and then, finally, kisses its taut bald head. Frank helps out by pressing her downward and now, she's doing it. She doesn't really need to move, because he's thrusting himself upward, holding her steady with his thick fingers, clutching her head with one hand and her breast with the other. She imagines the fur on the backs of his knuckles.

When Frank stiffens and begins to shudder and bellow, Reba looks up, fearful he's having a heart attack. Frank bucks upward, writhing. He growls through clenched teeth, "Swallow it, swallow it! What's wrong with you? Jesus God Almighty, fuck!"

Reba isn't sure what "it" is and when she bows down to slip the shrinking head back into her mouth, she can see the beads of Frank's discharge clinging to her hair, glittering in the moonlight.

Then Frank's face looms, creased with anger, his eyes bare slits, glimmering, malevolent. "Fucking bitch!"

The thing in her hand is not part of her lover's body. It's only the purplish brown penis of a boss who's wanted to fuck her for weeks. She can't hold back her tears of fear, anger, and they mix with Frank's cum, covering her hands, smearing her face. She doesn't care what he thinks. She cries as hard as she feels, raining sorrow onto Frank's crumpled dick. She can feel her mom's dead spirit watching.

Finally, weak and silent, she cleans up as Frank drives back to the bank's parking lot. She tries to read him, but he doesn't take his eyes off the road. I'm not what he had expected. He's angry at me. Maybe I should have tried harder? Reba mumbles she's sorry, but Frank only grunts.

The parking lot is empty and Reba's Honda stands alone, waiting for her. As she gets out of Frank's car, she wonders if she's going to be paid for the overtime, and if so, when exactly that overtime began and ended. But she doesn't ask and before she's in her own car, Frank is arcing his way out of the lot.

Billy's not home yet, it being Friday night. If Billy were home, he'd take one look at me and figure it all out. That wouldn't be good. Reba wipes off her makeup. Maybe this was a missed golden opportunity? Not necessarily for love, but for something more. Maybe being with Frank would have opened up possibilities? Frank is a man of the world. Maybe I fucked up?

Reba drops her clothes onto the bare bathroom floor, twists the taps on full and slips into the spray. As the water grows hotter, she stands with head bowed, unmoving and mute, a dagger of slick hair bisecting her thin shoulders. Lifting her face, she lets the flow tear at her lips, sandpaper her tongue and teeth. She slides the soap cake over herself, caressing the negligible mass of breasts, butt cheeks, legs.

This is me. This is all of me. There will never be more or less. Two legs, two arms, two breasts, a belly button, a head, a stupid face, a mouth. Everywhere I go, I take me with me. There's no way to escape. No one knows me but me. They think they know me by looking at me, but no one will ever know. Ever. My thighs, my ass, the soles of my feet. It's all I am and everything I am.

Reba dials the faucet ten degrees. Maybe I'll faint in here, fall down and hit my head and drown. That would be nice. I could slice my wrists so Billy can find me all red and runny and blue and floppy. Then he'd notice how I look. I'd love to see that. He thinks I'm a cunt, let him see it. A dead cunt. He'd miss me then because there'd be no one to fry his fucking chicken legs.

Reba racks back the shower curtain, her long outline vague in the steamy mirror. She wipes it bright again with a palm, startled by her own face. Look at me, nothing but a big stretched-out bird. Even my face is like a bird's, like an ostrich. Gigantoid mouth, gigantoid eyes. If they were any farther apart I'd be looking in two directions at the same time. Nothing but a plucked ostrich, that's what I am. Tits so small they don't even jiggle. Billy's right. I'm nothing but a useless skinny geek.

Reba tugs at her crotch hair with the hairbrush. Not even enough to shave off. Just a girl. Never be a real woman. Only good for blow jobs to freaky old guys. Why should anyone normal notice me? I'm nothing. I'm wallpaper. If I stopped moving, I'd disappear.

Reba fondles the teddies and thongs that Billy would never suspect she owned, stored in a Victorian wardrobe inherited from a long dead grandmother she's never met. The cherrywood veneer exhales an aroma of mothballs and mold. Why do I even bother? I'm not going anywhere.

The interior of the wardrobe door is papered with magazine clippings. Models, actresses and singers, wrapped in silk, bejeweled, coiffed, perfectly painted, a swirl of color and clear skin, blissfully suspended in a delicious syrup of movement and sex and cash. Their eyes say "You have no idea how good life can be!"

Outside her bedroom window, the night is black and still. No stars. No cars on the road. Even the peepers are silent. Reba runs a finger along the mullion dividing the panes. How many times have I touched this painted wood? How many times have I looked out this window? How many people have been born in this house, cried here, made love here, died here? I'm just one more.

In bed, Reba draws the pillow into her arms and nuzzles the cotton cheek. She settles onto her back and lets her hand find herself under the nightgown cloth. Here is a breast. A shape, so important. I'm not that bad, am I? My boobs are nice. Maybe not big enough, but I like them. What do I care anyway? I'm worrying about making some man happy I'll never meet. Fuck him! I'm a such a bad girl. If Billy only knew I did this! If any-one knew. I'm a sex maniac. Ugly and oversexed, what a great combination! Well, no matter. I am what I am. I can't help it. Think of nice things.

When she was little, before she was old enough for school, and long, long before death came to reside in her parents' hot bedrooms, before she understood that this house was old and sad, Reba would run down to the orchard in a homemade smock and take little bites from the green apples that fell all through the summer. In August, she would hurl them at her brother, or aim for the smooth tree bark, exploding them into green shrapnel.

When she was even smaller, she would dash over the tender springtime grass and the white apple blossoms would float like snowflakes into her upstretched arms. The bees would hum and zip over the white and pink and green. And again in the sweet, aromatic fall, the wasps would steal teeny nibbles from the ripest bits on each fruit. And then the dark leaves would turn curly and drop and she would race through the crispy piles.

On exactly what day did happiness end? When did it all turn into dry leaves? Don't think.

Everything smells of lilac as the petals drift down all around her. She gyrates in the heaps of fallen blossoms, letting them caress her bare skin, arms high over her head. The pink white petals swirl around her nipples, her armpits, her back, the insides of her legs. The leaves and blossoms and honeybees form thick streams, a Niagara crashing over her thighs, faster and faster. The hum of the bees roars in her ears, jet engines streaming down her throat, up into her belly, her asshole, running down inside her arms and legs, out to her toes and fingertips. The hairs at the back of her neck stand up. The universe resonates with the drone. Reba wants to pee and giggle at the same time. She lifts her arms even higher and then something, someone, grabs her by the hands and tosses her high up into the black sky and she's gone.

RICK SNEAKS OUT INTO THE MORNING LIGHT AND gathers up all the sunny Sunday morning stuff: newspaper, chive cream cheese, Nova, freshly baked bagels. Totes it back to the happy, happy family waking up in their sunny house. We will have a wonderful, happy family brunch in our wonderful family home.

Why am I mocking it, it is wonderful. A spacious, sunny, suburban domicile full of expensive plants, polished oak floors, black Japanese electronica, handsome bookcases and comfy furniture. Isn't this what I always wanted? This is the life I imagined in med school. A pretty, loving wife, two great kids, my own medical practice and a serene home with all the things it should contain. A great sound system. Thick handwoven rugs. Windows with views of leafy trees. A flat lawn. A barbecue.

On granite countertops, Rick and Laura slice lemons and red onion, lay out the thick pink pages of salmon and warm the bread in the chef's oven. Henry and Trina spiral through the house with nutty abandon, noodling like joyous background music.

Rick admires the determination and purpose with which

Laura prepares the food. He also likes how good she looks in a bathrobe, likes her plumped up like this, classical. She's still a piece of ass, but more than that, she's Laura, smart, focused, efficient, game. My wife. A hundred times more fun and sexy and good-looking than any of those humorless bitches and neurotics my friends married. Watching her slice bagels makes him horny. She glances at him, "What?"

"Careful, don't cut your finger."

"Stop staring at me, Rick. It's creepy."

"I was thinking how vivacious you look in that bathrobe."

"This? I was going to throw it out. And my hair's greasy as a pork chop. Kids!"

Like beagle pups, Henry and Trina flop and scrabble their way to the table, wrangling chairs like they'd spent their lives eating off the floor. They grab fresh circles of bread, poking at the oily fish with their fingers. Laura pours coffee. Haydn string quartets play softly under everything, which is perfect in its imperfection. Rick thinks, this is what it's all about. Happy morning.

Up late at the ER. The night had been uneventful until two in the morning when a guy in a suit walked in complaining of stomach pains. Before they could begin the workup, he suffered a massive myocardial infarction. Could not be revived. He died on the table. The wife called looking for him. Turned out she'd caught him smoking crack in the bathroom and had chewed him out about his drug use and he had become short of breath and she thought he was faking it. She'd told him if he wasn't feeling well he should get his ass to the emergency room. She even called the cab and that was the last time she saw him alive. Not only did Rick catch the patient, he had to spend an hour with the wife talking her down while waiting for the police.

This morning, Rick is suspended in a thick jell of fatigue. He needs caffeine and food. He is ready to indulge himself in the ambrosia of a New York City brunch. He sips his freshly brewed, freshly ground Dean & Deluca coffee and enthusiastically layers the fish and cream cheese on top of a bagel.

Laura says, "Save some for the kids." She says things like this all the time. She is the guardian of food. Guardian of proper behavior and posture. Guardian of tooth brushing and warm clothing. So why does it hit him so hard this morning? It isn't like he doesn't expect it. In his heart, he knew as he laid the last piece of fish on top of the white tufts of spread that he was pushing it. I shouldn't be eating all this. I'm getting older and cream cheese and Nova are not good for me. That guy last night was only four years older than I am.

Isn't it logical? Isn't that what I should be doing? Watching my health? I'm a doctor, if anyone should know that all this shit is bad for you, it's me. When I'm sixty, do I really want to be slumped in a wheelchair with a string of drool hanging off my chin? No, of course not. So Laura is right to be on my case, because she loves me. Plus she doesn't want to be caring for a vegetable, either. And I took a bit too much. The kids need to eat. Laura needs to eat. But I'm hungry. And Trina doesn't even like smoked salmon. Why can't I just have what I want?

The rightness of the morning disappears and in its place swirl clouds of irritations. Rick flicks the fish back onto the serving platter. It lies there, curled over, fragments of coarse pepper clinging. Spoiled. Everything is spoiled. And it's her fault.

Now Laura is saying something but Rick can barely hear her. "Well, not that much. You don't have to be ridiculous, Rick."

The clouds swirl faster, coalescing into a major storm system. Words come before he can edit them. "No. No. You're right."

"No, honey, take more. I'm just saying . . ." Laura's eyes are not on Rick, they are on Trina.

"I'm fine!" He sips his coffee. It's gone cold, it's too bitter.

"That's ridiculous. Trina, wipe your mouth." Laura wipes Trina's face.

"Mom!" Trina wriggles, collapses into a sulk. Laura returns

to her food, finds a forkful, lays it onto her tongue. She's forgotten the conversation already. Or is pretending to forget it.

Dark edges along the periphery. "What's ridiculous is that you're telling me, at forty-five years of age, how much food I can put on my plate."

"No, I'm not doing that, Rick." Laura reaches for the pepper. "Henry, sit up."

"Yes, you are!"

"I just said . . ."

Either Henry or Trina say "Dad!" Which one spoke? Aren't they all just the same person split in pieces? Or pieces of myself, like an arm or a leg?

"Rick, take as much as you want! Don't be a baby!"

"You know what? I've lost my appetite."

"Rick!"

Both kids definitely in unison now, more shrilly. "Dad!"

But Rick is up, moving with nowhere to go. Laura addresses his back: "So you're not having lunch?"

"I'm not having lunch." Just keep moving. Figure it out later. If I don't keep moving, I'm going to pick up a plate and throw it.

"But we just sat down."

"Dad!"

Rick rushes up to the bedroom. He sees a door, goes through it and enters a walk-in closet. Faraway voices call out, "Daddy!"

Close the door. Shut the light. Sit on the floor.

In the gloom with the shoes and the stored Christmas stuff and the boxes of wrapping paper, Rick doesn't give a shit about the fish. There are much larger issues here that need to be examined. Her presence. My inability to come to terms with her presence. Necessary, but chafing. Chafing and rubbing, hurting me. It comes down to this. A long time ago we fell in love. And we have remained in love. We have kids. And that's all good. But there's a problem. You don't stay in love forever, do you? What we have now is not what we had then. Now we're companions. Roommates. And I don't like her anymore. And she doesn't like me.

The family is an organism composed of parts. No. The family is an organization composed of parts. No. The family is a pain in the ass composed of parts. A state of being created by God to reveal how inept you can be. I spend time with the kids, but I don't like being with them. Why should I? My father never spent time with me. His father probably never looked at him twice. Ergo my father never really liked me. He endured me. Loved me from a distance. Maybe I'm a sociopath and don't know how to love my own family? I spend time with Laura, but we're not happy, not the way we used to be. Or pretended to be. Is familial love just a biological trick to fool us into nurturing what we've created? Then what? And if I weren't being a dad, being a husband, what would I be doing? I should write her a letter, that's what I should do. Tell her how I feel.

The midmorning sun leaks under the door, casting the empty computer boxes and hangered clothing into unrecognizable shapes. The scent of dust and shoe polish embraces Rick. Voices outside twitter, "Where's Daddy? Mom? Where'd Daddy go? Did Daddy go out? Is he hiding?"

Am I hiding? Not really. I could have stormed out of the house. Slammed a door. Grabbed the car keys and put some miles between me and them, between me and my life. Could have dropped in on the steak house down the road, knocked back a few Johnnie Walkers. But who needs all that drama? Laura would be worried. The kids would be filled with fear. "Where's Daddy?" "Oh, Daddy's down the street getting shit-faced." Never sounds good. The closet is a much better choice.

A space between his heart and the pit of his stomach cracks open and hurts. Why am I so lonely? How does it happen, in the midst of my happy family meal on a sunny Sunday afternoon that I am on the verge of tears in my suburban walk-in closet?

Am I overtired? Am I angry about something? Fuckit, just tell the therapist next week.

Eventually, since no one comes searching for him, Rick emerges. Voices rise from the backyard and he wanders down to the kitchen, spies the family from the window. He catches Laura's eye and it's devoid of emotion. He thinks, like a fish, cold-blooded. Why should she worry? I was just "acting out" and so she treats me like a child, she's ignoring me.

He watches them from the back door. Look, they're happy together without me. They don't need Daddy. Daddy is a useless appendage, a fifth wheel. I inseminated Mommy, fought my way into her and made her pregnant. I provided her with a home, provided her with a ways and means for bringing up kids and now I am a meaningless adornment to their lives. What is that Yiddish word Uncle Morrie always used to use? Schmuck—loser, knucklehead. The word means prick. Yiddish has more words for penis than any other language. Penis, prick, whatever. And then in med school I learned the German root, *Schmuck*, meaning, "useless ornament." Uh-huh. Here I am!

Laura has me figured. My ups and downs are just something to endure, like a rainy day, ultimately inconsequential. There are children to raise. There's a life to live. Q: "Who was that man you were with last night?" A: "That was no man, that was my husband."

Rick smiles in their direction, but they can't see him through the screen door. He wants to call out to Henry, to toss him the ball, but he can't do it. Henry will need a father figure soon. I wonder who's going to do the job, 'cause I suck at it. Maybe Henry would be better off without me? I could walk away, like my dad did. Solve the whole mess. Laura would find someone else, a better dad for them. A dad with nice breath.

The problem is Laura and I define love differently. I see it as something dramatic, urgent. She sees it as all the millions of molecules of daily life floating in between the big moments. Laura

could care less about the big moments. For her, all that's important is that we exist on earth together. That's all she needs.

Rick floats high in the sky and he sees them, way down below,
living, happy. He thinks, from out here in outer space, I can only
join you momentarily. After a while, it's just too much. And so I,
the Silver Surfer, must fling myself back out into the void. Bye!

IN THE CITY FARM-FRESH APPLES ARE SOLD UNTIL
Christmas Day. After that the sweetness fades and the peel goes
rubbery. This fall the days are bright and clear as Billy stuffs the
five- and one-dollar bills in a paper bag. He has enlarged his
assortment of country goods. On the collapsible metal table a
jumble of dirty-blond squash and shaggy rubber-banded carrots
lie next to a stack of kale. Behind the veggies he's arranged the
tins of maple syrup, each one affixed with a hand-lettered label.
Behind them, the dark clover honey, a chunk of beeswax trapped
in each jar.

With arms folded across his chest, Billy lectures the city folk
who dream of owning a country house themselves, a place where
they can cultivate their own patch of brown loam. They prize
their horticultural discussions with farmer Billy.

Q: "How do you get your carrots so plump?"

A: "Oh, well, you see, the secret is mixing some sand with the
soil."

Q: "What about nematodes?"

A: "Rotate your crops. Same thing with the squash vine mag-
got."

Q: "Is it ever too late to pick kale?"

A: "Nope, you just brush off the frost and she'll be all the
sweeter for it."

Q: "Are these apples organic?"

A: "Absolutely certified."

Billy lectures as Reba bags the produce. Then, as the satisfied customers wander off, he quips sideways out of his mouth, "Stupid sheep. If they thought about it for two minutes they'd figure out I'm full of shit. You know what their problem is? They'd go nuts if they didn't think there was a better place besides this human septic tank. They're not buying vegetables, they're buying a fantasy."

Billy rarely eats an apple and can't stomach kale. He hasn't touched a spade or a pitchfork in years, eats his lunch out of a McDonald's bag. He hates all veggies and hates all city people, calling them "kikes" and "spooks" and "queers" behind their backs. But he's a businessman, and his business plan includes making a good impression. So he lectures. He knows people are attracted by Reba's wholesome quality, so he insists she wear her dowdiest cotton dresses every Saturday.

Reba keeps an eye on the passing parade, wishing she could ask these alien folk about their interesting haircuts and tattoos, their pierced noses and lips and tongues, their glossy black shoes and the books they carry under their arms. How do you make a living? Where are you going? Are you students? Artists? Actors, maybe? A young man wanders by with his girl, who wears a jacket the likes of which Reba has seen only in magazines. They make a big show of how in love they are, hands stuck in each other's back pockets. The boy sneaks a look at Reba as they pass.

One Saturday while Billy is back sorting the van, a young guy comes up to the table, picks out an apple, lifts it to his nose and sniffs. He lobs the fruit back into the basket, picks out another and methodically feels and squeezes the thing like a pitcher warming up. On his chin, a barely visible wisp of a beard, like blond cotton candy. He nails Reba with his sky blue eyes, "You grow these?"

"Yes." Before she can stop herself, Reba pushes a lock of her hair behind an ear.

"Where?" Such an easy smile.

"Upstate." Reba fusses with the maple syrup, lining up all the tins in the same direction.

He picks up another and says, "Wow."

" 'Wow'?" Reba can hear Billy tossing crates in the van. Please Billy stay in there a little longer. "What do you mean by wow?"

"Well, you know, trees and shit. I mean, this apple didn't exist a year ago, then you grew it and here it is. In my hand. This amazing thing. It must be amazing to grow shit."

"We don't 'grow shit.' We grow apples. My family owns an orchard." Reba rubs her nose with the back of her hand, hides it in a pocket.

"Your family?" The smile grows wider.

"Me and my brother. My folks are dead." Just give him the facts. Don't make a big deal about it.

"Sorry about your folks. But that's nice. An orchard."

"How would you know?"

"Well, I imagine it would have to be nice. To grow things. To live on a farm. Getting up every day at dawn. Milking the cows, feeding the chickens, gathering up the apples. Fresh air. You must be really healthy. Sunshine. Blue skies . . ."

"Sky's blue here, too." And so's your eyes, but you're just fooling with me. Buy or go.

"Not blue enough. Plus up there you got all that wildlife. Owls and deer and things like that."

Reba smirks. "Deer suck."

He picks up another apple and studies it. "I never thought about it that way, but you know, you're right. Deer do suck." He says it like he means it and tricks a smile out of her. Cocky smart-ass.

Reba swallows away her smirk as quickly as she's let it slip out. "You buying that apple or just feeling it up?"

"Can I do that? Buy a single apple?"

It's one thing to be nice to an old lady or to the men with bright flowing scarfs around their necks, the ones who call her "honey" and "sweetness," the men Billy calls "faggots." But Reba has no patience for some pretty-boy pulling her leg. Giving me a hard time for the fun of it. Teasing me. "You want it or not?" He looks like a movie star.

"Can I have a paper bag, please?" He passes the apple to Reba, but she doesn't let him touch her fingers.

"For one apple?"

"Well, I want to save it for later. So I can savor it."

As sudden as a thunderclap big Billy is standing next to Reba. He barks, "Closed for the day," snatches the apple from Reba and flips it into its crate before turning his broad back on the shaggy-haired boy. "Let's get the goods into the truck."

The young man addresses Billy's rude shoulders. "Hey." Billy ignores him. "Excuse me. I want to buy that apple."

Billy turns and faces the boy. He grins, lifting his chin slightly. "You do, do ya? And what else do you want to do?"

The guy doesn't blink. "Eat it."

Billy's eyes go ten degrees colder. "Next week."

The guy shows his teeth. "What a load of crap."

A line forms on Billy's brow, as if he's trying to remember something, and in Reba's brain a movie begins to play in which a massive fist hurtles through space and pummels a very pretty face. She sees bits of teeth flying, and still the fist moves, ramming the fruit down the almost feminine throat. Reba thinks he sees it, too.

The young man relaxes. "OK, OK, dude. Don't get your balls in a bunch." His eyes say, "Fuck you."

Billy lurches forward and grabs a crate of Bosc pears. He hauls it up and away, just missing the guy's knees. Blue Eyes doesn't even have time to ball his fist. Tossing the crate onto his shoulder like a box of feathers, Billy turns his back on both of them and returns to the van.

Reba gathers the veggies into a waxed carton. Fifteen seconds pass before she dares to look up. The boy's eyes are brimming with laughter, fearless. Now she's sure the guy is nuts, or stupid, if he doesn't realize that Billy would split his skull just for the exercise.

The boy shifts slightly toward her, and Reba freezes, transfixed by his lunatic beauty. He's perfect, like an angel, like a painting in a museum. His skin is flawless. She wants to reach out and stroke his cheek, touch his hair. And then the apple is in his hand and he's trotting away through the crowd.

His lanky frame slips through the ebb and flow of the shoppers, gets swallowed up by it. Then Billy is back, the interloper forgotten, unaware of the theft, cursing out another crate. Reba grabs a bunch of kale. The culprit is almost out of sight, blended back into the customers. And then, just before he is eclipsed by the anonymous tide, he turns and, finding her eyes, takes a bite from the apple, and is gone.

That evening, after a meal of Popeyes fried chicken, Billy leaves the van alongside the park and locks Reba in. He says he needs a beer. She watches him lumber off, an angry black bear in search of honey.

The trees in the park have shed their leaves and in the early winter dusk, the limbs stand hard and simple, stark against the gray of the city's nighttime glow. The lady from the next table who sells the little containers of fresh wheat grass stopped setting up two weeks ago. Soon there will be no tables at all. The city in winter. Reba imagines cozy apartments where folks sit by stoked fireplaces reading books, playing chess, supping on homemade stew. She's seen the men in the park playing chess, other people reading on the benches. They all must go somewhere when it gets too cold.

In the shadowy back of the van the fragrance of apples and pears mingles with the faintest scent of spilled gasoline. This late in the year, this late in the day, it's not easy to see much inside the van, let alone read a magazine. And Billy bitches if she leaves the dome light on for too long. Besides, when she does, people can see her sitting inside. She prefers it like this, being invisible, watching the world go by.

As far as Reba can tell, there are always some people moving around the city, like motes of dust in interstellar space. They must be insomniacs. And now, in the early gloom of night, they dash past her observation post, going where? Home to families? To jobs? To places she can imagine but can't know.

The grease-stained alley beside a restaurant across the way shines white in the light of the street lamps. Like tiny phantoms, rats scuttle and nip at the pyramids of bagged garbage. Faceless figures clip along with determination or hobble lethargically, as if postponing the next bad thing. Or maybe they want to go slow in case someone has to catch up to them and let them know they'd just won Lotto.

Like sentries, dog walkers and surreptitious cigarette smokers make their rounds. Clusters of young men in open jackets walk briskly, chuckling and nodding at one another, probably more alive in this moment than they will ever be for the rest of their lives.

When lovers come by and embrace, Reba memorizes every gesture. She wishes there were more lovers. Lovers are the best people to keep an eye on because they're not waiting for something good to happen, they're making it happen.

About twenty feet from where she sits is a trash can. Since Billy split, Reba has counted seven people who have rummaged through that one can. And she has counted eight people who've stood sentinel while their dogs shit on the pavement, but only six who've actually picked up the shit. Two different guys have thrust their hips against the alley wall. Now a thin dark riverlet of urine traverses the sidewalk.

Battered blue and white police vehicles ease past every ten minutes. A silent ambulance with revolving lights floats by.

Three more rats. Chinese men on bicycles thread fearlessly through the erratic flow of traffic. And a guy who seems to be scratching himself limps off. Reba's figured out from her visits that he was probably shooting up into his leg. High above her, blinking dots of red symbolize unseen jets and helicopters.

It's hard to think of home when I'm down here in the city. Hard to imagine the farm is there at all, leftovers cooling in the fridge, oil burner clicking on and off in the dusty basement, cars swishing along the two-lane. And yet, it's all back there, even now.

Here in the city, while the apartment buildings loom, the multitudes do whatever they do. Way up there, in the blackness, one yellow rectangle of light.

Someone is up there now, maybe dreaming the way I am. Maybe someone I should know, or who should know me? Maybe someone . . .

A SNAP, like a pistol crack, breaks Reba's trance. Even before she wrenches herself around, she knows it's not a gun, knows it's someone rapping at her window. Fucking Billy, scaring me like that! But it isn't Billy. A male face only inches away, not one I know.

The street lamp backlights him, making him all silhouette, no face. Head nodding like a bobble-head doll as he hops from foot to foot. A flashy grin. And then she solves him, his white teeth splitting his face like the Cheshire cat's. Old Blue Eyes.

"Hey, whatchoo doin' in there?"

Reba says nothing. Old Blue Eyes makes a show of shrugging his shoulders, turns, and ambles toward the subway, letting her take a good look at his swimmer's shoulders, his tight butt. Men are tricky, Reba thinks. Especially men you don't know. He could have friends with him. Muggers. Billy has said it a million times, never open the door. No matter what. Not that she has any cash, Billy takes the cash. She thinks of Maureen. How frightened she'd be right now. But Reba isn't frightened.

Fear is not the issue, the issue is Billy's wrath if she fucks up. What if the van gets stolen? Or a case of fruit? What if I get myself raped? Billy will never forgive me. The guy stops to light a cigarette. He seems to be alone. She cracks the door.

"Hey. You scared the shit out of me."

He blows out a plume of smoke. "Oh, you're talking to me now?"

"Fuck you."

"Lady has a mouth on her. Look, that apple was good. I just wanted to see if you had any more."

"You owe me thirty cents!"

"OK." He takes three steps toward the van, reaches into his pocket, pulls out pocket change and holds it out to her.

Reba shuts the door. "That's OK, you can keep it."

He comes closer. "Why you locked up in this van?"

"I'm waiting."

"What? I can't hear you." Smokin'. Grinnin'.

She rolls the window down a crack. "I said I'm waiting."

He stands now so that Reba can see his face. He's fidgety and calm at the same time, turning every now and then as if to make sure Billy is nowhere around. In profile, his high forehead, strong straight nose, his jawline are like something out of a magazine.

He places his hands on either side of the window and leans into her, speaks onto the glass. "For the Second Coming? Or for your boyfriend?"

"My *brother*, remember him? The big guy? If he catches you here he'll kick your ass to kingdom come. Just for fun."

"And maybe I'll kick his ass . . . just for fun. This brother of yours, he ever been in prison?"

"No. Have you?"

"Not saying I have, not saying I haven't."

"Look, I don't care if you've been to prison or what. All I

know is, you can't stay here. You can have another apple, then you have to go away because Billy has a temper and he will hurt you. He doesn't care about prison or any of that, he's just very strong and good at fighting." Maybe this boy has a knife or a gun himself? Maybe he's dangerous?

"I don't want another apple." He drops his cigarette and steps on it.

"You asked me if I had any more." So beautiful.

"But I didn't say I wanted one. You shouldn't jump to conclusions. It can get you in trouble. I just feel good knowing there are more. Makes me feel secure. I'm the kind of person who wants to be sure that I can get what I want in an emergency. Because in this world, good things are hard to find."

"Right." She doesn't want to sound angry, but everything comes out that way.

"So, he just locks you up here all night?"

"Not all night. Just for an hour or so. He hangs out with his buddies and has a beer. Not that it's any business of yours."

"I don't give a shit what he does. I was asking about you. Kind of pathetic, you know, seeing you all imprisoned and shit."

"I'm not imprisoned. I can get out any time I want. Besides, he'll be back soon."

"Want to go get a beer with me?"

Reba rolls the window all the way down. "I don't even know you! I'm not going anywhere."

"That's about the dumbest thing I've ever heard. How old are you?"

"Listen, A, I have to guard this truck and B, they'll card me, C, Billy won't know where I went to."

"Look at me. Come on. You're smart. Look at me. What do you see?" He stops smiling. Is he being serious?

Reba won't meet his eyes, then does. "That's stupid." She feels high like the time she tried smoking one of her mom's cigarettes.

"Do you think I would plan some kind of complicated thing where I would steal an apple in the afternoon and then come by to the same place at night so I can, what, kidnap you? Seriously."

"I don't know. Yeah. Maybe."

"Dude, I saw your brother. I'm not going to fuck around. One beer. One."

"Don't call me dude. And listen, what's your name . . . ?"

"Dallas . . ."

"Dallas . . . look." She forgets what she's going to say.

"Reba, can I be honest with you? You're probably the prettiest girl I've seen in five years. I know you've got like a million guys in your life, but gimme a chance. Please?"

"Don't bullshit me, it's offensive."

"I know a place two minutes from here where we can get a beer. Come on. One beer. We'll leave a note, let Big Bro' know where we are. You'll be back before he is."

If they spend any more time talking, Billy is going to show up and hurt this guy. No reason to see his sweet face get all smashed up. "Ten minutes."

"Ten minutes. At most, eleven."

THE DOOR YAWNS AND BRUTAL GRAY WHITE BOUNCES off the unfinished wallboard. From where he's lying, Billy can see patches of spackle and tape where the workmen have left the job unfinished. Must have forgotten to get around to painting it. Wonder if they're orientals, too? A shiny poster for some kind of chink hair product is taped to the wall. Chinese. Or might be Japanese, how would anyone know? The only other things in the room are a small dresser topped with a lamp and the towel-covered table upon which Billy now lies naked.

The delicate black-haired girl gently shuts the door and the room returns to its peaceful dimness. Perched on the floor, the fake Tiffany table lamp warms the walls, creating the illusion of luxury. Billy sits up. The flimsy dressing gown of red satin embroidered with symbols, probably Chinese, like the poster, like her, slides off the girl's thin shoulders. In white panties, she leans over him and massages his shoulders and he catches the scent of jasmine. Her face is only inches from his, she smiles as she kneads him. Billy wonders if she has a brother.

"Lay back, I wash." As usual she's brought a small tray upon which lies a warm folded towel, like the kind you get in sushi bars. Which came first, the little towel in the sushi bar or the little towel in the whorehouse? She swabs his privates, her efficient determination reminding Billy of his mother cleaning the oven. Reba never cleans the oven. She wouldn't know how.

Billy can feel himself expanding in her tiny hands. She raises her eyes to him, wary. "How you feel? Good?"

"Um-hmmm. Sure."

"That's nice. Relax." Rub. Rub. "You work hard this week?"

"Yeah." No point in saying more. Over the past two months, Billy's figured out her English vocabulary is limited to about twenty-five words.

"I know. You need take it easy. OK. Good. You want massage?"

"Yeah. Massage."

He lies on the table, passive, inert, the way dogs at the vet's lie still, eyes open, just before they're put to sleep. He debates asking her for something besides a massage. Must be all kinds of things she'd be willing to do. But a massage is all Billy knows how to request. He's been told that it's safe to do that, because a "massage" is legal. On both sides. No law against him asking for one. No law against her giving him one. Any accidents that might happen during a vigorous rubdown are simply the results of human reflexes. He watches her expression as she manipulates his flesh. She's intently serious until she catches his eye. Then she smiles again, as if suddenly remembering to.

"You want Diet Coke? Mango juice?"

"No. No. I'm OK." Billy feels fat and helpless. "You're very pretty."

"Thank you very much. You also pretty, I mean, handsome. You handsome man. Big. Strong. Very big."

"Maybe too big? Fat. Big fatso."

"No!! You not fat. You strong. Muscle man." She giggles and brings her hand to her mouth. "You good man. I know."

But he is too big and he can't deny it. That's OK. Probably most of the guys who come here have something wrong with them. Probably a lot of assholes. She says I'm a good man. Probably doesn't tell every Tom, Dick and Harry that. What does being a good man mean to a hooker? Does that mean she likes me?

Billy wishes he could take her in his arms and kiss her on the mouth, but he's pretty sure that would cost extra. It's important to stay within the budget. And this isn't so bad, keeping things simple. He can watch her, get excited, get himself worked up. Only problem is, she has it down to a timetable, spending a specific amount of energy on his arms and legs and chest and then on to the inevitable.

Billy allows himself the luxury of thinking of this slim, dark-haired goddess as his girlfriend. Truth is, he's begun to think of her that way even when he's back at the farm. He's told the guys at the filling station that he has been "seeing" a girl in the city. And in a way, it's true. And it could be more true. I could take her out to dinner one night. Maybe see a movie. That's entirely within the realm of possibility. I could pay her to do that, too.

Once the apple business takes off, I can come by here with a lot more money. Whatever the expense, it wouldn't matter. I'd just pay it. Just tell the mama-san I'm taking her out for the

night. Why would she say no? And then when she knows me better, she might get to like me. Really like me. By being so noble
and pure and taking her out to a restaurant that's really nice,
maybe someplace in Chinatown. Bet if she is Chinese or whatever, she'd probably be impressed. Could order lobster in black
bean sauce, bet she'd like that. Then we could stroll around for
an hour or so, come back here and do this, too. She might even
let me kiss her.

Does she feel what I feel? She probably doesn't call every guy
who comes in here a "good man."

Next time I come by, I'll bring her a sack of apples. She'd like
that. Everyone likes fresh apples. She probably has an old
grandma somewhere in the slums of Chinatown she has to take
care of. She could bring the apples to the old Chinese grandma.
Do Chinese ladies make pie?

The girl is getting down to the special part, what the black
dirt onion farmer who had brought Billy by in the first place calls
"happy ending." She's been taking her time. But now she's
pulling and stroking Billy with the finesse of a milkmaid. I'm so
predictable. She knows something about me I don't even know
about myself. Wish I could hold back. Wish I could feel this way
forever. But here it comes, that moment when the whole thing
skids like a pickup truck on black ice, no way to control it.

Billy wants to grab her and press her warm skin against his.
Hold her close and not let go. Feel her tiny heart in her tiny chest
beating against his. Have that thing that everybody else in the
world has, even for half a minute. "Happy ending." Well, I'm
not the happiest guy in the world, but it's better than nothing.

BEER MAKES YOU ALL LOOSE. BEER MAKES YOU FEEL good and beer makes you pee. Beer is a good thing, probably the best invention mankind ever invented. Plus beer lets folks be themselves. Which is fun, especially with this Dallas guy. Because he kind of knows what he's doing and that's pretty damn cool. It's like watching an arsonist light up an old dry building. Whenever I open my eyes, he opens his. And they just get bluer and bluer. He also seems to be thinking what I'm thinking. Is that possible? Is there such a thing? Wait a minute. Stop. I have something important to say, but I can't remember what it is. "Your . . . your roommates."

Dallas pauses. "My roommates . . . ?"

"They'll see us . . ."

"We're only kissing." Dallas strokes her hair. Reba lets her jaw go slack as she kisses him. Like a guppy in a fish tank, she thinks.

"Are we? Oh, right." Reba is pretty sure they're doing more than kissing but she can't say exactly what that might be. Where has the cat gone? And where exactly am I? Still on the couch? Maybe I'm drunker than I think I am. Is that possible? Of course it is, silly. That's the way car accidents happen. That's how other things happen, too. Does it make any difference? No, it does not make any difference where the cat is or where I am or whether or not I'm drunk.

Dallas says, "Do you want to go into my room? Is that what you're saying?"

"Isn't this your room? I thought you lived here?"

"I mean where I sleep."

"I don't want to go to sleep. Wait a minute! Your room? As in bedroom? Where the bed is?" Everyone here is drunk. I'm drunk, he's drunk and the cat's drunk.

"Yeah, you wanna do that? Go there?" Reba can see a figure

over Dallas's shoulder. The figure runs his palm along the cat's arched back, then snatches it up and the cat says something, but Reba can't make it out. Dallas turns toward the stranger and says, "Dude."

The stranger, holding and stroking the cat, says, "I have to talk to you, man." Reba can't see his face very well.

Dallas says to Reba, "This is one of my roommates, Chud. His real name is Chad, but we call him Chud. Chud, this is . . . shit, I don't even know your name."

"Reba." Don't tell him your last name.

"Rena."

"Reba! With a 'b'!"

"Nice to meet you, Rena. Listen, dude, I still need to talk to you. When you got a spare minute."

Reba wants Chud to understand how to pronounce her name, but he's left the room. Reba punches Dallas in the chest. "You got me drunk, didn't you?"

"You haven't even had two beers, you can't be drunk."

"I don't know. It's weird out here. Your roommate is weird. Let's go to your bedroom."

"I don't want you to do anything you don't want to do. In fact, maybe you should be getting back."

"Don't tell me what to do! I'm tired of everybody telling me what to do. If I want to go to your bedroom, I'll go to your bedroom. If I want to jump into your bed and fuck your brains out, I'll do that, too."

Dallas manages a serious twist to his lips and says, "OK."

Reba floats in an enormous black cloud. It roils and silent scratches of lightning flash every few seconds. In the cloud are voices of young men arguing. The blackness reformulates itself into walls and windows and the horizontal surface upon which she lies. Not the floor. But like a floor. Low. Flat. A foam mattress. She rolls onto her side, reaches out for Dallas and finds cool, vacant sheets. She considers sitting up and the world slips sideways.

Reba waits for Dallas to return and touch her again. So far he's done almost everything she's ever fantasized about. He's stroked her face, kissed her eyes. He's put his fingers in her, put his lips to her nipples. He's even massaged her toes, lifted her legs up over her head and kissed her ankles. He's told her over and over again that she's beautiful. Too beautiful for words. He said that he adores her.

He'd hesitated for a moment when he figured out she was a virgin, but it was only for a moment, mere seconds, then without a word, he pushed into her. And it burned for a few strokes but it was OK. It was all OK. She's glad she'd had the beer. She's glad she'd come here. She's gonna be in so much trouble with Billy but that's OK, too. Billy will have just to live with the new Reba. Everything is gonna be OK.

When Reba wakes a second time, Dallas has not returned to bed and the apartment is very still. A bright light has been left on outside the door and specks of dust float in the silver air. Finding her legs functional, she hobbles over to her jeans and sweater, tugs her clothes on, runs her fingers through her hair, rubs her face and goes to find her lover.

Chud and another young man sit at the kitchen table passing a joint between them, sucking the smoke in turns and cursing softly. Neither looks up at her, so she crosses the room, finds what appears to be a clean glass and fills it with tap water. She crosses the room again, past the two young men.

"Looking for your new boyfriend?"

"Excuse me?" Don't look at them.

"He split." The kid who speaks has jaundiced eyes and a patchy beard that doesn't quite connect to his sideburns. Reba can't smell him, but she's sure he smells bad. It's possible this is the Chud-guy she met earlier but the boy sitting across from him also has the same matted hair, same tattered beard. Two stoned and ugly guys and the last thing she wants to do is have a conversation with either one of them, whoever they were.

The boy offers up the smoldering bit. "S'up?" He grins. His teeth are mossy.

The other mumbles under his breath. Reba can't understand him, can't understand the situation. She feels naked. Where's Dallas? She walks out of the room.

The cat is asleep on the couch, curled around the spot where she and Dallas had been kissing. She collects the beer bottles, then not knowing where to take them, lines them up carefully beside the couch. She wanders to the communal bathroom. Dallas must be there.

The room is empty but the framed mirror hanging on the wall reveals a girl with rat's nest hair and puffy eyes. An unacceptable look. She has no intention of letting Dallas see her like this. Clothes wrinkled, skin mottled with sleep and beer and sex. He's left a hickey on her neck. And she doesn't even know his last name. Reba smiles at herself. "Well, you got what you wanted." She hammers her face with handfuls of cold water.

Chud or the other kid, she isn't sure which one, appears in the doorway. With a smirk, he says, "You like coke?" She shoves the door into his ugly face. Through the door he says, "Dallas left, you know. He's gone. And he's not coming back."

"Go away."

"You're awesome. Please talk to me."

"No."

"You can stay here if you want."

"Fuck you!"

The toilet seat is cold and smudged with an unidentifiable substance. Was that there when I was in here before? She crouches over it, trying not to make contact. Suddenly she's crying and peeing at the same time. There's no toilet paper. She wipes her eyes with her shirt and her crotch with her panties. A smear of pink.

She sticks the panties in her pocket. Sneaks out the door and Chud is gone. She passes the sleeping cat and leaves.

Reba puzzles her way back to the park. The van is gone. A false daylight from the vapor lamps saturates the mounds of cloth and cardboard heaped on the park benches. She gets lucky and finds an empty bench. Billy will be back sooner or later. Or maybe he's already back home, abandoning me, trying to teach me a lesson? I should call him. But he might be asleep by now. Plus I don't want to get yelled at. Better to stay put for a while.

A young woman who smells like mouthwash plops down next to Reba. "Got a smoke?"

"No. I don't . . . uh, no." Reba expects her to move on and find someone else, but she doesn't.

"That's what they all say. 'I don't smoke.' Listen, you smoke. In your heart, you smoke. I see it in your eyes. So if you're not smoking yet, you will. Never say never, baby. You know what I'm talking about?"

"OK. Yes." Reba turns and searches the vacant streets for Billy and the van. She can feel the lump of underwear in her pocket.

"You OK?"

"Yes." Reba faces the young woman again. She isn't all raggedy like the bums Reba has seen wandering around in the early morning when she and Billy unload the van. The kind of people Billy ridicules. This one has nice eyes.

The woman is shaking her head. "You can't win." Reba nods. "You know what I'm saying? What are you, nineteen, twenty? It's just starting, kid. Just starting. And you know what? Once it starts, it doesn't stop. Like a wheel going round. You think you're working the system, but the system's working you. Look at me, I'm twenty-four."

The woman looks older than twenty-four.

As if illustrating what she's saying, she points across the street. "He just walks out of the bar, you know? Leaves me there, drink in my hand. One minute, he's got his arms around me, lighting my cigarette, next, he's gone. So what am I supposed to do? He's got the keys, he's got everything. So I wait. I wait until the bar closes. What do you do with somebody like that?"

"Maybe you shouldn't go out with him anymore?"

The girl-woman laughs a raspy, cynical laugh much older than twenty-four years. She's missing a molar.

"You got any money on you, kid? Couple a bucks?"

"Not really."

"Oh, I'm not asking you for money, sweetheart. You think I'm asking you for money? Babe, I wouldn't do that to you! We're in this together. No. I'm just saying, if you had a buck or two, we could split a pint."

"Pint?"

"Wine. And not that Mad Dog. None a that shit. Good wine. Half bottle. Nice."

"I don't think the liquor stores are open this late."

"When there's a will there's a way. Look, we each throw in two bucks, we can have a little warmup. Whaddya say? Unless you're in a rush."

"I'm not in a rush."

The woman smiles warmly at Reba and Reba thinks, Billy will find me sooner or later, what else can I do? She takes out two dollars from her jeans pocket and hands it over. "I didn't get your name."

"Jean."

"I'm Reba."

"Reba, if you have another buck I can get a much nicer vintage."

"Well, let me see," Reba counts her cash. Jean snatches a dollar and makes off into the gloom. She approaches a man at the far end of the park who reaches under some shrubs and passes a package. Jean begs a cigarette off the guy and he lights it for her. Returning, she unwraps the brown paper twisted around a pint of Wild Irish Rose. She sits and smiles again. "I even have little paper cups. How's that for living?" She blows a stream of smoke up into the black underside of an overhanging branch.

"Great." Reba thinks, I can do this. They drink the wine.

Reba's head is heavy, she wants to lie down on the bench. But that would be so rude. Overhead the sky is turning brighter, even though here in the park, a mosaic of bright synthetic glow and pitch-black darkness covers everything. A chilly breeze flows through the shrubs and benches. The wine salesman at the other end of the park has left.

Jean's eyes are closed, young under all the makeup. But not as pretty as Reba had first thought. Her lips are thin and her nose is too thick. She looks like she's dressed to go to a party. Her perfume smells like something Maureen would wear to work. This woman is a complete stranger to me, but here I am sitting next to her, like we're best friends.

Jean's eyes flicker open and register displacement. She asks Reba, "What time is it?"

Reba checks her watch. "Five thirty."

"Fuck. Better get back to work. He'll kill me if he doesn't see me out there. You OK? You need anything?"

"I'm fine. I think. My brother's going to show up pretty soon."

Jean makes her way to the avenue. As if she's timed it, a car slows down and stops. Jean leans in to the driver, walks around the front of the car and gets in. The car drives off. Reba tucks her bag under her head and curls her legs up onto the bench.

A SCRAPING ECHOES THROUGH THE PARK AS A STOOPED figure in a frayed tuxedo drags something past the bench where Reba sleeps. A whoosh of fear and her eyes open. Billy has not found me. I am in the city, I am alone, as vulnerable as a deer being chased by coydogs. As vulnerable as . . . she completes the thought . . . as a girl alone in the city. In her pocket is a ten-dollar bill and a handful of change.

The dawn's silvery orange paints the buildings, cars, the worn asphalt and the street signs, even the few people propelling their way through the frigid air. The glowing street lamps hang in there, but it's a new day and it can't be stopped.

The ad on the pay phone promises CALL ANYWHERE for twenty-five cents a minute. She picks up the receiver. She dials. The phone in the farmhouse rings. Once. Twice. It'll be better if Billy yells at me on the phone. Gets it out of his system. Before it can ring a third time, Reba hangs up. If I don't want to talk to Billy, why am I calling him? There'll be plenty of time to take my knocks.

The ache in her belly charges the lightness in her heart. Shouldn't I savor this moment, not spoil it? Just pretend that Billy said it would be OK to spend a day on my own in the city? So here it is. The day. Hungry. Food.

A poster on the plate glass window of the McDonald's advertises a ninety-nine-cent egg-and-sausage breakfast. Reba goes in. In the restroom she scours her face. Someone has pasted a sticker onto the mirror and someone else has scraped it off, leaving a white circle in the corner. Someone else has scratched their initials into the glass. No paper towels, only hot air. It takes eight punches for Reba to dry her face.

A large woman in a blond wig prances into the restroom, stops and stares at Reba. Reba thinks, I'll fight you, sister, if I have to. But the woman looks away and Reba finds a stall two doors down, while the woman clacks around the washbasins. She's obviously waiting for me to come out so she can stare at me some more. Magic Marker lettering is scrawled on the enameled divider, so twisted Reba can't decipher it. This must be what it's like to be in a foreign country. When Reba emerges, the woman is gone.

Juggling a slippery plastic tray, Reba finds a seat along a wall. Including the city tax, breakfast has set Reba back two bucks.

It's good to get something warm into my gut, even if I have to eat it alone. Take-out coffee is better than no coffee. Any minute now, Dallas or Billy will walk in. I know it. I can feel it.

As Reba shoves her pile of crumpled napkins and cardboard into the trash bin, a cherubic man calls out to her. "Excuse me? Miss? Miss?"

"Are you talking to me?"

"Yes. I, uh, I'm sorry. Paul Yorkin. I was wondering what agency you're with?" He's short and bald and his teeth aren't so great. His smile looks forced. Kind of like the Lucky Charms guy. What is he? A leprechaun.

Reba says, "Agency?"

"Elite, right? They're supposed to be sending over all the new girls, but I haven't seen you yet. What's your name?" He squints slightly and his smile grows.

"I think you have me mixed up with someone else." This guy thinks I'm one of those limousine prostitutes.

"No I don't. I've seen your stuff. I know I have. For bebe, no . . . Aldo? You're on the billboard in SoHo."

"Uh, my stuff? No." Through the plate glass, the world out on the street is accelerating.

"Uh . . . *Mademoiselle,* last month, the piece on hand-knit sweaters. And, um, the Macy's print ad last week, right?"

"I don't think so." She towers over him and he's forced to look up to meet her eyes. He seems overheated in his bow tie and suit jacket, pulling a white handkerchief from his pocket to swab his wide brow. He's only slightly overweight, but his head is very round and he makes Reba think of an overgrown baby.

"You saw Gisele's layout in *Vogue Paris* this month? You saw it, I know you did. Mine. Prada campaign, mine. So listen, please have your agency, who are you with, Monique? Have her give me a call? Or maybe if you're in the neighborhood, you could drop off your book?"

"I think you've mistaken me for somebody else."

"Well, that's a very big mistake. How tall are you?" The man's eyes are the kindest she has ever seen. His face glows with sincerity. He's either the nicest man in the world or a con man.

"I don't know!"

"You're at least five eleven."

"Don't remind me. My family's a freak show."

His eyes glitter with delight. "Listen. Here's my card. I'd love to snap a few pictures. Bring in a stylist, the whole bit. Would you be up for that?"

"You mean for cash money?" She scans the card. It says "Paul Yorkin—Paris—Milan—London—New York" and a phone number. No addresses. Just a phone number.

"Money? Uh, no, no money. But I'll make a trade with you. I'll let you keep a few photos for yourself. If you like them, you can get them reprinted. Who knows? I'm just . . . it's unbelievable that no one's shot you yet. Are you new to New York?"

"Not really."

"I see. Uh-huh. All right. Well. Look. Uh . . . what are you doing right now? I don't want to lose track of you."

"Why?" I believe him even though I shouldn't.

"Well. I figure no time is better than the present. My studio's just around the corner. Very convenient."

"You can't take my picture right now, I've been up all night. I'm a mess."

"If this is you as a mess, I can't wait to see you when you're in good shape. I mean, you look terrific. Really, really terrific. And I love this cotton thing you have on. What is it? Diesel?"

"I don't know what it is. My brother makes me wear it."

"Listen, we don't have to make this into a major production. Just, uh, come by, wash your face, brush your hair, great hair by the way, and we'll just snap off a couple of rolls. Uh . . . it's totally cool. My assistant Adam will be there by ten and it's just a few blocks away. I mean, unless you have somewhere you're going. I'm sorry, what did you say your name was again?"

"Uh . . . Rena. R-E-N-A."

"Rena. Great name. Terrific name. Rena."

"Where is this place?"

"Literally around the córner. I shoot for everyone, *Vogue*, *Cosmo*, lots of editorial."

"*Cosmo?*"

"I had five pages last month. The furry hats."

"You took those pictures?"

"Of course! I wouldn't be caught dead in this friggin' place, but I had a big argument with those jerks at Coffee Shop two days ago and they banned me."

"Banned you?"

"They won't serve me until I apologize to the girl behind the counter and I refuse to, so there you have it, McDonald's coffee in the morning. Listen, I have to get to the studio, so what do you say? Come on up, it won't take long, I have people coming in at twelve so we can only grab a few shots." He wipes his brow again and smiles. Reba thinks, *Cosmo*. Furry hats. Cool.

BILLY STUDIES THE LIFE CYCLE OF THE PINHEAD BUBBLES rising through the amber to sudden death. Fucking whores. It's because I went to the whores again, because I screwed around. I knew that sooner or later something bad was gonna come of it. If this had happened when Dad was alive, I would have gotten the strap. But Dad is gone and now she's my responsibility. Damn.

Six hours ago Billy was orbiting the park, nursing a half-pint of Mr. Boston Peach Brandy. He figured to roll up from behind Reba and scare the shit out of her. But that hadn't happened. Instead he found himself negotiating a neighborhood of narrow lanes lined with cars parked bumper to bumper. Rusty fire escapes cantilevered off the facades of the brick walk-ups. Dark people stood in doorways next to trash cans with their lids chained together.

Under the bright shadow of a yellow and red awning, two nut-brown men tracked Billy as he got out of the van. He stepped past them into the bodega. One man flicked a cigarette into the gutter. The other chuckled.

Inside, the place was dense with sagging shelves of canned black beans, Kitty Litter, rolls of toilet paper, bottles of Mr. Clean and Odd Job. On the floor topless cardboard boxes lay loaded with plantains, sweet potatoes and shriveled green peppers. In the far corner stood another Latino playing a video blackjack machine, his right foot resting on a case of Malta. Sawdust had been strewn on the floor and the sharp scent of pine cleaner filled the air. A skinny cat with a scabby ear strolled by.

Two men stood barricaded behind a scuffed sheet of bulletproof plastic. One had a trimmed moustache and both wore fedoras. Behind them on a shelf, fitted in between the Pepto-Bismol and the pads of Lotto tickets, a small black-and-white TV spouted garbled Spanish.

For lack of anything better to do, Billy pulled Dallas's note from his pocket. One man, the one without a moustache, turned to him. *"Si?"*

"A girl come in here?"

"Girl?" On the TV screen a fat man was embracing a chesty bleached blonde.

"Yeah, like me. White. Tall, but skinny. Kind of pretty."

The companion mumbled something that sounded to Billy like "Ag-wa."

The man said, "No." He eyed the scrap of paper in Billy's hand. Billy felt his face flaring. "What you need, *papi?*" The man was relaxed, almost kindly.

"I just told you. Looking for a girl." More staring. "Listen, you speak English?"

"No girl here, *papi*. See?" His eyes flickered and died.

The men who had been standing in front of the store joined in. The guy at the video blackjack game stopped playing. Billy thought, I'm too tired for this shit. My back hurts. Fuck them. He waited. One of the men from outside said, "What's the problem?" But he wasn't talking to Billy, he was asking the men behind the counter.

Billy measured his speech, as if spelling it all out to a mentally handicapped person. "The problem is, my sister, she went off on her own and I'm asking you, *have-you-seen-her*?"

"Your sister?"

"That's right."

"No, man, we haven't seen your sister." The man who spoke followed the English with a few words of something, maybe Spanish, and the others chuckled, eyes crinkling.

Billy stepped up to the man at the video poker machine. "How about you, Chief, you see a girl in here?"

"*Que?*"

"Aw, fuck you all." Billy remembered he was wearing steel-tipped work boots. Kick that grin off your greasy brown mug.

The man from outside stopped smiling. "Hey, my friend, no swearing in here, you know?"

"Fuck you, too."

"That's not cool, man. You wan' us to call the police?" Now they didn't seem so smart-alecky. Now Billy wondered what he was doing in this smelly little grocery.

"I'm just asking for a little help."

"And we told you, man, we have not seen your *puta* sister." Someone snorted. Another chuckled. "That your truck out there, *flacco*? You should keep an eye on your truck."

Ugly brown fuckers. Greaseballs. Nosepickers. Fuck you. I'll come back here with my shotgun and take that grin off your ugly brown face. Billy left.

Outside, Billy pulled himself up behind the wheel and slammed the door. A shiver thrilled his spine, followed by a starburst of anger. I'm going to slap that bitch silly when I find her. He finished his bottle and threw it out the window as he drove away. Fuck 'em.

He drove around for another hour, ending up back at the farmer's market. Fatigue coated him like a layer of grease. Outside the van, the city lay motionless, its clamor lowered to a surflike drone. Billy fell asleep behind the wheel. Around four AM he roused himself, started the van and drove.

As he passed the meat market, a transvestite called out like Billy was the last man on earth. He gunned the engine and slid out onto the highway. A city of whores and spics. Someone should incinerate the whole fucking mess. Shouldn't even be down here in the first place. And where the fuck is Reba?

The sharp squirt of a police siren blanked Billy's thoughts. There they were, in his rearview, right up on him, lights spinning, red-white-blue. More. Always more shit. Billy pulled over.

The cops hung out in their cruiser for ten minutes before one emerged and came up alongside the van. As the cop wrote out the ticket for running the light, Billy realized he was sober again, so he pushed it. "My sister, she's missing."

The cop glanced back at his partner, who was in the cruiser running the van's plates. He pointed his flashlight into Billy's eyes. "What sister?"

"My sister."

"Why don't we do this, sir: just step out of the vehicle, keep your hands in sight?"

The officer ran the beam of his eighteen-inch Maglite over the contents of the van. "Anything in there doesn't belong in here you wanna tell me about? An unregistered firearm, for instance?" The other cop strolled over. The second cop rested his hand lightly on the butt of his gun. Maybe the computer had spit out something on the van. Billy thought, they are armed. You cannot run. Just answer the questions.

"You been drinking?" The second cop. Looks pissed off.

"I had a beer four hours ago. Listen, we come down here to work. She left a note and I can't find her." These guys are white, they'll help me.

"Uh-huh. This address here on your license, this where you're from?"

"Uh-huh. About three hours upstate."

"Well, sir, you better get back up there before you get into any more trouble." He handed Billy the license, registration and ticket. "Drive safely."

"What about my sister?"

"After twenty-four hours you can call in a missing persons complaint, sir, but I wouldn't hang too much on that. She'll show up sooner or later. How old is she?"

"Twenty."

"Uh-huh. Well, there you go." The other cop smirked. Fucking cops. Cops and niggers and whores and spics. Fucking Sodom and Gomorrah. Fucking cesspool. Septic tank shithole full of steaming shit. Fuck you. Unstrap that Glock and I'll kick your stinking ass. All of you. Creeps and bums. Creeps and bums.

At the kitchen table, Billy sips his beer as the world flows from the shadows and congeals. Down on the road, the intervals between the hum of the passing cars shortens. People heading for church. He takes the smallest sips now, fizzy white flashes popping along his visual periphery. Don't fall asleep, Billy! Because Reba is going to call and damn soon. She's probably not hurt. She always keeps the door of the van locked. No. She just strolled off, maybe to see a movie and then, idiot that she is, got lost on her way back.

This is the problem with women. They have all this good stuff, their prettiness, their warm boobs, their hair, their sweet soft hands. But they can't think logically for shit. Persist in getting themselves in trouble. And they do it knowing full well that if the trouble gets bad enough, some guy will always come and save their ass.

Think I'm gonna save you. But what if I'm not there? Did you ever consider that? What if you got caught up in something you can't get out of, and I'm not there to bail you out? The kitchen walls stand dumb, Felix the Cat ticktocks, Billy flips his empty into the bin and finds another. Bitches. Excuse me, but that's what you are. Nothing but trouble. Pretending to be stupid and weak, so some dumbbell will want to protect you. But what if you go too far?

This is the problem. They walk around so sure of themselves and they don't even know why. They don't know why they have power, they just know they have it. Like that time she thought I'd gone off to work and she left her bedroom door open a crack while she changed. Standing there in her little bra and panties. Those long legs of hers and the curve of her backside. Got hard, despite myself.

Locked the door, but as soon as I finished the deed, the shame started to eat me up. Couldn't believe what I'd done. Couldn't believe what I'd thought. The worst, most perverted thoughts about doing it with my own sister. My own sister, naked, spread for me, begging me. Begging me. "Please don't hurt me, Billy. It's my first time!"

Sometimes, Billy couldn't even look at her. But the more he tried to avoid watching his own sister, the more he had to. Found himself sneaking glances while she cooked for him, while she cleaned the house. And she only grew more beautiful. She blossomed, even if no one understood that she had, he did. And as she did, it got worse and worse. Leaving her undies around where he could find them. Prancing around the house in a bathing suit.

This is why I have to protect her, to keep her safe. This is penance for transgressing against her. If I can use all of my strength and mind and will to shelter her, then maybe eventually, my sin will fade. And above all, never show her any affection, because she might take it the wrong way. And even if she didn't, the tiniest grain of love might develop and grow into something horrible. Don't ever touch her. Don't ever smile at her.

The old walls glow with the hue of morning. Billy lays his head down onto his thick forearms, turning his face so he can keep close watch on the beer bubbles. He waits for the phone to ring. He thinks, I should whip her. She deserves to be whipped. He shuts his eyes and sleeps.

LIGHT TRAVELS INVISIBLY THROUGH THE AIR AND COMES to rest upon a surface—cloth, a jewel, skin. It streams through the tall loft windows, it pulses out of the hot halogen bulbs, or flares off shimmering office towers blocks away, reflecting sunlight a million miles old. Fill light, soft light, key light. Boxes of light, doughnuts of light, balloons of silk light. Light bounces off the brilliant aluminum-skinned umbrellas. Rim light, backlight, eye light. Light as palpable thing, shaped and sculpted, aimed and trimmed. Present and absent, echoed and burning. Illumination that lasts almost a full second, or that bursts with a pop, leaving only the tiniest trail of a sizzle tattooing the retina.

Adam holds a black meter up to Rena's face and calls out cryptic numbers to Paul. Paul spins dials on his camera and then, almost absentmindedly, snaps as the strobes pop one after another. Polaroids are yanked and flipped onto countertops and apple boxes. More huddling. Rena, with scoured face and brushed-out tresses, frail and looking slightly lost, stands alone on an enormous sheet of paper that loops onto the loft floor like a royal train.

Adam shifts the skeletal light stands and reflective sheets of white board and makes sculptures Rena can't understand. She tries to smile. If she were standing here without her clothes she could not feel more naked. No one says a word to her. This is a big misunderstanding. In another minute a TV camera crew is going to jump out from behind a wall. Ridiculing me, the farm girl, the knucklehead. "Surprise, it's all been a big joke!"

Paul abruptly scrunches his brow into his viewfinder, then looks up as if angry, as if to glare at her. He stares through her. He wipes his forehead. Rena is hungry again and her temples throb. Fatigue migrates up the insides of her skull like a toxic fungus. When she was washing, there was a spot of blood in her jeans. Is she still bleeding down there? Was that boy touching her only ten hours ago? This isn't working out.

"Do you like music?" Paul is bent over a set of Polaroids, checking them with a loupe. A wizard fishing through his box of spells.

Rena catches herself biting a cuticle. Her mouth is dry, gluey. Why are they torturing me like this? I'm ugly and too tall. Obviously, this guy Paul is bored to shit. Now, he wants to stop and listen to music. His assistant is grinning at me like a blond monkey. She says, "Look, I should probably get going. I'm supposed to be meeting my brother."

"Rena? Honey? Just keep your shoulders straight, face the window and then turn your eyes to me. No, keep your head turned. Just your eyes. Yeah, that's it." He still isn't looking at me. "What kind of music do you like?" Like a doctor when he hits your knee with the little rubber hammer. As if he doesn't really care.

"I like dance music."

"Oh, so do we. Adam?"

Adam puts aside the Leica he's been loading, strides to a mini-sound system scattered into a corner of the loft. He squats over a pile of CDs. His bleached yellow hair is cut short and ragged and he is incredibly skinny. On his T-shirt is emblazoned: PIG BOTTOM. And so far, he hasn't said a word. For twenty minutes Paul has been barking orders at him and Adam has done what he's told. Adam's smile is stiff, like the grimace of a beaten animal.

"You know what would be great, Rena?" Paul is studying her. He pesters his camera.

The exhaustion gnaws into her leg muscles, but she wants this, and she's screwing it up. She says, "I'm not really good at this. I'm sorry." She catches a scent of Dallas in her hair. The memory of the night grabs her like a demon, stroking her all over, blowing its sweet breath over her belly.

"No, darling, you are. You are. I know you are. You just have to relax. And listen to me when I say something."

"How do you know I'm good at this?"

"When I saw you eating that Egg McMuffin. I could tell just by the way you move your mouth. Now listen, honey, just pretend you're at home, in your bedroom or whatever and just, you know, dance. Can you do that for me?" The music wells up under Paul's words. Moby.

"Just dance?" Reba likes Moby.

"Like we're not even here. You're alone. Dancing by yourself. Like you do in your bedroom. You know what I mean?"

How does this guy know I dance in my bedroom? One thing is for sure, I'm not in my bedroom right now, I'm a million miles away from it, just like I always wanted to be and maybe this isn't going to last, but fuckit, here it is, dance to it. The Moby girl is calling her like a siren. Just dance and let this guy throw you out and go home to Billy and let Billy holler. And then you can go to bed and sleep. But for now, fuckit, dance. She opens her eyes and sees Paul and Adam watching her and it's all so stupid. Suddenly she can't stop laughing. And now Paul is smiling, too! And then she says, "No. Not like this!" and she covers her face, peeks out and he takes her picture again!

"That's very nice, Rena!" He's shouting over the music.

"This is so retarded!" She thrusts her arms by her side in frustration, Paul takes a picture. She points at him. "Stop!" He takes another picture.

"No, you're wrong! It's wonderful. You're wonderful. You're doing just fine. Just keep moving. Dance. Let the music get inside you. And then don't forget to look at the camera. Eyes, it's all about your beautiful eyes."

He's telling me he likes me. He said, "Wonderful."

The strobes flash, saturating her with blinding whiteness. She moves and moves again, Adam cranks the volume and she lets it all go. For the second or third time in twelve hours she's having feelings she can't identify—a combo platter of fear, excitement, depression and confusion.

But the camera doesn't know feelings. It collects the movement of the muscles and the eyes, records the shadows of structured illumination and tells a story in chapters $1/250$ th of a second long. If a girl is laughing, that's the story. If she's got wonderful hair and she's laughing, then she's laughing about something wonderful.

"You were such a good girl! You want to look at the digital stuff? Adam, show Rena the digital."

Rena peers into the back of the camera. It doesn't seem like much but it doesn't look terrible, either. "I'm not so bad, am I?"

"No, you're not. You're very pretty. We'll develop these and see what we've got. I think they're going to be super. Really wonderful." A buzzer sounds. "Fuck, they're here. Rena, leave me a number and I'll call you tomorrow. OK?"

"I don't have a number. I'm . . . I'm moving."

"Oh, shit. Then you have to promise to call me tomorrow, OK? Please don't forget?" His voice rings hollow, promising nothing.

"No, I mean, of course not. And thank you."

Voices echo from the tiny elevator outside. Paul greets them. "Hey! Look who's here!"

A throng of young women and men invade the room. As Paul

flies past Rena he gives her a peck on the cheek, "Tomorrow," then disappears into a back room. The new people give Rena the once-over, but no one says hello. Slicing kiwis and mangos in the kitchen, Adam seems to have forgotten her. So Rena leaves.

She lets the pathways of the city determine her bearing. I'm one of them now, the people I used to watch from the farmstand. Most of them know where they're going. Do I? Rena passes a woman flopped down on the filthy sidewalk, her back against a wall, head bowed, a piece of cardboard in front of her. What does it say? "I am sick, anything helps. Even a penny."

The nice leprechaun is just fooling with me. Screwing with my head. What do I think, I'm going to be a model? Ugly girls don't become models. Stupid fucking girls don't become models. But still, I could stay here. I could become one of these people. I could be like that girl on the bench in the park. I could do a lot of things, I don't have to go home. It isn't home anyway. Home is where the heart is and I don't know where my heart is. I could stay here. The city will take care of me.

A sunburned boy ambles by. He asks Rena for a cigarette. He's shoeless and shivering. His pupils are minuscule, his skin raw and crusted with crud. Rena says she doesn't have a ciga-rette but before she's finished her sentence, he's moved on, mut-tering. He'd never actually looked at her.

RICK ABANDONS HIS FAMILY. AS USUAL, HE'LL DRIVE, find a place to stop, get out of the car and smoke a cigarette. Laura always smells the tobacco if he smokes in the car, so he has to get out. Not many things make her angry, that does. He'll have his cigarette and come home with some sort of wretched peace. Why am I so nuts? The smallest thing pisses me off. Why?

Last week it was the lint in the dryer, this week it's a burned-out lightbulb in the bathroom.

He finds himself in the old suburb, blindly zeroing in on his parents' crummy split-level. Mom sold it years ago. And now good old Dad lives in Arizona behind the walls of his gated community, where his other children and his other grandkids come visit. Dad reinvented himself a long time ago, minus Rick and his mother, and it makes him happy.

During his own visits to the desert, Rick makes a commitment to spend one whole afternoon with his father. This usually means driving around, hitting golf balls, drinking. When they depart the compound Dad waves to the security guard, a black fellow from Haiti. Probably doesn't even know the guy's name. Doesn't matter as they roll out into the day, Rick knows his dad feels secure. His life is composed of rituals: rinsing off the car with a garden hose, stocking up on frozen food and toilet paper, watching HBO, folding the laundry, fretting over the high electric bills, schtupping his wife, maybe.

Rick and his dad chop their way through a short round. Rick can beat the old guy now, but it doesn't make any difference. They both know who's the better golfer, the better man. They both know who has the hairier chest, the bigger biceps. In the clubhouse, Rick gets wasted on whiskey and soda and expounds on intra-abdominal pressure and its effects on hemorrhoids. The kind of practical medical advice he's expected to give the old man when he visits. After three stiff drinks, the ride back to the gated community is a pleasant blur. As they enter, Dad waves to the Haitian guy and Rick waves, too.

Contemplating the cacti and the shiny parked Mercedes and Chryslers within the complex, Rick thinks of his mom living alone in an overheated apartment building next to a Dunkin' Donuts. She doesn't drive anymore and uses a laundry cart as a walker on her way to the supermarket. She eats a lot of donuts, doesn't have cable. Rick makes a point of visiting her once a month to partake of her lousy cooking.

Rick's parents of today are nothing like the parents Rick knew growing up in Bergen County. That mom and dad of childhood past were not white-haired and feeble but volcanic and stubborn. They were spirited, hard-drinking people who prosecuted arguments with religious fervor, screaming and yelling and slamming doors so hard the little house shook. The place itself was just a kennel for mad dogs and Rick made a run for it as soon as he could get a driver's permit.

He drove away to college and never came back. Years later, when he feels confused, he returns and lets the toxic fumes of his childhood osmotically infect his memory. Memories are known quantities, like old friends, familiar. He thinks to himself, yes, pain. But interesting pain. And mine. The one thing I really, really own.

When Rick was small, boys from down the street would come by and say, "Can Rick come out and play?" When they got him alone they would punch him in the head or kick him in the balls. When he'd complain to this mother, she'd say, "Tell your father." When he told his father, the old man would lecture him to go back and hit them first before they could do their damage. One day, as he was being taunted, Rick jabbed a fist into the nose of one of the "bad boys." While the kid cried and bled all over his jersey, an older brother slapped Rick in the face until he fell to the ground, then kicked his ribs and made him eat dirt.

In Rick's old neighborhood, when it snowed, the plowed drifts by the side of the road turned gray within hours. In the spring the beetle-gnawed trees lining the streets would not bud and leggy weeds infected the lawns. No one cleaned up the dog shit. With its splintery telephone poles and patched asphalt, the neighborhood discouraged happy thoughts. Rick's crappy little house with its torn window screens and blistered green trim was like a set in a movie about disadvantaged people.

The only respite was the sky blue ranch house across the street. The cheerful tint would buoy Rick up. It said to him, "Happy people exist, they live across the street in that blue house." In fact, the people who lived in that house were Catholics and before Rick was five he had made the association between the sky blue of the house and the Vatican. He knew that inside that house, the air didn't stink of canned air freshener and Winstons the way his mom's did. He knew that their furniture was new and unbroken. He knew the parents were usually in good humor, always busy. And the little girl who lived there, Louise, was very appealing. Like her folks, she was always smiling. She had a scrubbed, clean look and she wore fresh clothes every single day.

Until Rick was six, before his neighborhood pals began to beat his ass regularly, Louise was his only playmate and the two children spent hours tripping around her neat patch of lawn or exploring the ancient railroad tracks that ran across a field behind the subdivision. They were equals, she and he, colleagues in their nascent world of lost teeth and scraped knees. Rick knew she was smart because she could tie her shoes months before he could. Rick was very happy when he was with her. In fact, he was as in love with her as he would ever be with anyone.

A mangy hedge grew alongside Rick's house. It had been planted there to cover the mystical electric meters. Invisible to casual passersby, a slender dog path ran between the house and the hedge, creating a perfect hiding place for Rick and Louise. They spent hours in their "secret place."

Rick knew Louise was more than a friend. She was a girl, and Rick had heard interesting things about girls. So Rick bribed Louise with his prized possession, a small cherrywood pirate's chest. In the chest lay trinkets he had collected from the bubble gum machines at the supermarket. Ornate tin rings, baby Troll Dolls with crazy hair, plastic charms for a nonexistent charm bracelet. Rick let Louise take her pick in exchange for one precious favor.

And so, behind the privet, where no one could catch them, little Rick took his first step down the long winding road of feminine mystique. He would squat so his eyes were only inches from the navel of his little girlfriend and watch as she wrestled her diminutive trousers and cotton panties (freckled with miniature blue blossoms) down over her white thighs.

The texture of the combed cotton, the blue printed flowers, the scent of fresh laundry burned onto Rick's memory. And of course, the soft flesh, unblemished. The essence of femininity. The essence of beauty. Vulnerability. Softness. Mystery. As Rick knew intuitively, this precious perfect thing was it—the apple in the Garden of Eden. This was the central problem of the female, the puzzle of the girl, the nexus of all mystery, the conundrum to end all conundrums.

Would he be punished for this evil deed? Was someone coming, would he be caught? But no one knew. No one saw him seeing her, examining her, playing doctor. A lone robin redbreast hopped among the dandelions, cocked his head. Maybe this was Louise's Catholic God-man keeping an eye on things? Could someone's God cross the street if the sin were bad enough?

Six months after Rick learned Louise's secret, she moved away, as if to get back at him. From then on, it was all about fists and dirt-eating and Rick missed her very much.

Now Rick sits in his car in the midst of the older and poorer neighborhood. He thinks, I loved that little girl. No, better than that. She was my friend. But he can't remember how it felt. The neighborhood is strangely empty today, refusing to entertain him. He starts the car and drives home to his wife and children.

A YOUNG MAN WITH SILVERED DESIGNER SUNGLASSES cocked atop his gelled hair steers Rena into his boss's office. Leaded-glass windows frame a stately sycamore under which the city traffic crawls. Classical cello bleeds into the room, absorbed into the thick white carpet, the heavy drapes. There are at least six sprays of red roses. And on the enormous glass coffee table stands a crystal vase choked with white lily stalks. The scent of the flowers compete with aromas of coffee, cigarettes and perfume.

A woman in a muumuu is poised by the window talking on a phone. She smiles at Rena. On her desk lie enlargements of Paul's photographs. When Rena reaches the center of the room the woman hangs up and floats toward her, eyes twinkling. She takes Rena into her arms. Under the silk, Rena can feel the soft pillowy folds of the woman's flesh. Despite her heaviness, she is possessed of the most lovely, perfectly made-up face. Like a porcelain doll, thinks Rena. The woman in the muumuu draws back, takes Rena's hand and says, "Hello, there, little girl!"

Rena says, "Hi."

"I couldn't wait another minute to meet you!" Her wholesome scent reassures Rena. "Would you like some coffee? Some water?"

Rena says, "Water," and the young man with the gelled hair leaves the room.

Marissa eyes Rena with an expression of hunger. She says, "Wow." Rena grins with embarrassment. "Paul told me, but seeing you in person. Wow."

Rena had washed her hair at Paul's, he lent her clothing left behind by clients. Adam helped her with her makeup. They let her crash in a back room. "What did Paul tell you?"

"He didn't have to tell me! The pictures tell me. Did he show you the pictures?"

"Yes."

"We're going to have a great time together."

"That's good. I think." Rena laughs.

"Have you been signed before?"

"Signed? No. Nothing. Ever. Before."

"And where's your family from, Rena?"

"Upstate."

"Upstate. Wonderful. I love it up there! Some great friends of ours have a place in Columbia County. Do you know Columbia County?"

"Sort of. Not really."

"How old are you, Rena? I'm sorry, please sit down." Marissa sails over to a long white couch strewn with Moroccan pillows. Rena sits, trying not to touch the fragile-looking array.

"I'll be twenty-one pretty soon."

"Oh, you look so much younger! That's wonderful! So we won't need your parents to co-sign."

"Um. My parents are dead."

"Oh, darling. I'm so, so sorry." Marissa takes Rena's hand.

"It's OK. So, um, are you saying you have a job for me?" Marissa continues to hold her hand and Rena wonders if she's a homosexual like the guy with the gelled hair.

"Oh, I think there will be lots of work for you. Paul really captured you, but now that I see you in the flesh, I think we can keep you occupied. Are you going to school, have a job?"

The console on Marissa's desk beeps and a nasal voice announces, "Marissa, it's Randy."

Marissa pauses, calculates, releases her hold, presses a button on the console and says sharply, "Tell him I'm running out and you can't catch me."

"He says it's important."

Marissa picks up the phone. "Hi." She's sweet again. She nods her head, listening, keeping her eyes on Rena. She lights a cigarette, miming an offer of one to Rena, who shakes her head no. She inhales deeply, gushes smoke and says, "Not possible. I don't care, Randy. Because with her you attract all the others. Deal first or no go. No. OK. Gotta go."

Marissa hangs up and beams at Rena. She says, "I can't believe how beautiful you are. You are nothing short of perfect."

Rena feels confusion. "No, I'm not."

"We'll see." Marissa stubs out her cigarette as if angry at it. "So you were saying you go to college here in the city?"

"No. Actually, I . . . I'm sort of free at the moment."

"Taking some time off. Good. Well, I think it's time you got busy."

"You'll hire me?"

"Hire you? Darling, we're an agency. We send you out. We take care of you. More. How's your living situation?"

"Living?"

"Do you have a place?"

"Not really. I've been kind of staying with friends." Don't tell her that Paul let me stay at the loft.

"We'll help you with that. We'll help you with everything. We're going to have a great time. First you'll do a few go-sees. Just with the best people. Paul already loves you so he'll give you some work. But he's very high end. I don't want you learning the ropes with him. You should start with some easy stuff. Generic catalogue. Just to get your feet wet. You'll have so much fun, you'll see. Does that sound nice?"

"Yes." Rena exhales and her face grows hot. Oh, God. Emotion. Don't cry. Don't cry in front of this nice woman, you look ugly when you cry.

"Good. Anthony will bring in the papers. Let's get that out of the way so we can start booking you. Sound good?"

"Yes. Uh . . . Marissa?"

"Yes, dear."

"One thing?"

"Anything."

"Do you have a bathroom?"

"Please!" Marissa opens a small door in the corner revealing a small powder room done in pale blues and browns. Rena heads for it.

"Rena?" Rena turns, thinking, wrong move. "No drugs. Right? I don't have to say that, do I?"

"Uh, no."

"I'm sorry. It's been a messy year. Kate. All that. You know."

"Yes." Rena says this as if she knows what Marissa is talking about.

Another bathroom, another mirror. Rena checks her hair, her makeup. I look good. I look very good. And I won't have to stay at Paul's anymore. She's going to take care of me. Oh thank you God. Thank you Jesus. I'm going to make you proud. I am the girl who can do it. Right here, right now. In the city, I am going to do this. I am going to be a model. This lady might be crazy, but why not? My eyes are nice. I knew that already. And my lips aren't bad. And I'm blond and tall. That's what they want, right? As long as you're not actually ugly. Maybe in New York they have a different standard. Want a different look. The white trash look? Who cares? Doesn't matter. Here I am. Here I am. Rena smiles at her reflection. My teeth are good, too. See?

Within the hour Rena is signed to a three-year personal services contract. The agency takes care of all her needs. Marissa finds her a place to live on the Upper East Side with two other girls who model for the agency. She's issued a small expense allowance and instructed where to buy clothes, buy makeup, where to go for dry cleaning. Appointments are made for facials, waxings, hair conditioning, manicures and teeth bleaching. Finally, she's handed a miniature TV set as a "welcome aboard" present, an empty portfolio for all the clippings she'll soon have and a Dolce & Gabbana knapsack for her "go-sees." She can use Paul's pictures for the time being. It's almost overwhelming.

Before the week is over Rena is so busy, she doesn't have time to go on "go-sees." A friend of Paul's gets her into an editorial shoot about head scarves for *Teen Vogue*. Marissa finds her a job down on Grand Street doing a flyer for a New Jersey department store. For that she has to wear a nightie and a cotton jersey. Marissa forbids underwear ads, says Rena is too special for that. On the following Thursday Rena gets a paycheck for $750 minus taxes and her allowance, almost double what she and Billy ever made at the farmstand.

Rena figures she'll call Billy on her day off, but there is no day off. She doesn't call Frank, either. Probably burning bridges, but some bridges should be burned.

A month in, she celebrates by buying two bottles of wine on her way home. She plans to share it with her roommates, but no one comes home that night.

She wakes up at four, the bedroom lights dazzling, guffaws gurgling from the little gift TV. Rena's first thought is, oh god, I still have my makeup on! Get out of bed and wash your face, girl! She staggers to the bathroom, gets everything off and collapses back onto the bed.

Morning. Saturday again. All the girls sleep till noon, if home. Rancid and foggy, Rena pads around the hushed apartment and finds the phone. She dials the number while she sips juice. After five rings, she gives up. Relief flows with the reprieve. Then concern. Where the fuck are you, Billy? Maybe you're here in New York, at the farmstand? Of course, it's Saturday, that must be where you are! Rena swallows four extra-strength Excedrin and showers. Head throbbing, she finds an empty cab on the street.

Using the cab as vantage point, Rena circles the old spot. The guy who sells the whole wheat bread is there, but there's no sign of Billy, no sign of the van. The place feels abandoned, too cold. If Billy isn't at the farm, and he isn't here, where the hell is he? She calls the house again and lets the phone ring ten times. No one at home.

The train ride along the empty river takes up the rest of the day. The cityscape of buildings and pedestrians, storefronts and honking traffic, falls away and the sight of one lonely barge propelling against the dark current tranquilizes Rena. By the time the train creaks and hisses into the station, she's napping, pretzeled into the hard seat. She finds a driver finishing off a late lunch of cheesesteak and fries in the back of his cab and gives him directions to the farm.

As they pass through town, the guy lights a cigarette and cranks the window. Probably has a freezer full of frozen venison at home. Rena wants to tap him on the shoulder and ask, "Have you ever heard of a girl named Reba Cook? Do you know where I would find her?"

Here it is. Still here. The gravel drive, the lawn, the back steps. Rena gets out of the cab, runs up the steps and knocks. Nothing. She puts her key in the lock and oddly it still turns. She takes a breath as she enters and it all rushes back, but with the added scent of winter heat. Burned black residue stains the stove enamel, the sink is crowded with glasses and beer bottles and the counters are cluttered with empty KFC cartons and gray, dry wing bones. Black grains of rice lie sprinkled over gnawed scraps of hand soap. Mouse shit. Sorry, Billy, I'm not going to clean up your mess.

Upstairs, evidence of Billy's life minus a sister is scattered about like crime scene trash. In the corner of the bathroom, a musty towel molders where it has been kicked. The bedroom floor is littered with underwear, T-shirts, socks and beer bottles. Under Billy's bed lies a stack of *Maxim*s and a mound of crumpled Kleenex. The thick aroma of his skin rises up off the yellowed sheets.

In the bathroom Rena turns the tap. Three floors beneath her, the well pump clicks on, sucking and pushing aquiferous water up to her. The furnace grumbles, heating the water. Outside, a breeze waffles at the windowpanes and a scraping branch screeches like a tiny witch along the siding of the house.

Rena checks the window, looking for rain. A dim, overcast day. Sunset will be here soon. Then only blackness. Wouldn't mind being out there. In the black, in the nothingness.

In her dad's closet Rena finds a scuffed Samsonite suitcase

and into it she packs her clothing, makeup, hair dryer and CDs. She leaves her boom box in Billy's room and drags the suitcase downstairs, pausing in the kitchen, thinking maybe she should take the frying pan, too. Felix watches, swishing his tail in irritation. No more cooking for now.

The cabbie fits her luggage into the sooty well of the trunk and Rena asks him to wait five more minutes. He shrugs, returns to the front seat, folds his arms over his chest and shuts his eyes.

By the time she gets to the orchard the tops of her shoes are soaked with the evening's dew. She stands still in the center of the arbor and waits, her breath trickling out into a white vapor. This is the best thing about this place, to be able to stand completely still, lean way back and let the clouds drift over your head as the breezes sift through the trees. Most of the foliage has fallen and leafless twig fingertips cling to the summer's mummified brown apples. The chickadees hop from branch to leafless branch, chiding her.

Rena calls out "Billy!," willing her brother to appear. Only the frozen quiet answers. She thinks, this is the world. It cannot be destroyed, it will always be here. It doesn't miss me when I'm gone and it doesn't care if I come back.

THE PILLS IN HIS POCKET RATTLE TO THE RHYTHM OF his step as he makes his way down Broadway. He claws them out and tosses them onto the ground. The beat keeps clicking in his head. Like rocks in my head. Like a bad motor. Monkey mind-controllers. All part of the system. How can you beat it? No answer to that one. Feet hurt. Need food. Always need food.

No point stopping at the police station to complain, they don't want to hear it. At first they did. Even took some notes.

But after a month or so, they'd had enough. Too busy. Told me they were going to lock my ass up again if I didn't get lost. So I got lost. Can't fight city hall. Then the van got towed. Tried to file a stolen vehicle report. They laughed at me, told me to go to a detox. Bunch of niggers and spics anyway. Who needs them?

I know they don't like the way I look. I don't like it, either. But I didn't choose these clothes. They're not my clothes. This sweatshirt's pink, for god's sakes. The pants have a drawstring. I hate drawstrings. Sneakers way too large. Damn things keep slipping off. All worn through on one side. White socks all black. Holes. But where am I s'posed to wash 'em. In a mud puddle?

Reba sent checks to the house. Never been so drunk in my life. Brainstorm: have the checks forwarded to a mail drop in the city and then I won't have to do so much traveling.

I knew what she was up to. Maureen at the bank showed me in a magazine as hard as that was to believe. But you call the agencies and no one knows nothing. Told that one rude lady to go fuck herself. Then couldn't get through anymore. Somehow the word got out about me and that was it.

Hang around in front of the buildings, watching the giraffes coming and going with their photo albums under their arms. Try to look for Reba, try to get up to the offices. But those modeling agencies don't like guys hanging around their lobbies. Understandably. Next thing I know, I'm arrested. Spent a weekend in the so-called Tombs. That's when the van got towed. That's when I started drinking spirits. One thing leads to another. And so here we are.

Got to prioritize. First of all, it's important to keep moving, to circulate, keep an eye out. If I just keep walking, I'm bound to run into her sooner or later. If I could find Reba, she'd buy me a nice lunch. The homies picked my pocket when I took that nap on the train, so no money, no ID, no nothing. Luckily, there's those other homies who buy the checks off me. Ironic. Like iron. Like a hammer to the head. Iron to the head. Maybe that's why I have a headache.

But a man can only walk so much, drink so much, hang out in diners for so long. Even the massage parlor won't let me in. Girlfriend gone or they said she was gone. Besides, who needs a "happy ending" anyway? Just need a place to lie down.

Learn how to sleep on your feet. Learn how to use newspaper to keep warm. Sometimes you just don't know where you are. Woke up in the airport that one time. Took all day to get back to the city. Even with money, the hotels won't have me. Fuck them.

Stick a bottle in the pocket and keep moving. That's all. What else can a man do? When I get tired, I lie down wherever I am and take a catnap. Cheaper and simpler. Fuckit. No hotels. No front desk. No attitude.

Almost saw her that one night, five o'clock and dark already, and there she was in the crowd. Shouted but she just kept walking. Followed, called out her name, but she pretended not to hear. Everyone looking at me like I'm some kind of bum.

Next night, wait in a doorway for her to pass by. When she sees it's me, she'll be happy to see me. Can't expect her to turn around every time someone calls her name. And I'm ready to forgive her. We'll go home and she'll be able to sleep in her own bed again. Maybe we'll even have a little homecoming party.

She must have taken a different route. Figures. But the cops, they knew exactly where I was. This time I get stuck in the locked ward at Bellevue. Injected and strapped down. Won't tell 'em my name so they take my mug shot. Plow my brain with Haldol, Lithium and Prozac. Fingerprint me while I'm lying stoned on the table. Another thirty days down the drain.

Morning. The cold gets you moving as soon as you wake up. Gotta unstiffen those joints. Get coffee at that church. No soup till noon. Stand in line with all the assholes and misfits. The smell's enough to drive a man crazy.

When I find Reba she'll get the van out of the tow pound and we can go home. She can talk to the cops and find out where it is.

They'll listen to her 'cause she's a pretty girl and the cops like girls. I know they're afraid of me. That's the fact. And they should be.

It's OK. I know where the bathrooms are. There's a map in my head. And AA meetings are always a good place to find a cup of coffee and a cookie. Five or six spoons of sugar, lots of milk, good as new. Almost. Soup, coffee, the odd buttered roll and you're in business. An egg salad sandwich and things are better than good. In every lobby and subway stop they're watching me. But they're not as smart as me. They're used to the others, the smelly ones, the fucked up ones.

Need the exercise. Gained too much weight in that place. Sitting around all day with those lunatics pigging out. Mashed potatoes and vanilla wafers will do it to you every time. Wouldn't mind a plate of mashed potatoes right now. But no way am I going back to that place. Sitting in a circle, staring at your own white socks under the black rubber sandals. That foot-powder stink on everything. Powder and puke. And the spades with their prison muscles, itching to fight. Or worse, fat and zoned out on meds with those dark TV circles under their eyes, pulling at their crotch all day.

Not to mention the women in that place, bitches every one of them. My one buddy in there, that Irishman whose mother died ten years ago? He said that one of the nurses sucked cock. But I don't want none of that. The pills take care of the urge. It's enough just getting up in the day, feeling like someone wrapped your head in Saran Wrap. Knees like wet loaves of bread. Hate those pills. Where'd I put 'em, anyway?

So wait a minute, what was I thinking about? The market. Should take another walk through the market. Maybe someone will recognize me. Well, with my new walking diet, I lost a lot of weight. First I weighed too much, now I don't weigh enough. That's life, isn't it? A balancing act. Always trying to get it right. And you never can.

My so-called friends. Wouldn't even say hello to me. Goes to show. And someone has the balls to sell apples on my spot. If those cops weren't there, I would have done something. Explained the facts of life to him. Guy looked Jewish. Figures. I established that spot, got people used to coming there to buy my apples, organic heirloom apples, and now here comes the Hebe cashing in. Should have kicked his ass. But the meds, there's an empty spot where the anger used to be. Funny.

That's OK. The money will be here soon enough. Find Reba, get home, pick some apples. Except maybe there won't be any apples. December isn't really good apple-picking time except in South America. Or do they even have apples there? Somewhere, somewhere it's apple-picking time. Probably always apple-picking time somewhere. Somewhere there's always someone doing something different than this right now. Somewhere, someone's happy. Breathing. Sleeping. Somewhere Reba is breathing. Somewhere. Somewhere, something is something. Somewhere.

SCARY THINGS BECOME NORMAL, SAFE THINGS BECOME scary. Easy stuff becomes difficult, difficult stuff, like walking down a runway in front of a zillion people is too easy. The folks I thought were important are nobodies, the silly men and skinny women I thought were nobodies, run the world. And everybody lies. And I make ten thousand a month.

What do I know now? Valentino. Oscar de la Renta. Ungaro. Lanvin. Missoni. Issey Miyake. Herrera. Louis Vuitton. Balenciaga. Gucci. Klein. Prada. Sander. Dolce & Gabbana. Viktor & Rolf. Lagerfeld. DKNY. Tracy. Lang. Boss. Westwood. Smith. Fendi. Givenchy. Rykiel. Sisley. Dior. Comme des Garçons. Kors. Galliano. Matsuda. agnès b. Alfaro. Alaïa. Blahnik. Polo. Nautica. Cartier. Lancôme. Tiffany. L'Oréal. Clinique. Chanel. Coty.

TAG Heuer. Bulgari. Winston. Jade. Rolex. Hermès. J. Crew. Nordstrom. Spiegel. Lands' End. Just Silk. Banana Republic. Gap. Sears. Kmart. Macy's. Bloomie's. H&M. Target. Fred Segal. L'Occitane. Tootsie Plohound. Abercrombie.

Nivea. Schick. Kotex. Tampax. Oil of Olay. Prell. Neutrogena. Wrangler. Adidas. Puma. Vans. Levi's. bebe. Aldo. Guess. Fossil. Skechers. Hard Candy. French Connection. Otto. Dr. Martens. Oakley. Swatch. Diesel.

Coco Pazzo, Nobu, Ivy Bistro, Balthazar, Indochine, The Whiskey, Bains Douche, MK, Bowery Bar, Bungalow 8, Lot 61, Mercer Kitchen, Pastis, Standard, The Dresden, Bouley, Kate Mandolini, Bar Marmont, House of Blues, Viper Room, Moomba, Cipriani, La Quinta, Zen Palate, Time Cafe, Fez, The Delano, Coffee Shop, Fashion Cafe, Industria, Hard Rock Cafe. The Viceroy. I get in everywhere.

The Hamptons, the Azores, Boca, Vegas, Bryant Park, Bermuda, Canyon Ranch, Beaver Creek, Aspen, Costa Rica, Puerto Vallarta, Kaleakala, Cap d'Antibes, Positano . . . Harley, Ducati, Beemer, Caddie, Hummer, Rover, Lamborghini, Mercedes Coupé, Lotus, Maserati, Porsche, Porsche, Porschessssssss, yeah.

And Johnnie Walker Black, Jack Daniel's, Tanqueray, Absolut, Jägermeister, Smirnoff Ice, Stella Artois, Lafite-Rothschild, Source Perrier, Hennessey VSOP, Cristal, Dom Pérignon, Perrier Jouët, San Pellegrino, Veuve Clicquot, Glenlivet, Stoli, Grolsch. Lattes, cappuccinos, espressos, bitters. Camel Lights, Camel Reds, Marlboro Lights, Newports, American Spirit, Kools, Luckies, Players, Dunhills, English Ovals, Gauloises. Mescaline, shrooms, windowpane, blotter, X, Special K, poppers, Valium, Librium, Xanax, Klonipin, Vicodin, hash, sens, cocaine . . .

THE STRETCH SLIPS INTO THE TRAFFIC LIKE A SLEEK
black shark. Pissed-off hands-free drivers hammer their horns in
the screeching wake. The other girls blab on their cells, squeal-
ing with phony hilarity, long legs squirming. Rena props herself
against the black glass, a broken-necked swan, the sparkly L.A.
night traffic sizzling outside clouding sky blue eyes, crowding her
perfect skull. Honking and revving all around like geese, a flock
of Beemers and Suburbans escort the dream mobile. Like bees.
Like a zillion bees. Are there honeybees in L.A.? The place is
jammed with flowers, must be bees somewhere. Flowers planted
around every strip mall, in every yard way, on every median,
guarding the hotel, scenting the lobby, the halls, the suite. Are
the blossoms still out there at midnight? Do the bees ever taste
them? The label could say "Pure Hollywood Hills Honey."

The world filters through prisms of mascara. Out on the pavement, broken glass and mirror shards mark the latest smashup,
like a spray of diamonds, a sixty-minute memorial to someone's
fucked-up life. Gigantic pink faces on billboards, illuminated rectangles of ego and desire loom. Is that me up there? I know I'm
somebody, 'cause everybody's looking at me.

Beneath the adamant traffic lights, the sad Mexicans with
their plastic net sacks of oranges have gone home to their arroz
and beans. In their place, a scruffy black man cajoles the guilty
and plays his lanky beggar's comedy, hip-hop car-to-car clutching a scribbled-on chunk of cardboard that reads: "I haven't
eaten for two days. I am HIV positive and can't work. I had to
give my dog away. Any and all contributions are welcome."

What's-his-face (Who are these guys? Agents? Producers?
Rock stars?) is buddying up with the chauffeur, his new best pal,
urging him to take the stem. He leans through the glass guillo-
tine. "Smoke it! C'mon brother! One hit!!!"

"No, man, no, man," chuckles the driver, "no, man, I'm driving, I'm the driver, I'm in charge of yo' safety." Fake-laughing it off. The freaked-out whites of his eyes visible in the rearview mirror.

"C'mon dude!" The tormentor sucks on the pipe. "See, it's easy." He winks at Rena. Like: We're all in this together. We're party people, living large.

The chauffeur struggles. "Look, in the day, in the day, I did all that. But I'm driving yo'." Rena understands where the guy's coming from, even if the knucklehead with the pipe doesn't. This guy is an ex-addict. Got sober, got himself a job as a driver. He just wants to be left alone to drive the damn car.

An SUV packed with black kids slides past and the thump of the bass vibrates through the limo's doors. "We're all driving!" shouts the witty agent-producer-fashionista-whatever. Skip, his name is Skip. Skip takes another hit off the stem. Rena remembers now. Skip is the one with the gun. In the club Skip bragged about the chrome-plated .38 tucked under his waistband and all the girls tittered and called him "Mac Daddy." Skip calls out to the driver, a thin black kid wearing a silly cap. "Dude, were you ever in a gang?"

"Let's not get into that. I'm going to school now."

"Hey everybody, the driver was in a gang. Dude, take us to the hood!"

"No, no. Now, you all relax back there, leave the driving to me. Gotta get you to your party."

"Dude, I'm telling you, take us to Compton! We'll drive around. See the brothers."

Skip is grinning at Rena. Having the time of his life. Drugged-up asshole. We're all drugged-up assholes. You know where we should drive, Skip? Let's drive back east to the farm. You can meet my big brother, Billy. Come on back home with me, Skip. Big brother Billy'll teach you a thing or two. He'd be more than happy to show you his gun, more than happy. Blow your skinny treadmilled ass to kingdom come, dig a deep dark hole under the old apple trees and bury your drug-riddled bones.

But Skip won't let it drop. "Come on, man. What'sa matter, you afraid?" Skip gives her more eyes. She knows what's coming. Touching me all night. Letting me know he's claiming me. Taking charge. I know what he wants.

Billy. Where'd you go, Billy? I know you're out there somewhere, just like I'm somewhere. Everyone's somewhere until they're not anywhere anymore.

Martinis and coke. Martinis and coke. Martinis and coke. New apartment, no more filthy roommates. Airports and hired cars. The Brits. The Frenchies. Milan runway. Italian guys with their motorcycles. Long, long fucking days in Paris. Five-hour makeup. Greek islands. The Caribbean. Saint Bart's. Nevis. Martinique. So good at it now. So good. Everyone says so. So fucking good. Been to Greece twice, Italy three times, including the Milan shows, the Caribbean ten times, Los Angeles six. I've hung out in the Hamptons, worked in Paris, got laid in London.

Where's the club? Where's the couch I should sprawl on to? Gimme the boys. Gimme the boys. Never thought I could laugh so much. Flash, flash, laugh. Now I know how to show my teeth when I laugh. Now I know how to hold my head high and toss my hair. Hold a drink. Give eyes. Give more teeth. Swing my arms when I stride the catwalk, while all the old postmenopausal ladies in pearls and black stare at my nipples and pussy and ass like hungry vampires. Want to drink my blood, don't you? 'Cause it's the fountain of youth.

Jump in the turtle pond, everyone's skinny-dipping. Hey, Billy? Hey, BILLY, you FUCK! You wanna go sell some apples?

I'm here, I'm really here, with the shutterbugs and stalkers in their dirty parkas toting their autograph books. Treating me like I'm a big deal.'Cause I guess I am. That's me up on that billboard, Mom. See? 'Cause I'm special. 'Cause I'm PERFECT.

Marissa always says so. That's why I'm in this big stretch limousine, with all these crazy people.

Soon I'll be in Skippy's hotel room where the sheets are starched white and crispy and the towels are changed two times a day. Where I can call for massages and pick at thirty-dollar salads all sprinkled with flower petals and wrap myself in the softest cashmere.

So Skippy has a gun and Skippy has an eight ball and Skippy will have a hard-on by the time everything collapses into shit tonight. Wants to be a man and put it someplace. He'll expect it. Grabbing and fussing like some kind of spastic molester. By the time everything winds down to blackout, what difference will it make? I'm doing it.

AT THE PARTY HE THROWS FOR RENA'S TWENTY-FIRST birthday, Paul pulls her into the darkroom to show off some fresh contact sheets. He lights a joint and they check out the prints, not a bad shot in the batch. He kisses her in an innocent way and she kisses him back. They finish the joint and go back to the party. Someone says to Rena, "Where you been?" And Paul's wife says, "Paul, could you please carve the turkey?" Paul's little girls, dressed in black velvet and lace, run in and out like midget Elizabethans.

Luc has stopped by with his new girlfriend. Rena and Luc had sex three times. Once was in the middle of a bridal gown shoot. And here's Andre who did the punk-rock layout for "Fashions of the *Times*." For that Rena had to paint her fingernails black and wear thick kohl under her eyes. It was fun.

Everyone is in the biz. Like a huge dysfunctional family. For this party, the claws are retracted and when people smile, they mean it. Paul will not invite anyone who is not "nice" and so the party emanates real warmth. For half these folks, this is the only family they've got.

Rena finds a good spot on the couch while the gathering whirls around her. This is not a pickup scene, so when a sorrowful-looking guy in an old corduroy jacket flops down next to Rena, she thinks: I know he's cruising me but that's OK. It's kind of pathetically sweet.

The minutes tick by and he says nothing. Rena asks him why he's at the party and he says he works freelance for *POP*, the new British magazine. She tells him she's on page forty-eight and he seems surprised. He tells her he's a novelist and pays his rent by writing two thousand words about the city for each issue, adding that he's already run out of ideas. He says he hates parties, hates the scene, even hates the magazine. He has a novel to write and no money.

His name is Fred and unlike the gangs of smiling people at this party, he doesn't smile. Rena tells him that it's her birthday and she has been modeling for almost six months now. He says he's sorry to hear that and Rena can't tell if he's joking. Then they sit in silence, watching the commotion of the party gyrate like a big lopsided machine.

Rena asks Fred if he would like to get something to eat. He says he isn't hungry. Three cigarettes later, he asks her if she would like to come to his place. He says, "I'm not asking for anything more than that. I can't stay here another minute, but sitting next to you is calming me down. Excuse me for being so forward."

Rena thinks, I'm being bad, but the party's boring.

Fred lives in a Brooklyn neighborhood caught between epochs. Corroded chunks of nineteenth-century industry jumbled and bent sprawl in the dead ends. The old railroad tracks lead nowhere, rotting docks no more than submerged blackened stumps. Monstrous redbrick warehouses loom vacant and dark, waiting to be made into new quarters for the nouveaux riches. A pattern of cobblestone lies under layers of asphalt, like exposed muscle beneath flayed flesh. Rats scurry in packs, thick, sleek and fearless.

Fred does not live in a loft. He lives in a tiny apartment on a side street only a few blocks from the water. The cramped flat is cluttered with books and newspapers. It is underlit, but not repulsive, imbued with the sweet smell of tobacco and old paper. The place has a view to the street and before the windows two battered armchairs face one another. Between them is a small coffee table littered with ashtrays and stained china cups.

Fred leaves Rena and fusses in the kitchen. Books cram every shelf, every horizontal surface. Rena decides it would be stupid to ask him if he's read them all. She picks one up and flips through it, doesn't bother to scan the words. Used to get A's in English Lit. Hah. Now books are something I carry on to the flight and never get around to reading.

On the street below people pass like yellow ghosts. Dead leaves freeze onto the damp asphalt. Fred returns and smiles at her for the first time as he hands her a coffee cup. It smells like burned rubber and holds no more than a spoonful of black liquid. For a moment she thinks she might have made a mistake. The gooseflesh rises on her forearms.

The two sit facing each other in the armchairs, again saying nothing. Fred doesn't return Rena's smile. Rather, he picks a book off the stack at his side.

In the dim light, Fred reads out loud. " 'I would not allow a person to damage her soul in order to love me; I would love her too much to allow her to demean herself.' " He says, "Kierkegaard" and Rena nods as if to say, "Of course."

"Rena." He stops, pauses, starts again. "I slog around in that toxic fashion sewage because I don't mind being destroyed doing what I have to do to get what I want. But you're not like all those cretins at the party. "

"I'm just—"

"—wait, let me finish. I can see that and I can feel that. But see, just because I can see that, doesn't mean that I'm not a motherfucker, too. Because I am. I tend to hurt people. It hurts me when I do it, but I can't help myself." Fred sits back.

Rena says, "First of all, Fred, you don't know me, even though you think you do. You can't see what people are like on the outside. And second of all, I'm a pretty good judge of people and I don't think you could hurt a fly." Should I tell him about Skip in L.A.? Or my three-night stand with Luc? Or Frank. Or Dallas? No. Don't tell him anything.

"Well, give me time, baby, give me time." Fred suddenly howls with laughter, frightening her.

Rena lifts her cup and finds it is empty. She places it down on top of a book. "You think I haven't run into my share of jerks? I'm not stupid. I get what that's about. I get it."

"I know you do. Why do you think I invited you here?"

"Maybe I'm a motherfucker, too."

"Oh, I bet you're a real heartbreaker, huh? Bodies strewn all by the side of the road. I'm sure. Someone as beautiful as you, it's unavoidable."

"I don't know about bodies. But I have my nasty side."

"I'd love to see it."

It's Rena's turn to smile. "Be careful what you wish for."

"I'll tell you a secret. You're the first woman to enter this flat since I moved in."

"Yeah, right." But it's clear that no one comes here.

Again, Fred laughs his wolf laugh. "Do you know why that is?"

"You're gay?"

A weary chuckle. "No. It's much better than that." Fred taps the ash off his cigarette and closes his eyes for a moment before speaking again. Later when Rena thinks of Fred she remembers his pregnant pauses and is sure he had been doing it for effect. "See that little bit of tinfoil on the table? A harmless bit of trash.

But that harmless bit of trash is my master. It rules me. Because I chase the dragon's tail. You know what I mean?"

"No."

"That's why I had to run from that party. And that's why I'm stuck here. My shit's here. I smoked some in the kitchen while I was fixing the coffee."

"Drugs?"

"Not drugs. Please. Heroin. The king. All these assholes on coke and X, babbling like monkeys, feeling each other up, thinking they're something special. It's like they're committed to triviality. They want to live nothing, think about nothing, it confirms how they really feel about themselves. Heroin is not about any of that. Not at all."

"Are you addicted?"

"Everyone's addicted. Don't you have to eat every day? Piss? Shit? Life is an addiction." He smiles sheepishly. "Sorry. I'm sounding stupid."

"Well, you're kind of depressing me, I think." Rena thinks of the leaves stuck to the wet street beneath the window.

"I'm sorry. I didn't mean to fuck with you."

"So why did you ask me up?"

"You should run back to your friends now. Thank you for making my night perfect. I'll think of you and it will be a very happy memory."

"Hey, you don't have to make it so complicated. I like hanging with you, too. I get worn out by all the knuckleheads."

They sit not speaking for another moment. Fred breaks the silence. "Rena? Would you mind if I, you know, smoke in front of you?"

"Smoke? No, of course not, I smoke."

"I mean . . . you know . . ."

"Oh. No. Whatever you want, it's your house."

Coming to life in a way Rena hasn't seen all evening, Fred

digs a tiny envelope from a crevice in the wall, slips a square of tinfoil out from between the pages of a book and in moments, is sucking the white fumes up off a blot of bubbling black, as intent as a jeweler cutting a diamond. When every bit of smoke has been sucked away and only a dry crust remains, Fred leans back in his chair and gazes at Rena with such a thorough look of love she has to turn away.

His voice is hollow as if from underwater. He says, "Would you believe that I pray? I do. Every day. And I have to apologize, because I'm so selfish. I prayed for you to show up in my life."

"Yeah?" This guy is so great.

"I'm sorry, but it's true."

"Stop saying you're sorry! It's nice being here. I feel like we've known each other for a long time."

"Another lifetime, maybe? Ancient Egypt?" And Fred laughs his sardonic laugh. He closes his eyes. "I am the answer to no one's prayers."

Does he want me to leave? "It's getting late," she says.

"Oh, no. I can . . . wait a minute, can we just sit for a moment?"

"Sure . . ."

"And could you do one thing for me?"

"You want to smoke some more?"

"No. Well, yes, but not right now. I was going to ask, could you hold my hand?"

Fred closes his eyes again. Rena leans forward and touches him. The flesh is absolutely still, pulseless, like Dad's the day he died. Yet it is warm and she feels his fingers twine into hers. Then very slowly, Fred brings her hand to his lips. He does not open his eyes.

They sit like this for minutes. Rena's shoulder aches, but she doesn't mind. She searches his face to see if he's fallen asleep until he says, "I'm not asleep," and opens his eyes. He lets her fingers slip out of his. "I'm sorry. That was so nice. You have the hand of Beatrice."

"Yeah? Who's Beatrice?"

"A girl. No one. Forget it. You know, I love the feminine presence. But for me it's different. I don't have the normal impulses."

"That's not such a bad thing, believe me."

"I'm sure the world wants to get as close to you as it can."

"That stuff you smoked. Is it good?"

"This?" He pinches the empty envelope of drug between his fingers.

"Could I try it?"

"Famous last words."

"One time?"

"I have a better idea. Stay here tonight with me. We'll hold hands all night. Would you do that?"

"I have a job in the morning at six. It's already one now. It wouldn't be a good idea not to show up for work."

"A responsible girl. Funny."

"You're pretty funny yourself."

A veil descends between them. "The first thing you see every morning in the mirror is beauty. What can that be like?"

"You're pretty beautiful yourself. Except I wish you weren't so sad."

"Listen. I have to see you again. I'm not sure when. Promise me that when I call, you'll come? No matter what? Even if you have a new boyfriend, whatever. Even if you're married. Even if you're dead. You have to come. OK? Promise?"

"OK. It's a promise."

Fred starts to get up, but Rena stops him. "It's OK, you don't have to. I'm cool on my own. I carry Mace. The real stuff."

Fred eases back into his armchair. "Thank you. For visiting."

Rena kisses him quickly on the lips and splits.

CRACK 'EM WITH A FINGERNAIL, THE STINK OF THE blood, fuckin' lice. The colder it gets the harder it is to dig 'em out. Plus I smell like shit. Shit and that other smell. Like cheese. I smell like a piece of cheese with shit in its pants. Vodka's the only thing that cuts through it.

Encrusted and hallucinating, Billy wanders, scolding the street lamps, pissing in the shiny enameled doorways of the rich, rummaging Dumpsters. The cops take one look at his size and beat him down, make him kiss the pavement. It's raining billy clubs. And the sidewalk is a cold, hard bed. But anything's better than being stuck inside with the loonies.

If I could find the van I could get back to the farm. It's always something, isn't it? A world of hurdles. Hurdle-world. No money. With money, even the Koreans let you in to buy a candy bar. No money, you're not getting in anywhere. Guy points a gun at me. Blabbing at me like a monkey in heat, how am I supposed to know what he's saying? Just walk away. Walk away. And in this city, there's plenty of money. People drop it on the street, problem is, it takes all day to find it. Quarters, dimes, pennies lots of pennies, once in a while a crumpled dollar bill, might as well be a twenty. But don't let anyone see the money, because the others are always out there, always trying to frisk the pockets. Sleep during the day is the best thing. Tired. Hard to stay awake. Waitin' all night for the Burger King to close, just to get the lukewarm fries.

And how's a guy supposed to sleep anyway with rats sniffin' my asscrack and kids stickin' firecrackers up my goddamn nose? People walkin' their dogs right past my face! Just everybody step back. Step fuckin' back. Way back. Another good reason to stay away from water. Stink-factor. Touch me, touch my shit. Who said that? Someone said that. Someone also said, go to the soup kitchen. But you can't just take whatever they hand you! Who knows what they're serving out of those pots? I saw mouse pups in there. Water bug larvae. Baby snappin' turtles.

Get a couple of bucks together, pick up the cans and bottles, bottles and cans, a real egg salad sandwich is a possibility. Salt and pepper. Maybe a cup of coffee with half and half. Ten packets of sugar as long as the chink-o doesn't see. Who knows? Who can know if he can't think? Air horns blowin' my ears out. Bike messengers going the wrong way on a one-way street. Bunch of foreigners delivering chop suey. Baby strollers. Dogs, sniffin' and barkin', pissin' and waggin'. And the spooks and the Jews. You can always tell a Jew, 'cause he's the one giving the free advice. "Why aren't you working? Young man like you?" Just me give me the money, Abraham, I don't need a lecture!

Billy nabs a rolling canvas bin from the garment district, keeps a change of clothes, bottles and cans for deposit, blankets, cushions from a discarded couch. And of course the Reba archive. The collection has grown cumbersome but when something's essential, you gotta make do.

He spends most of his day moving from one recycling mound to the next, searching through the bundled magazines and newspapers set out by the curbside. Collecting Reba, now called Rena. The perfume ads, the department store ads, all of it. Even the swimsuit ads. If I don't do it, who will?

Billy studies her now under a blanket tent, deep into the night, like a Talmudic scholar, his flashlight illuminating her saintly, virtually naked self. He surprises himself when the jism spurts out from his clenched fist. How'd that happen? The little devil, making me do bad things. Of course. You can't escape the devil.

My own damn sister. But what can I do? Forces beyond my control. When I see her looking at me like that, I can't hold back. I love her like a brother, but that's the problem, isn't it? She isn't really Reba anymore, is she? So it doesn't count, does it? Where's my bottle?

Billy emerges from a blackout, frozen solid to the sidewalk.

He can't peel himself up off it. His spilled blood stains the ground like solid black syrup. The pain needles its way into his fingers, his toes. He groans.

Fucking cold. Like someone's stomping on my fingers. Need a drink. A pint of wine right now and I could go to sleep. Fuck! Like having my legs in a vise. Isn't freezin' to death supposed to be sweet like fallin' asleep?

Billy flops his head sideways, tearing a patch of skin off his nose. He smells the fumes of a car idling nearby. The frozen exhaust drifts by his face, inches from the ground. It's only feet away. Shut off your damn headlights!

Billy goes blind. He screams again, pushing up hard against the frozen swill and blood. Paralyzed, no movement. Pisses his pants and feels the damp warmth become more numbness. Turning again, he squints his eyes and can almost see past the brilliance. There's the car, two silhouettes watching him. Warm inside, they don't want to be bothered. Then the door pops, and someone is standing over him. "Buddy, get up."

"Fuck you!" It comes out, "Fuh-ya!" Billy doesn't mean to say "fuck you" but that's what comes out. What he meant to say was "Who are you?" or "Help me." But it comes out "fuck you." Fuck you is easier.

"Yeah, well, you stay out here any longer you're gonna lose the tips of your fingers or maybe your nose. You might even die, you understand that, pal?"

"Fuh-ya."

"Look. I'm not touching your scabrous ass. We called EMS."

"Fuh-ya."

"Dude, you keep telling me to fuck myself, you're gonna hurt my feelings. Now it's either the men's shelter or the island, which is it gonna be?"

"Shah."

"What's that? I can't understand you. Say it louder."

"Fuh-ya."

"You speak English?"

"No." Urine ice crystals are forming around Billy's testicles, biting into him like giant lice. He sobs.

"All right, dude. Ambulance will be here in a few minutes. Hang in there, try not to croak on us."

Coming out of the blackout, Billy finds himself standing in line at the shelter, drool all soaked through the front of his shirt. No cops. Might as well stand in line, at least it's warm. But even if they let me in, which they probably won't, not gonna be here long. I know the drill.

A tap on his shoulder. "Hey, big guy, keep it movin'. Don't want to be here all night."

Behind Billy stands a cocoa-skinned muscle-bound fireplug with a black moustache, five four, five five at most. Guy has a gap in his front teeth and bloodshot eyes. Unlit cigarette cocked behind his ear. For a second, Billy thinks of old Frank Decker, then realizes that this guy is probably a Negro and Frank is probably white. But maybe I'm wrong about Frank, come to think of it. Maybe this is Frank, for god's sake! "Frank?"

"You retarded or something? Move your fat ass, son."

Billy croaks, "Don't touch me."

"I'll touch you all I want, motherfucker. Don't you be telling me what to do." The fireplug glowers at Billy.

"Fugoff nigger."

"Believe me, you don't want to be telling me none of that shit. You know what I'm sayin'?"

Billy turns his back on the little guy and steps forward two feet. The guy nips at his heels, like a poodle. A poodle looking to be beat with a stick. "You smell like shit, you know that, big boy? You smell like dog shit. You been lying in dog shit? Or maybe you been eating dog shit. You been eating dog shit? Or maybe eatin' your old lady who is full of dog shit. Is that true? Is your old lady a pile of dog shit?" Billy sniffs through his beard. It's true I do stink. So what? Good. A shove nudges Billy from behind and

Billy stumbles forward. He ignores it. Another shove. "Go on, get outta here, stand outside, dog shit. Go." Shove. Shove.

Billy turns to face the little guy. "I said don't touch me."

The fireplug knits his fireplug brow. "I touch you all I want, motherfucker. Big fat stinky honky motherfucker. Smell like somethin' dead." The line is long. The security guard at the front can't hear the little guy. The other men shuffle away, making space, tracking the tormentor and tormentee with sideways glances. "Stinky!" The little guy laughs, smiles at his compadres, then thrusts out with another shove.

Billy turns, swings. He clocks the poodle fireplug full face and the little guy drops like a sack of sand. His head hits and the cigarette bounces off his ear, rolls away. The fireplug stays down. Billy turns his back one last time and takes a big step forward, muttering to himself, "Troublemaker."

The security guard walks over. "You." Billy faces away from the guard. "Who hit this guy? Hey you, chief, you hit this guy?" The guard is prodding Billy with his nightstick. Billy leaves the line and walks off into the night.

"Fuck you," he thinks. But he doesn't have to say it.

RICK STANDS NAKED BEFORE THE MIRROR. LAURA HAS gone to visit her mom for the weekend. Taken the kids. Rick's waited all week for this and now here it is and he's alone in the house and so far all he's managed to do is take a shower and stare at his naked self.

He cups his scrotum and juggles his balls. He thinks, I'm shrinking. They're no bigger than cocktail olives now. And look at those arms. Like sticks. Neck like a turkey, chest flat as a pancake, virtually concave. Clumps of hair in the drain every morning now. And it's been years since I could make out the fine print on the medication bottles without glasses.

This is how it arrives, like a hyena hanging out on the fringes of the herd. Waiting for the weak one. Because death is patient. It waits for fragility. And it doesn't have to be physical weakness, it can just be a lack of desire, a lack of will. I've seen it at the clinic. You have to want to be alive, want to exist. Maybe I don't want to be me anymore, maybe I don't want to move forward anymore. So I get weaker and weaker and poison invades my tissues, toxifies me while I am unconscious, inch by inch while I sleep.

Because I am dying (Did I ever want to live?) I have lost my need for sustenance, including sleep. The absurdity of accomplishment becomes obvious. I don't even need lust. My seed-shooting period is over. I've done my job dispersing my genetic code. Time to wilt like a cut rose, wither and turn brown. Infidelity is an aberration, an anomaly. Women flirt with me out of boredom. There won't be any more adventures in my life. It's time to find a good walking stick and a sun-warmed park bench.

Rick gets dressed and wanders out to the backyard. A spring breeze slips through the budding maples and the iridescent clouds scud over a star-blotched void. The windows of the neighboring homes emanate TV-blue light and the moon hides behind the thick foliage, leaving shadows like tar pits over the lawn. Rick lights a cigarette and smokes. This is my yard. My house. My lawn. My dirt. I own the dirt all the way to the center of the planet. That's got to be a lot of dirt.

The cigarette tip glows like a signal from a distant friend. Everything falls into place and Rick can't recall what's been making him so anxious. He lets the butt fall onto the unseen lawn and crushes it into the cool leaves of grass.

Domestic dialogue echoes off the walls of a nearby kitchen.

Rick wanders to the edge of his acre and watches. The bodies of his neighbors swim through the fish tank glow of their home. The indistinct voices refuse to adhere to their movements and gestures. Are they arguing? Or just being emphatic?

Rick steps over the property line and enters their yard, fairly certain they have no dog. The border of shrubs and trees makes him invisible. He steps closer, and the sound synchs up with the moving mouths. What are these people's names? Ed and Jane, I think. Moved in about six months ago. No kids, no way to know them. Never bothered to visit and introduce myself. Why should I? They'll be gone soon. Ed is rarely home. Jane comes and goes all day in her Beemer, cell phone stuck to her pretty head.

Tonight, Ed is wearing a button-down oxford and his tie is loosened. Jane snatches dishes from the dishwasher and sorts them onto shelves, into cupboards. She's sexy because she's thin, taller than average, possessed of slightly droopy, full breasts. Her hair has been streaked blond like almost every woman's in the neighborhood (every woman this side of the Hudson, probably). Her face holds no emotion, as if restraint is a positive trait. Ed, also tallish, also coolish, gives the impression of what? Having piles of money? Balls the size of lemons? How old are these people? Late thirties? Why don't they have kids?

Although he can hear them, he still can't understand what they're saying. Ed keeps repeating something about "over there." And Jane shakes her head, "No." Whatever it is, it seems important to them. Or not. Maybe they're going to adopt a child from South Korea. Or maybe they're discussing politics. Or maybe they're trying to decide what they'll be doing next weekend. Or maybe they're planning to rob a bank.

Abruptly, they leave the room and Rick guesses they are heading upstairs. Maybe they're going to their bedroom, to fuck. How does that joke go? "What's foreplay for a WASP? Answer: Drying the dishes."

Rick finds a set of stairs leading from the patio flagstones up to a cantilevered sundeck. Breathless, he creeps up the stairs, and now, much more exposed, crosses the deck and peers into the sliding glass door of the second story. Ed and Jane wander around like sleepwalkers. Rick steps away from the house into a patch of darkness. He observes the couple with the detachment of a Kinsey Institute researcher.

Ed and Jane strip to their underwear. She applies cream to her hands and leaves the bedroom. Ed pulls off his boxers and stretches out on the bed. Fools around with his flaccid penis, pinches a nipple, stares at the ceiling. What do you see up there, Ed? The penis flops to and fro, to and fro. What is taking Jane so long? Is she getting out the handcuffs? Lubing the sphincter? No. Here she is! Naked and sullen, almost defeated. She lies down beside her husband. A perfunctory kiss. Then she flips her hair, gives Ed a little shove and when he lies back, takes him into her mouth. Her butt is angled toward Rick, he can just make out the fellatio. He sizes up Ed's member. Pretty average.

If Rick had planned it, it couldn't have worked out this well. The perfect voyeuristic moment. He focuses on Jane's wonderful buttocks, discovers he's tumescent, unzips and starts to play with himself. Three human animals move rhythmically toward climax.

Rick's semen spurts out over the deck railing. Oblivious to Rick's contribution, Ed and Jane are still at it, helpless and pale, nothing like the people in porno videos. With no awareness of their participation in the ménage à trois, they begin a frenzy of awkward spasms. As the energy drains out of him, Rick recalls a nature show he once saw on PBS. Something under water. A jellyfish or a prawn, reflexively spritzing its goo into the frigid brine as friendly kelp wafted to and fro.

Finally, Ed whinnies while Jane's glazed eyes aim directly at the spot where Rick stands. They lie still and Rick feels pity for them. Feels pity for himself. Feels pity for every dumb prick and cunt on the planet. He sees that he's left a few drips of jism on their cedar deck.

Rick descends from the porch, crosses his yard and returns to the familiarity of his own well-lit home. As he steps back into the tenderness of his own space, he feels the pinch of his dried cum glueing the tip of his dick to his underwear. He thinks, I should call Laura.

LANDING IN NEW YORK, RENA FINDS THE MESSAGE FROM Fred on her voice mail and grabs a cab to his place. He greets her in an unbuttoned dress shirt and a pair of old trousers. He holds a lit cigarette, and wipes his nose on a sleeve. His ribs are visible. His feet are bare.

Three days before, Fred's drug dealer, Barry, was busted as part of a citywide crackdown and without his drugs Fred has been cycling through a course of fevers, sweats, vomiting and diarrhea. Rena moves in, stays overnight, nursing him with chicken broth and whiskey and fetching him cigarettes. The next day, while Fred retches and moans inside the locked bathroom, Rena checks her voice mail. There are six messages from Marissa wanting to know where she is.

Rena likes taking care of Fred. Likes being alone with him. And during moments of clarity, he reads her passages from his history and poetry books. He shows her Du Camp's Egyptian photographs and Man Ray's nudes, sketches by da Vinci, paintings by Arthur Dove. He recites lines from Hesse's *Steppenwolf* and Baudelaire's *Flowers of Evil* and Durrell's *Black Book* and Henry Miller. She sits by him and says nothing while he smokes.

Fred gets a phone call. Hanging up, he tells Rena that she has to go on an errand, that it's a matter of life and death.

Twenty minutes later Rena stands before a white brick apartment building in the East 30s. An instant after pushing the little black button, she is buzzed in. In the black and silver lobby, a shriveled woman emerges from the elevator leading a small dog dressed in a tartan vest. Rena slips in just as the doors creak shut.

Rena can hear the metal clicks and slides of multiple locks as the front door is unsealed. Barry sports a comb-over and a long-sleeved shirt buttoned at the wrists despite the dry heat pulsing from the cast-iron radiators. He drags a kitchen chair out for Rena, its leg catching on a curl of lifted linoleum. A raccoon-eyed girl enters from the back room, raking her fingers through her hair. An abandoned carton of beef chow fun sits leaking on the table.

"Uh. So you're a friend of Fred's?" Barry glances back at the raccoon-eyed girl as if she were his partner in the interrogation.

"Yeah." Rena tries to meet Barry's eyes, but he won't allow it.

"How do you know Fred? If I may so ask?" With nervous gusto he chews a nail, spits it out.

"We met at a party. About a month ago." A reek of insect repellent and steam heat. Barry's girlfriend does a little shimmy, rubbing her bum against the wall.

"Oh. A party. That's interesting. A party, really?" Barry picks a piece of lint off his shirt and sniffs it. He doesn't notice the cockroach skittering past the toe of his cowboy boot, or if he does, can't be bothered squashing it. He smooths his shirt and grins fiercely.

"Yeah." Rena glances at the girl.

"Oh, this is Gigi, Gigi, this is uh, what is it? Rifka?"

"Rena." Neither the girl nor Barry look Rena in the eyes.

"Rena, right. Rena is in your old business, Gigi. She's a model too. How 'bout that, huh?"

Gigi scratches at her upper arms. "Barry? Stop fucking with my head? Please?"

"Fucking with you? No one's fucking with you, Gigi. You're the one fucking with me. I thought you came by to wish me well. But that's not the case, is it? And you know what? I'm tired. I've just spent four days in a stinking cell with a bunch of crazy unwashed lowlifes. Living on bologna, mayo and stale white bread sandwiches and cartons of fucking Hi-C. So don't tell me I'm fucking with you. All right? Don't tell me that. Right now, I'll do what the fuck I want. You're lucky I'm even standing here, my sweet. So, here's the deal, I'm not keeping you. You can go any time you want."

"Just lemme have a taste, Barry." She tugs at her hair.

"You had a taste. How many tastes do you want?" Barry fondles the bulb of his nose, his forehead glossy with sweat. "You don't see Rifka here asking for a taste."

"Scumbag." Gigi glares at the floor like a petulant four-year-old.

Barry leers toward Rena and confides, "My own fucking girlfriend is calling me a scumbag. How about that, Rifka? Can you dig that? And you want to know why she's calling me a scumbag? I think you can appreciate this, because she's a fucking junkie, that's why. She's a fucking junkie ho. My own girlfriend. Hurts me to say that, but it's true. That's the kind of situation you get yourself into when you do what I do. No one really loves you, they only love what you can do for 'em. So let me ask you this, Rena, Rifka, whatever-the-fuck your name is, is Fred like your boyfriend?"

"I don't know. No. We're friends."

"Friends. Uh-huh. Like the TV show. And you're copping for him. And what? You a weekend chipper? Gigi used to be a weekend chipper. Gigi used to be a lot of things."

"Barry, shut the fuck up! I'm gonna go, I swear."

"Go. Who's stoppin' ya?"

Rena's cell phone rings. As she lifts it out of her jacket pocket, Barry grabs her hand. The fingernail on his pinkie is untrimmed, his palm moist. "What's that? Who's that? Don't answer that."

Rena glances at the little screen. "It's Fred. He probably wants to know if I got here OK."

Barry snatches the phone and brings it up to his mouth. He

pushes the answer button but says nothing. Rena can hear the murmur of Fred's voice on the line. Gigi paces by the front door.

"Barry, come on!" Gigi squats down, rises, then squats again. Her frenzy is bleeding into Rena. Rena's stomach begins to ache.

Barry tells the phone, "Yeah, she's here. Does she have the cheddar?" Barry scrutinizes Rena as he listens to Fred. "No, I did not ask her. We were just making small talk, man. I didn't realize you had just met her. She could be anybody." Another pause for listening. "Uh-huh. Uh-huh. But that doesn't prove anything. She could be Florence Nightingale and a New York City detective at the same time. It's possible. Anything is possible. Believe me."

"*Barry!*" Purple bruises run the length of Gigi's forearm.

"That's Gigi. Gigi. My friend, you met her. Listen, Fred, I understand, I understand your turmoil, it is understandable given your circumstances, but you also have to be aware of my situation here. I just left Rikers ten hours ago. Dig? Caution is also understandable. Uh-huh. Well, here, you talk to her."

Rena takes the phone. "Fred? Are you OK?" Rena won't meet Barry's eyes. "I'm fine. No, I am. Uh-huh. OK. Right. Are you sure? All right. Yes. I'll tell him." She clicks off and stands up. "He says I shouldn't hang out here, I should leave."

"He didn't say that. No way did he say that." Barry blinks like there's something in his eye.

"He told me to bring the money back and he'll come by himself."

"He's too sick to go anywhere." Barry bites a lip, plucks an eyebrow. Gigi tugs her hair. Rena can smell Barry's B.O.

"That's what he told me." Rena is heading for the door before she realizes she's made the decision to leave. At the door, she faces a puzzle of locks.

"Barry!" Gigi the human timepiece marks the half minute.

Barry says, "Let me see it. Let me see the money." He takes a step toward Rena.

Rena stiffens. "You're supposed to have a package for Fred. You give me the package and I'll give you the money."

"Barry! I'm gonna throw up!" Gigi is on the floor, rocking back and forth, her palms shoved between her thighs.

Barry pauses for the first time since Rena has entered the apartment. "You tell your boyfriend, what goes around comes around. I get fucked with here, I call my friends. You tell him that." Barry steps into the back bedroom, ignoring Gigi, who leaps up to follow him. Rena doesn't move. A dog barks outside the door, clawing the hallway tile. The door is locked. Couldn't leave even if I wanted to. Rena checks the clock on the stove and sees that it's broken, tries to estimate how long she's been standing there when Barry returns with a fist-sized package wrapped in brown paper and cake-box string. He drops it onto the kitchen table. No sign of Gigi. Barry says, "Money."

Rena hands Barry the envelope from Fred. He tears it open and counts quickly, almost breathlessly. Rena's banking days tell her he's holding a thousand dollars in his hand. The muscles in Barry's face relax and he says to Rena, "You wanna taste? On the house?"

"No thanks." Gigi has disappeared.

"Don't make me suspicious of you." He counts the money a second time.

"I don't use it."

Barry stops, looks at her like he's seeing her for the first time and says: "Hang out in a barber shop, sooner or later you're gonna get a haircut." His smile radiates real warmth.

"Yeah, well, I don't need a haircut tonight. I get 'em free at work."

Barry moves toward the door, "Rifka, you're always welcome. Come by any time. Now that we know each other."

Gigi gropes her way back into the kitchen, finds a chair and collapses into it, seemingly oblivious to the world. But when Barry unlocks the locks, she lifts her head and croaks, "Bye! It was nice meeting you, Rena." Rena hears the locks clicking into place on the other side of the shut door.

Sixty seconds after Rena reenters his apartment, Fred has the drug in his lungs and in his bloodstream. The gaunt sick look fades and he smiles. With the greatest gentleness, he lights a cigarette, takes a deep drag and lies back into his armchair. He gazes at her with dilute good cheer and says, "I think I love you."

"Yeah? That's nice." Rena feels herself blush.

"You saved me. You lifted me up."

Rena reaches out and strokes his head. He doesn't shrink away so she comes closer and wedges herself next to him and throws a long arm over his shoulders. She kisses his ear. "I want you to be well."

"Oh, I'm very well, thank you."

"Do you want to eat something? You should."

"Eat? No, angel, not right now. No. I just want to inhabit this moment. You know how sometimes there are moments you wish would extend in all directions forever? That's this moment, right now. Everything fits together, everything makes sense."

"It's weird. I feel that way, too."

"Rena . . ."

"Yes?" She snuggles into him.

"No. Never mind." He reaches out to tap the ash off his cigarette.

"What?"

"I was going to offer you some. Would you like that?"

"I'd love to do anything with you. Dance with you. Sleep with you."

"All that and more." Fred scratches his nose. The cigarette smoke curls around the two of them.

"Then I would love it."

Fred taps a pinch of dope onto a tinfoil scrap. He heats it and as the white vapor rises up he holds it under her perfect nostrils.

"Keep it in for as long as you can." Rena inhales, and as she does, she's struck by the flawlessness of Fred's cheekbones, his jawline, even his ear. He is a god. She lets one hand stretch downward along his thigh and feels tenderness bloom like a flower in her bosom. Fred is speaking again. When did she shut her eyes? "More?"

She looks up and finds a facade of love like nothing she has ever known. No. She did know it, once. It's the look Jesus had when he ascended to heaven. She smiles in assent and Fred and she share another blot of drug. He lowers the tinfoil as the smoke curls up out of his mouth, brings his arms around her and kisses her.

Rena twines her legs around him, braiding herself into him completely. This man is my missing parts, what I have needed for so long.

In the morning, over black coffee and cigarettes, Fred asks her about her work. She says she's lost track of it. He tells her that's a bad idea and insists she call Marissa, claiming illness.

Every night she returns. During the day, she books editorial with French *Vogue,* and *Cosmo* and an ad with Lord & Taylor. She's booked for the spring shows in New York. She's booked for a possible cover. By the end of the month she's in the Bahamas with Luc, and before coming back, she hops over to Saint Bart's to shoot with Paul. Everything is very right. Everything fits together, like Fred said, finally.

RICK WAITS AT THE GLASS AND IRON FOYER DOOR AS A man in ink-smudged blue traverses the faux-marble lobby. Pausing for a moment behind the thickly painted wrought iron, he scrutinizes Rick, then drags the heavy door open, huffs back to his post and his sports page. The guy has seen Rick dozens of times, but there is no nod of recognition. Rick finds a seat outside Edith's very exposed office.

From behind the door come funereal voices. It opens revealing not Edith but a snuffling thickset woman, who daubs pink tissue to her eyes while Edith strokes her back. They hug, oblivious to Rick at waist level. He tries not to overhear the snatches of their adieu. ". . . I just don't think I should call her, Edith, you know what I'm saying?"

"I know. Let's talk about it next week." Edith is nothing if not efficient. The stroking has ended. The urging away follows.

"I feel so sad." The kitten refuses to leave the teat.

"Next week. Bye." Edith's gimlet eye catches Rick squatting like a toad outside her door. She nods him into her confessional. "Go ahead, Rick. I'll be right with you." This is said firmly, as if Rick has been eavesdropping intentionally. Rick knows the drill. Edith runs hot and cold. The expansive warmth he's just witnessed comes in carefully measured doses.

In the gloomy den every item—the curtains, the walls, the couch, the table, is a shade of brown. Edith is the third therapist Rick has tried, and it has become obvious that the reigning aesthetic demands that therapeutic space possess deep shadows, frumpy furniture and something hanging on the wall from the late-Berkeley school of macramé. Somber books by Adler, Sullivan, Fromm and even Chopra are lined up within a chocolate-colored bookcase. A needlepoint proclaims "Let the Child Lead." (Stitched by a patient? How is he/she doing now? Is he/she happy, sad, mad or glad?) On the coffee table, a box of tissues lies next to an economy-sized bottle of Excedrin, a miniature clock and a stack of business cards. A set of auburn pillows and a grief-worn tan quilt lie jumbled on the couch. Thick drapery covers the lone window, absorbing any light entering from the airshaft without. The room is as still as a burial vault.

Rick figures the eerie atmosphere is intended to stir up scary memories. That's what this place is, isn't it? A pain factory? Wake the childhood pain from its slumber, then chop off its ugly head. But why would I do that? No need to go looking for trouble. Better to let lying dogs lie. All that's needed is someone to talk to, even if it does cost a $150 an hour. Rick is perspiring. He peels off his jacket and drops down onto the couch.

Edith reenters, her Mona Lisa smile unreadable. She settles into her armchair, brushes a thread off her sleeve, peers at Rick and with the chill of a Nurembergian prosecutor, begins: "How are you doing, Rick?"

Rick has already decided he's not going to answer that question today. Not going to give her the satisfaction of seeing him squirm. Because, of course, I'm not doing well. If I were doing well, I wouldn't be here, would I? I'd be someplace else, happy. So you already know the answer to your question. It's a dumb question. Answer a dumb question with a dumb answer. I'll just say fine. See what she does with that. Of course, she'll know at once I'm lying.

Rick hears himself say, "I'm good. In fact, since confessing all those things last week, I feel like, I know this sounds absurd, my 'inside' self is more connected to my 'outside' self now."

Edith adjusts her cocoa-colored knit shawl. "Well, that's wonderful. It's a good feeling to make progress, don't you think?"

"I peeked into my neighbors' windows while they were having sex and masturbated onto their cedar deck."

Edith's expression does not flicker. "And how did that make you feel, Rick?"

"Like a goddamn pervert. No. It made me feel good. Made me feel ecstatic. I don't know how it made me feel because I don't know how I feel about anything."

"What do you mean by that statement?"

Rick fingers a golden pillow tassel. "Which one?"

"You choose."

"Look, I'm just saying, I mean, what motivates a man to do something like that? It's not normal. Right? Or centered or whatever. But I did it because I want some anarchy in my life, you know? It's like if I don't do something crazy, I might go insane."

"It's not uncommon to think the way you do. Especially for someone your age. It's called a midlife crisis. You'll get over it. We all do."

"No. I don't accept that. This isn't that." The anger is thudding in Rick's chest. Tell her. Tell her about anger. "Look, I'm angry because things were very difficult when I was a kid. My father behaved all wrong. He hurt my mother. He hurt me. I know everyone has things to be angry about, and I have plenty to be thankful for. It's bullshit to complain. It's futile. It's just a feeling. I want to complain to someone, so I complain to you. But the problem isn't something that can be fixed. There is no fixing. It's just life. Life goes on. It's like when you play a record, the needle's in the groove and one note follows the next. But for me, it's like the record's skipping. And I'm not that happy about it. And what's worse is that it used to be good. I have some memory of that. But back when it was good, I didn't know it was good, I didn't realize it was happening. That pisses me off, too. And now I'm nostalgic for the old place. Except that when I was in the old place, I wanted something else then, too. Why can't I just say to myself, 'I love Laura. I love the kids. I'm very lucky.' I'm an asshole for not being happier. Tell me I should be happy."

"Maybe you don't want to be happy. Maybe it's easier being unhappy."

"Maybe I'm just selfish. I have such a good life. I should have gratitude for my good life."

"Should?"

"Aw, come on, Edith, you know what I'm saying!"

"What are you saying?"

"Don't you ever feel that way?"

"What way?" Edith gives Rick her best beatific inscrutable Buddha smile.

"The feeling that you want to rock the boat, bring it all down in shambles around you. Destroy your life and start all over?"

"Everyone feels that way at some time or another. You wouldn't be human if you didn't."

Rick inventories the items on the little table before him: the tissues, the business cards, the clock, the lip balm. Why does she need lip balm? He looks up and of course Edith is watching him. Or pretending to be watching him. She's probably thinking about something else. Her dog's eczema, maybe. At least she isn't asleep. Rick feels the pillow in his hands. I'm twisting the pillow. The pillow is very resilient. Probably designed to be mauled. A therapist's pillow represents so many things to so many people.

Edith breaks the silence. "What are you thinking right now, Rick?"

"That you never give me a straight fucking answer."

"It's not my life, Rick. It's your life. You have the answers for your life. If you think I'm going to sit here and tell you you should leave your wife, I won't do that. But if you tell me you are planning to leave your wife and children, I will ask you why you made that decision."

"And that's supposed to help me?"

"You know what you want. But perhaps you are afraid to take what you want. It could be freedom, but it could also be a desire for a deeper love with your family. Everything comes with risk."

"But if I think I want something, but 'really' want something else, how will I ever find out what I 'really, really' want? I mean this could go on forever."

"Obviously you're in some discomfort with whatever plan of action you've currently engaged in, so you have to reconsider that plan. Unless you like being in pain. So, Rick. How do you feel right now?"

"Edith, I don't think this is getting us anywhere."

"Us? You're the patient, Rick."

"Me. That's right. One more predictable assortment of needs and wants and quirks. A source of amusement."

"I'm not amused by your pain. I think the answer is right on the tip of your tongue. You just don't want to say it."

"And what's that?"

"You know. I don't."

"I don't know! Fuck!"

"Tell me about your mother, Rick. Are you angry at her for letting your father do what he did?"

"No. Here's your money. I don't need to do the whole session. And don't put me down for next week. This is stupid and I feel stupid for doing it and I'm sorry I've been wasting your time. Well, you get paid for it so I guess it's not a waste of your time."

"Rick—"

"No. Here's the deal. I hate my life and I want out and you can't do anything about that. And what's worse, I have a life that's better than 99.99 percent of humanity's, so I'm an asshole for hating my life. But you know what? I hate it anyway. I want something I can't have and that pisses me off. And you can't get it for me because I don't even know what it is. So I'll see you. I know it's not your fault, but on the other hand, I doubt you'll ever break the bad news to me that I'm an unhappy, depressing loser and always will be unhappy, so I will say good-bye." Rick is crying.

In the lobby, the doorman doesn't look up. I could have murdered Edith and the stupid doorman would be clueless. The perfect murder. Why doesn't Edith come running after me? She should beg me to come back. Assure me everything is going to be all right. But that isn't her job, is it?

On the street, Rick bumps into a mentally handicapped delivery boy. Packages spill onto the sidewalk. Rick halts but does nothing to help the guy, who is mumbling to himself as he stoops to collect his parcels. The guy tries to get things right again, as if it all were a performance for Rick's benefit, an absurd ballet.

People rush past, someone kicks a fat manila envelope, keeps walking. Anonymous packages scatter among anonymous feet.

Rick watches the confused guy. He can barely find an address. That's me, thinks Rick. I don't know where the fuck I am.

IN SAINT BART'S THINGS ARE PERFECT. EXHAUSTED FROM a long day out on the boat, everyone dog-paddles ashore to meet up with the caterers. They end up sitting Indian-style on beach blankets, cracking spiny lobsters and drinking beer. Reddened and wasted by the sun, the other girls and the crew eventually drift back to their rooms to smoke dope and watch *Survivor* on satellite TV. Rena and Paul remain on the beach, sedated by the sand's memorized warmth, splitting a bottle of Haut-Brion. Last month in Nevis everyone had been bitchy and irritable. But Lands' End pays big bucks so today the sky is wide and blue.

In an atypical burst of energy, Paul trots down to the lapping surf and wades into the lagoon's bathwater. He waddles farther until he's barely visible, then shouts something Rena can't make out. In the half-light of the slow winter sunset, naked under her sarong, she strips down and joins him. It's like being a kid, in the days before sex, before all the bad stuff, innocent and naughty at the same time. She thinks, Paul is my dad now.

The amniotic water laps her breasts, soothing and voluptuous. Paul bobs in the dark brine like a luminescent dolphin. With a silly smile on his face he slips up beside her and takes her into her arms. They kiss. The kiss of an uncle for a child. And there's his thing wagging in the tidal current. So what?

Rena drifts away and Paul floats onto his back spitting jets of seawater into the air like the spouting baby whale he is. Rena makes a show of laughing. Why should she take him seriously? She doesn't want to take him seriously, why spoil it?

In the torchlit twilight they towel off, Paul huffing from the exercise. All this swimming has been an expenditure on his part. Rena can't help herself, she comes up to him from behind, gently fits her arms around his thick waist and lays her head on his shoulder.

Later, at a reception thrown by the hotel, fortified by several brandies, Paul says, "These snowbirds think they're special because they can hang out with the New Yorkers and brag about their backhand and their handicap." He grabs Rena's hand and they retreat to a balcony overlooking the black and silver sea. A monstrous pink moon. "Isn't it sublime? And completely wasted on these fools. Like everything. Pearls before swine. I work so hard, and who sees it? What's the saying? If a tree falls in the forest and no one hears it, does it make a sound? The clients only want impact. So who am I doing this for? The women under their hair dryers in Duluth? The fashion queens in Miami Beach? I create a dream. But what's the real dream, Rena? If we can't see it, touch it, who can? I make dreams for all those poor souls out there, but who makes dreams for me?"

"We dream our own dreams, Paul. We live our dreams. I do."

"Do you?" Paul is handsome in the evening light.

"I think I do. I used to dream about doing what I'm doing right now. And here I am."

A sea breeze caresses Rena's cheek and she inhales as Paul leans into her and says, "You are so beautiful." He kisses her behind the ear.

"So are you, big guy." She thinks, when Paul kisses me, I feel good. I'm happy right now. Right this second, I am happy. I like being touched.

Paul says, "Marissa called before dinner. You landed the Nordstrom contract. Don't let her know I said anything. She wants to tell you herself."

Rena reaches for her wine, drains the glass and flips it into the blackness below their feet. "I knew I'd get it."

"Yes. But listen, keep the exclusive contract to two years. No more. There's gonna be a lot more where that came from. You can go all the way. I've always seen it in you."

"Marissa knows what to do." Beneath them the surf is a long piece of fabric ripping.

"Listen! You are precious. You are alive. Don't trust them with your soul. Don't trust them with your happiness." Paul has slipped an arm around her waist.

"I trust you."

"Thank you. Your loveliness saves me every day." Paul is flush with drink. "You are a flower. An incredible flower. Do you know why a flower is so beautiful, Rena?"

"Why?" Over Paul's shoulder, their host is trying to catch her eye. He's been flirting with her all night. He's hot and he knows it. She keeps her focus on Paul.

"Because it wants to be pollinated. Everything in you, Rena, every molecule wants to be pollinated. That's why they want you, because you are the thing itself, the thing that draws the bee to the flower."

"You are so full of shit! Who wants me?"

"The men. The women, like Marissa. The buyers. The editors. The industry. They want to devour you. They want to possess what you have. They'll use you up and step over your corpse when they're done with you."

"Well, I'm not going to let them use me up. Whatever that means. Besides, I get paid pretty fucking well to get possessed." Rena nuzzles Paul's shoulder.

"Problem is, I want to possess you too, my dear."

When the door clicks behind them, they hug, swaying. This is all he wants, to know that I'll say yes. He's so fucked up he'll fall asleep and won't even remember I ever came to his room.

Paul does not fall asleep. He strokes Rena's hair, caresses her arms and legs, leaving her breasts for last as if they were sacred.

She doesn't stop him. It's as if it's his body, too, he knows it so well. So tender, so careful. When has anyone been this careful with me? This is a kind of love, right? Affection is love. Paul's touch feels more like a mother's than a man's.

When he climbs onto her, his volume is soft and delicate. The whole enterprise isn't wrong, it's just different. A brother and sister making love. And Paul's wife is far away and we're only making each other feel good. We're friends, good friends, taking care of each other. Just this one time. It's nice that there is something awkward about Paul, he isn't sure of himself the way that Dallas and Luc were. He's like a big dumb puppy.

Even so, when Paul finally comes, panting and flushed, Rena's relieved it's over. A long day is over. Sun, swimming, drinking, she's asleep before he has rolled off her.

In the middle of the night, she wakes. The candle is guttering. Paul snores with the depth of a happy man. She pulls the covers over him, thinking how much like a giant baby he looks. It feels good to lie next to him, it feels safe. She lets the tropical air nudge her back to sleep. Through the open window the moon has risen, no longer pink and huge, but high and blue and small.

ELEGANT AND GLOWING, PAUL AND RENA SNUGGLE AT Balthazar and Pastis and Nobu, sip Perrier Jouët at midnight, nibble beluga in the back of the town car that waits for them wherever they go. At gallery openings Paul boldly holds her hand as the crush of cologne-scented cognoscenti grin and burble. Paul is providing entertainment for everyone. Showing up in public with a girlfriend is dangerous and fun and great P.R. He introduces Rena to his chums, CEOs and movie stars, almost all of whom he's shot. Rena doesn't want anyone thinking she doesn't truly love Paul, so she links her arm through his and squeezes it against her side.

Rena thinks: I make five thousand dollars an hour now, give half to Marissa, send some to Billy, spend the rest. Everything is different. Everything I thought I knew I have to forget. Life works different here. It's a big game and you play the hand you're dealt. You work it. I'm working it. So Paul's my boyfriend, so what?

I'm no longer just another pretty girl. I'm an "important new face." With my Nordstrom contract, with all the new jobs, I am in the eye of the fashion storm. Marissa calls me on her cell phone ten times a day. Tells me how to play my hand. Marissa says, "You have to want it." And I tell her, "I want it and I'm going to get it." Marissa tells me I have to be smart. I have to play for keeps.

Rena stops by Fred's place every few days. He never leaves the apartment now. Wakes up early, his bowels loose, the world colorless. When he hasn't stockpiled enough of Barry's dope to get him through, he's forced out to the street at six AM with the rest of the stone-cold junkies, cops his drugs, runs home and is nodding out by eight. Rena finds him back in bed in the late morning. She brings take-out coffee, they munch on honey-dipped doughnuts and gossip. Fred entertains her with stories of scary street dealers wielding rusty golf clubs. He tells her about anonymous slots in anonymous doorways of rotten buildings. Fred probes Rena relentlessly for details about her sex life with Paul. He revels in the romantic ineptitude and self-consciousness. Rena feels guilty when Fred makes fun of Paul, but Paul's nasty, too. She thinks: everyone's nasty. That's part of the fun of the life I'm in now. We dish, we gossip, we backstab. But nobody means it, really. And I have a secret weapon—Fred. I always have Fred and he's my true friend.

Paul insists that Rena keep her eyes open when they make

love. Sometimes he can't maintain an erection even after he's inside her and ends up masturbating while she lies there next to him. After sex he drinks until he passes out. Or if he manages to stay semilucid, he makes long confessions about his miserable teen years and how girls couldn't even conceive of dating him. He tells Rena he dropped a lot of acid in those days, smoked a lot of pot. He says he had wanted to kill himself until he discovered photography. Rena tries to stay awake during the confessions, but she always falls asleep.

Paul books her for sessions as often as possible and they enjoy lazy days in the Caribbean and Mexico and the Hamptons. At first, Rena ignores interest from other guys, but then, out of perversity or boredom, she starts to spend more and more time with the narcissistic straight male models. The danger is fun. The sex is meaningless. There are motels and hotel rooms everywhere.

In Quintana Roo Rena gets caught making out with Larry, a Calvin Klein "boy." Larry's so fearful of incurring Paul's wrath that everyone, even the makeup guys, conspire to convince Paul that Larry is gay. Rena thinks, "Yeah, I'm being bad, but who's good? Nobody."

Rena, in addition to assignments, seeing Paul, seeing Fred and seeing whomever, has her schedule packed by Marissa, who has Rena make an appearance at every opening and function she can find. She crams four shows of Bryant Park runway work into one day. Marissa drags Rena around to six art openings in one Saturday afternoon. Every charity benefit, every new club is a must. Marissa tells Rena, "I want people to ask 'Who is that girl?'" To that end, dating Paul is a good thing. Rena's bookings hit gridlock and this forces her base rate even higher.

One morning in Barbados while shaking off a wincing hangover Paul discovers that his wife, Annette, is divorcing him. He spends all morning on the phone, sucking down endless soda and bitters, trying to find his lawyer while Rena watches TV and eats Cap'n Crunch out of the box. Paul's cozy house in Sag Harbor and the Central Park apartment (six pages in *Architectural Digest*) are at stake.

Things get worse when Annette figures out that the affair has gone on for almost two months, that she's been in the dark while everyone else knew. Paul's lawyer tells Paul to stay away from Rena but Paul books Rena every chance he can and sees her more than ever.

The legal fees eat up Paul's assets. The studio gets sucked into the whirlwind of Annette's fury. She places a lien on the rights to his copyrighted photography. Paul's doctor gives him a prescription for Xanax and he begins each day drinking and continues until he passes out. One morning, Rena arrives for a job and finds him in his studio, trying to load a camera by himself.

"Where's Adam?"

"Fired his ass. Everyone. Fuck 'em."

"Where are the other girls? The client?"

"I don't know."

The loft echoes, empty. The sun streams in from the high windows. Paul won't meet her eye, continues to play with the camera. She's alone with him. She says, "Paul, I'm here to work."

"We're going to work. We're going to work. Don't you start giving me shit, too."

"I'm not giving you shit, Paul, but there's nothing happening here."

"That's what you think." Paul abandons the camera on a stool and fiddles with a strobe. It pops repeatedly. "I'm working. I'm dealing with it. There's a shoot here today."

"Paul, you're drunk."

"Whatever."

Paul finds the Stoli and sucks from the bottle. Rena comes up behind him and touches his shoulders. "Paul, I care about you so much."

He turns and buries his face in her shoulder. She holds him, little Paul in his mommy's arms. Then, head bowed, he leads her by the hand to his bedroom in the back. She sits on the edge of the bed and he begins to kiss her and she lets him. He unbuttons her blouse, yanks her jeans off, her thong. Naked, she waits for him as he gets his pants open. Smothered under his weight Rena knows he's too drunk to get hard. After five minutes he stops moving. His breathing becomes even. She extricates herself from his slack body, gets dressed, and leaves him passed out on the bed.

A few days later Paul comes by Rena's apartment. When she opens the door, he lurches in and scuttles into the bedroom. He has mud stains on his suit, he reeks of wine and weed.

Rena follows Paul. "What are you doing?"

"Is he here?" Paul smacks his lips and wipes his brow with his handkerchief.

"Who?"

"You know who." He can't catch his breath.

"Paul, come back when you're sober. Or better, don't come back. This is getting really boring."

"Fuck you. Wait. I don't mean that. Listen, I need you, Rena. Things are getting really crazy with Annette."

"I told you to apologize to her. Did you do that?"

"I love you. I know you don't love me, but I love you. I want to take care of you. You need me to take care of you."

"Actually, I don't, Paul. I need you to leave."

"Let's get married."

"You're already married to Annette!"

He winces like an animal caught in a trap. "This isn't fair."

"Paul, we had our fun."

"I lent you money when you were homeless! I took care of you!" His flushed face goes slack, tears gather in the corners of his eyes.

"You know I'm grateful, Paul."

"I don't care if you're grateful. I want to be with you. And I'm being crucified for it."

"Things change."

"No."

"It's better this way."

"Don't hate me, Rena." His eyes roll large like a steer's just before slaughter.

"Paul, it's time to move on."

"No." Crying, full-bore, head hanging.

"Yes!"

Rena places a hand on his shoulder, but when he looks up at her, his face is twisted and wet. He lurches away. She tries to touch him. He shoves her. "You fucking bitch. I am one of three top fashion photographers in New York. Do you think it's some small thing that I chose you? That I ruined my life for you? What are your priorities? What do I mean to you? Nothing? Are you hollow? Are you heartless? I think so. Here's the news: without heart, you'll never make it. Without a heart, you're just good bones and a pussy. Not special. Nothing. Not special. Just a cunt."

Rena slaps him, and he falls to his knees sobbing. A blubbering child, fleshy and miserable, glossy with booze sweat. Snot drips from his nose. She tries to pick him up but he won't, can't, stand up. He smells bad, like garbage that's been left in the heat. My god, Rena thinks, he's wet himself. She leaves him there, on the floor. That night, when she returns, he's gone.

THE DRYER-WARM SWEATSHIRT, THE ZIPLOC BAG OF scrubbed plums for the ride, the car registration, the Post-it note with the real estate agent's phone number, the map of the Eastern Seaboard with the route highlighted, bottled water, extra sunglasses, a wad of cash. Oil and tires checked. Seatbelts checked. "Did everyone pee?" No answer. Finally the Explorer's doors thunk shut, the air conditioner is set on high, and the vehicle eases back out of the drive. From his vantage point on the flagstone walk, Rick tracks Laura's negotiation of the SUV bumper past the delicate shell of his Maxima. "Call me as soon as you get there!"

The windshield tint obscures Laura's pursed smile. Is she concentrating on steering or is she pissed off at me for not sitting there beside her? Probably both. But it's just One More Thing, isn't it? An accretion compressed under its own weight, like soul coal, her resentment means nothing because there is nothing anyone can do about it.

In the backseat, Trina and Henry hang over their Game Boys oblivious, like puppets with their strings cut. Laura barks and they raise their Super-Mario-blinded eyes and comprehension dawns: Daddy is not driving the car! He is illogically standing on the front lawn, without them, left behind in their big house while they go on a fun vacation. They flap their hands good-bye, crazy as rabid poodles, the temporary insanity a welcome distraction from the vibes pinging back and forth between Rick and Laura. Finally, the car has slipped too far, its windows glazed white with summer light, impervious. The vehicle drifts off through the depths of the shaded street, as anonymous as an ocean liner cleaving the green sea. It turns right and disappears.

Rick examines a fallen chunk of rotten maple branch lying on the lawn. It's good to remain out here a little while longer, in case Laura has forgotten something. If she has, she will see me in the middle of the front yard, the loyal dog standing guard. I will stay right here until Labor Day when you return with darker skin and lighter hair. That's the deal, isn't it? The family has fun and I do penance. We'll talk on the phone every night and I will gripe about work and the city heat, and you will tell me about the frigid sea and the farmstand corn and the perfect peaches.

The street remains vacant, so Rick ambles up the brick steps. Inside, he stumbles over a mislaid brown paper sack of snorkle masks and flippers. First topic of discussion for tonight's phone call. A visit to the pricey surf shop that smells of rubber and coconut oil to buy replacement stuff. Rick runs the numbers and calculates the outlay at about a hundred bucks. A small price for freedom.

Rick's house is cluttered with sheet-draped furniture. Like a Chekhov set, he thinks. Laura has arranged this going-away present. Painters are coming next week. Nothing like a bunch of hulking, non-English-speaking Polish guys wandering around your house at the crack of dawn to keep you straight and sober. Her position, of course, is that the house is going to be empty all day while Rick is at work, so this will be the best time to get it painted. Rick is pretty sure he has relatives who died in Poland during the war.

The windows glow with the deep color of the maples, the sun-saturated flat lawns, the rhodies and peonies only now dropping their last pink blooms. The light enlarges the volume of the house. It's a good house, but Rick has never thought of it as his own. Many families have lived here before my family. Probably many more will follow. Who knows how long we'll stay here, or who will take our place?

He slips off his Top-Siders and pads into the brilliant kitchen. Why does it need to be painted? Why does Laura insist on this endless regeneration? Is she bored? Probably. The hum of a neighbor's lawnmower wafts through the screened windows. My kitchen, he thinks. My stove, my fridge, my plates, my cutlery. That's why people don't get divorced. Don't want to lose the props. Isn't that what the black kids call it? "Props." Even if it is all make-believe, it's a home. It's a home that symbolizes home. And I'm a husband and father who symbolizes a husband and father. I'm a man who symbolizes a man.

Rick finds a carton of juice in the fridge and sloshes a cold dollop into a clean glass. Laura bought this glass. Selected it, considered it. Harvested it and tucked it into the warp and woof of our nest. Spill. The ants will have to take care of it because I'm not wiping that counter. And so it begins. Ha! He gulps the cold sweet liquid in two swallows and burps. I could light a cigarette right now if I wanted to. Right in the middle of my kitchen. Laura's kitchen, but mine now. I could gorge on a pastrami sandwich over the sink, let the fat juice dribble off my chin into the drain. Leave beer bottles on every horizontal surface. Fart. Take a dump with the bathroom door wide open. Fucking pee on the fucking floor.

I could have an affair! The thing Laura would least suspect me of doing while she's gone. Smoking, not lifting the toilet seat, yes, but fucking around? Never. She doesn't think of me that way. She knows what I am. A dependable, reliable, money-earning, ball-less husband.

Did she ever really lust for me? Would she have wanted my cock if it hadn't been loaded with children? Does a woman ever want a cock the way a man wants her to want it? Look at gay guys. They do what men really want to do. Fuck each other like goats. Right? Well, some women obviously like to do that, too. Or pretend to want that. Just not the ones who want kids. Or just not Laura. Or just not Laura with me. Maybe with someone else. Not me.

Is it hormones? Fatigue? No. She just doesn't like me anymore. Maybe she loves me. But she doesn't like me. She's angry at me for everything I've ever done, for everything that anybody's ever done. We were friends once. We were allies. But we're not allies any-more. We're enemies. No, worse, we're diplomats from foreign countries. We go through elaborate rituals to keep the peace, for-getting what it is we want from each other in the first place.

Rick roams the house picking up socks and towels and toys. He gathers up the morning newspapers, sorts them neatly and drops them by the basement door. Well, fuck her. I don't like her, either. I live in a black hole of domesticity. Household appliances, kids' school clothes, sneakers, just plain fucking food. How do you spend three hundred bucks in a supermarket? Oh, but she's got an answer to that one: "You try shopping for this family, you'll see." The credit card bills come to four figures every month. And I come up with the money to pay them. I hold up my end. But it never ends. Prescriptions. Movies. Chess matches. Magazine subscriptions. Flowers. Underwear. P-T-fucking-A dues. Hey Laura, get a real job why don'tcha?

Does she ever bother to consider what I have to do to get that money? How much time the clinic takes up? That it's a business? Cash in, cash out. Insurance companies, suppliers, bills from labs, rent. The phones alone. The air-conditioning. The law firm I had to hire to chase bad debt. Laura thinks all I have to do is hang out with patients, hold their hands and gossip. And the money arrives, just like magic. I should sit her down with the accountant for just one afternoon and open her eyes to the shenanigans of the claims adjusters and the patients who move and leave no forwarding address, show her the tax forms for Zoe, the limitless billing from the labs, the fees from the cleaning company. Or those plant people who take care of those fucking plants in the reception room. The plants she said I had to have. Never thought about what they'd cost. The bills from the accountant who cuts the checks to pay the bills.

But she'll just start listing how much laundry she does in a week, how she has to shuttle the kids to the doctor and the dentist and the orthodontist. How she has to wait for them after school, how she has to endure the other mothers doing the same thing. How the cleaning girl is unreliable and has to be followed around the house. How she has to watch the yard workmen, the dry cleaners, the grocery boys, everyone. And she's right. I know she's right.

If it weren't for the kids, we wouldn't be together anymore, that's obvious. And who are these kids? Organisms. Issue. Fruit. That's all. Manifestations of DNA composed of muscles and bones and fat, self-conscious and fearful, each created with a built-in timer. They will endure for about seventy years, then die and decay just like I will die and decay. Of the billions of people who exist on this globe of saltwater and dirt, my two kids are genetically related to me. So what? There are probably lots of people who are genetically related to me and I don't even know their names, let alone "love" them. I can "parent" Henry and Trina all I want, they're gonna be who they're gonna be, with or without me. Did Dad ever give two shits about what was going to happen to me in the future? If I were hit by a truck tomorrow, they'd get over it and still be who they were going to be.

Rick has one of Henry's T-shirts in his hand. It smells of boy. I miss them more when they're not around. What kind of love is that? Conceptual children. I love them most when they're close but not too close, or sleeping, or in school. Whenever I'm actually with them, I want to get away from them as soon as possible. They're kids. Lovable but annoying. Like a jigsaw puzzle you can't be bothered figuring out because the picture is so obvious.

Maybe by being apart for a while, we'll realize we miss each other. Or not. And if in the fall things are still like this between Laura and me, maybe we'll go to a couples counselor. God, listen to me. Couples counselor. Put on the fucking blindfold and get up against that brick wall. Like I don't know the steps: counselor (talk it out), Prozac (calm it down), Viagra (get it up) . . . whatever you have to do to endure. Already on the Viagra. For what that's worth.

Hey, Rick, just hang in there and wait for the kids to grow up, wait for the body to stop having so many urges, wait till the fight goes out of you, wait for retirement. By which time you will be so beaten down by a compromised life, so old and decrepit, that you will be more than grateful to have a warm body to clutch in the middle of the long, dark, painful, good night.

That's the deal, isn't it? Compromise so you're not left alone. Gather up a nest egg and wait it out. And then, impotent and postmenopausal, me and Laura will spend our last days clucking and fussing about how we miss the kids, take afternoon forays to the supermarket to cash in those coupons and reminisce about how nice that trip to Tuscany was?

Just get on that old conveyor belt of life, pal, enjoy those golden years and reserve your space in the assisted community (with the attached Alzheimer ward), where you will wander anonymous corridors until you lose your mind completely. Senile and incontinent you will lie in bed day after day after day, a few photos of unrecognizable grandchildren taped to the wall beside you, TV set aflicker, a world spinning on without you.

And then one night, after the volume of the TV sets is lowered for restless sleep, the shit and piss of your cellmates swabbed away by sullen Caribbean blacks, Celebrex and Plavix and Synthroid merrily coursing through your veins, your heart will hit the pause button and stay paused. And by then, everyone, especially you, will be happy to see you go.

Rick fishes out a brittle packet of cigarettes hidden behind the stereo and lights one. He lies down on the couch in the TV room, and thinking he might want to catch the ball game later, finishes half a beer and falls asleep. When he wakes, he makes a show of jumping up, brewing fresh coffee and looking for more chores. He tidies and sweeps the garage. Wipes off the lawnmower blades. He considers cleaning the gutters and stops for another beer.

Bottle in hand Rick trots from room to room yanking windows open, letting the leaf-cooled breeze into the vacant house. It's early for dinner but he orders moo shu pork from the joint downtown and eats it while watching the Mets lose. He leaves the greasy cartons on the coffee table and takes a ride to the center of town for ice cream. He stops in the smoke shop, scans the dirty magazines, too intimidated by the Pakistani who runs the place to buy one, instead buys a fresh pack of cigarettes and heads home. He makes one more circuit of the house, mulls over jogging, doesn't, takes an easy bowel movement and a hot shower, smokes another cigarette and hits the sack early. As he falls asleep he thinks, It's so much easier when she's not around.

A house finch yodeling outside his window greets him as he opens his eyes. Six fifteen, and he's wide-awake. Buoyant, he showers, fries up some eggs, postpones jogging one more time and takes a long walk instead. He spends all day organizing the attic. He drinks two more beers, thinking, I'm the kind of guy who is energized by booze, and falls out on the couch. He wakes up from the nap hungry. He liked the Chinese food so much, he orders it again, joking with the delivery boy as if they are old friends. Sunday fades in happy isolation. He could call old acquaintances, the ones he complains about never seeing. "Hey, my wife's out of town! What's up?" And what would we do? Go to a movie? A strip club? Have dinner? Why bother? I love being on my own.

Rick calls Laura and she says she's happy to be at the beach, that she wishes he was there with them. But Rick knows she's relieved to be away from the stress of dealing with his moods. He complains weakly about all the patients with summer colds. It's a game they are playing, happy to be separated but not copping to it.

For the rest of the week, Rick manages to rise with the sun and get to work before Zoe. He clears his desk. He carefully reviews all the lab reports. He digs out back issues of both the *Journal of the American Medical Association* and the *American Medical News* and reads them over his lunch, something he hasn't done in years. He's more easygoing with Zoe and she seems to appreciate it. He compliments her on her tan. Since many of his patients are gone for the summer, his workload is light and he's back home before sunset every day. He roams the house, sniffing for damage or theft. The painters are making slow but even progress.

Every morning Rick does fifty sit-ups and twenty-five push-ups. One night he avoids TV altogether, reads thirty pages of a novel by someone named T. C. Boyle, gives up, calls Laura and ends up on the phone with her for forty-five minutes. When Laura tells him she's been meditating and that Rick should try it, he says he will. Henry comes to the phone, gives his dad the sandcastle and ice-cream report, and hangs up before Rick can say good-bye. Rick meanders out into the backyard, places himself under the canopy of stars and smokes a cigarette. He thinks, I'm such a lucky guy.

Friday night arrives and Rick decides to take in a movie. But he never gets there. Instead, he strolls the twisting streets of Greenwich Village. Everywhere he goes he sees couples holding hands, kissing, laughing together. He enters a lounge and sits at the bar, waiting for an interesting woman to come sit next to him just so he can tell her how much he misses his wife. It happens all the time on TV. It's a way to get laid, right? Isn't that what I want? To get picked up and go home with a stranger?

When a bony-faced queen tries to strike up a conversation, Rick finishes his drink and leaves thinking, I miss Laura. Back home, he tosses his keys on the kitchen table and they echo off silent walls. Why doesn't my family come running in? Why isn't Trina grabbing hold of my legs and shouting, "Daddy, we missed you so much! Mommy said we had to come back and get you!" Why aren't they here? Why aren't I there?

Rick finds a bag of stale chips shoved behind the cereal boxes, stowed in a halfhearted attempt at discipline. He grabs four beers, uncaps them and lines them up on the coffee table. He flicks on the TV and finds himself watching a movie called *Sleepless in Seattle*. Tom Hanks's wife has just died. Rick notices the red light of the message machine blinking and his heart leaps. There's one person on this cold, cold earth who thinks of me. Why can't I appreciate that?

In the first blush of dawn, Rick finds himself on the couch with a sour stomach and blocked sinuses. His jeans are strewn with oily potato chip crumbs. In his gut a restlessness, an anger is building. He roams the house, fuzzy. Go up to bed, Rick. Just go to bed. Go-to-bed. I can't go to bed, because to go to bed just means sleeping, then waking up again. And what will I do tomorrow, I mean today, Saturday? I'm tired of cleaning.

Rick finds a bottle of whiskey in the liquor cabinet. He knocks back a shot. The pudding in his head shifts and throbs. He downs another. He lights a cigarette. "Yes, the house will stink of smoke, Laura." He hears his own voice reverberate, unanswered. So what? He has an urge to go find a bar and get into a brawl, but it's five thirty in the morning.

What if I call an escort service? That would be interesting. Even if I don't do anything with the girl. Just sit her down and tell her about my fucked-up life. Or tell her about my fucked-up life and then have sex with her. That could work. But then I'd have to kill her. And myself. An option. The whiskey kicks in.

In his study, Rick slides open the bottom drawer of his mahogany desk. In the rear, "secret" compartment, are two videotapes. The first is called *Faces of Death* and it catalogues fatal accidents, suicides, murder. Footage of people shooting themselves in the mouth, dying in car collisions, exploding, burning, all caught on video. Why do I keep this? Posterity? The second tape was given to him as a joke by a best friend's wife on his fortieth birthday. It's a collection of vintage porno featuring John Holmes a.k.a. "Johnny Wadd." Rick thinks, in a few years Henry will be old enough to know what this is. I'll have to find a better hiding place. On the other hand, pretty soon I can throw it out because I won't know what to do with it.

The Johnny Wadd tape delivers the full spectrum of cheesiness, from the orange-tinted lighting to the oscillating psychedelic wah-wah soundtrack. Rick likes the hippie girl Johnny is plowing and before he can hold himself back, he's coming. Waves of ecstasy roll through him as the moustachioed Casanova slides his stem in and out of the spaced-out chick. Rick thinks, what a waste. Beautiful girl like that. Then he thinks, I guess girls didn't shave their pussies in 1970. Then he thinks, wonder where that girl is today? Probably a Republican home-maker in Orange County. Then he thinks, I'm such an asshole. For a few minutes he doesn't move, letting the blobs of cum cool on his stomach. He smears the gray puddle with the tip of his fin-ger, making a perfect circle around his navel. The stuff exudes a familiar smell that's weirdly reassuring. Rick wipes his belly with his underwear and, bare-assed now, flips off the VCR with the remote, leaving the TV screen empty and blue. He curls into a fetal posture and falls asleep on the couch, dragging the cushions over his body in lieu of a blanket. He dreams deep dreams, farts unconscious farts and luxuriates in the warmth of his own gas.

RENA LETS THE TERRY-CLOTH ROBE FALL OPEN AND inspects the faint stubble on her legs as she addresses the cell phone. "What are you telling me, Marissa?"

Marissa says, "They decided to go brunette."

Outside the hotel room window, birds hop in and out of the flowering red hibiscus. Rena can hear the garden workers spray-ing down the ferns and flowers, Spanglish mingling with the birdsong and traffic hum and the last of the morning's humidity. She lights a cigarette and says, "That's such crap." Rena thinks, I'm so over this L.A. thing. This con game. The perfect weather, everything's a big deal. And all they do is lie.

"Sorry, honey." Marissa's voice is clipped and cool. Probably flipping through photos as she speaks. Things are different now.

"That cover was mine. I was due." The hairs on Rena's legs are growing stronger and sharper. Shaving turns leg skin into a weapon. Time for a wax.

"I agree. What do you want me to say?" Does Marissa sound

far away because she is far away or because she just doesn't care?

"I want you to say I have the cover." Rena finds a miniature bottle of vodka in the minibar and drains it. It tastes wrong. She feels sleepy. It's ten AM.

"I can't say that, honey. Next one. You're going to get it."

"Does this have something to do with Paul?"

"Don't even go there."

"Paul is best friends with those guys."

"It's not worth it, honey. Listen, Tuesday, I've got you in for a session for H&M. Stay away from salt this weekend. You're flying tomorrow, right? No sundae on the flight."

"Fuck H&M. I need a cover. I'm spinning my wheels, Marissa."

"You made twenty thousand dollars last month. That's not spinning your wheels."

Paul is doing this. It has to be Paul. The editor's assistant had called her directly, all wound up, saying she had to cancel gigs, be ready, absolutely no haircuts. The designer himself called Rena. Everyone called. Everything was set but the actual session.

"So who's shooting this? Have they decided?"

"I haven't heard. Listen, Rena, I ordered a car for you. It'll be there in twenty minutes. Go to my spa. Put some mud on your face and relax. It's on me. We'll talk Monday, OK?"

Rena is treated like a star the minute she walks in. She's ushered to the special rooms, worked on by the top girl. As she lies on her stomach, waiting for the masseuse, she hears chatter outside the room. Paul Yorkin is shooting the fall cover with Angie. Has to be the same one. Of course. So I lost the gig. Without a cover I lose my spot. I will become second rate. Once you lose your momentum you're dead. Marissa lied to me. Fuck her. Fuck them all. I didn't ask for this. They dragged me into this, especially Paul.

On her way out the twittering girl at the counter wants an

autograph and Rena explodes, "You don't even know my fucking name." The girl looks hurt, so Rena promises to send a
photo, signed. She lights a cigarette and someone comes running
at her, shouting, "No!" Rena escapes out the door.

I should call Paul and chew him out, but what's the point?
He'd only gloat. Or worse, try to start something again. Fat
fuck. It's not my fault he left his wife, that he's unhappy. Now
he wants to make me unhappy. And why? Because he "loves"
me? Bullshit. He's as selfish and piggish as the rest. So he ruined
his life. Who cares? He'll get another girl. Another girl he can
fall in love with. Have babies with. I never loved him like that.
Never did. Couldn't. I tried but I couldn't. That's all. Not my
fault. Shit happens.

She calls Fred. But Fred sounds distant and preoccupied,
absorbed in his readings or just stoned.

On her way back to the Four Seasons, Rena buys a liter of
vodka, hangs a DND on the door, puts a DND on the phone,
draws the curtains, clicks on the cable, and zones out on confessional talk shows for the rest of the afternoon. She wakes up
dizzy with no idea of the time, calls room service for two pots of
coffee, drinks one cup, gets back into the vodka and orders the
pay-per-porno. What would I do if I ever met a man with a dick
as large as the guys in those films? Doesn't matter, I'm not fucking anybody anymore. The porno world is just like real world,
full of big dumb pricks.

By four in the morning she's eaten every Famous Amos
cookie, the Pringles and the Mason jar of cashews in the minibar. She falls asleep in the bath, cell phone in her hand, calling
Paul's voice mail and hanging up.

She wakes when the concierge rings her room to tell her that
her driver has arrived. A half hour later she's made it to the
lobby, where she chews out the front-desk girl over the inciden-
tal charges. The driver takes her bag and she chain-smokes all
the way to the airport. Her damp cell phone isn't working.

On the plane she drinks a bottle of Beaujolais and lets the businessman next to her make goo-goo eyes and dumb conversation until she finally shuts him down by asking about his wife. Then using the overpriced in-flight phone, she calls Marissa, her favorite haircutter, her favorite makeup guy. She calls every bar and every restaurant until she finds Adam and then insists he stay on the phone until she lands. After an hour he says he has to get off. She finds Fred and now he sounds happy to hear from her, ready to engage. She asks if she can come by and he says he would love to see her. Could she pick up fresh fruit and flowers on her way?

The captain cheerily announces that they are ahead of schedule but Rena knows from the cyclic roar of the engines they are stacked over the airport. When they finally land there is no gate available, and when they do find a gate, there are no personnel to wheel the ship into the ramp. She tries to find Adam again and is told by two different flight attendants to stop making calls. She falls asleep under the thin airline blanket while everyone on the plane files off. The businessman sheepishly wakes her and hands her his card. She shoves it into the barf bag. Her cell phone is completely dead as she walks up the ramp off the plane.

The limo driver waits at the bottom of the escalator with a sign that reads "Coke" instead of "Cook" and she thinks, that would work. She hands him her bag and they walk out to the parking garage in silence. In the car she lights a cigarette. The driver says something and she snaps, "Don't talk to me," cracks the window and glares at the other limos and cabs flashing by. The LIE is a parking lot and they are stuck for another half hour. The city skyline lies cushioned in a gray haze.

When Rena arrives in front of Fred's building, she remembers he asked for fresh fruit and flowers. She rolls her overnighter around the corner to a twenty-four-hour Korean fruit stand. She finds kiwis and a grapefruit and a bouquet of gladiolas. Under glaring fluorescent light, the foreign-born men who run the place seem harried and distrustful, unmoved by her glamour. When she gets back to Fred's building, he doesn't answer the buzzer.

She has his key, so she lets herself into the building. It is late, the unventilated stairwell close and hot. The apartment is dark and quiet, too. Fred is under the covers in his bedroom, asleep. For the next hour, Rena arranges flowers, cleans up the little kitchen. She feels useful for the first time in a while and it occurs to her that she wouldn't mind being Fred's wife, taking care of him, cleaning his house, feeding him. She takes a break to smoke a cigarette, strips and gets into bed with him even though she's on West Coast time and is bound to be awake all night.

He looks so gone when he's asleep. Younger. He's let a piece of fluff grow on his chin and it makes him look like he's from a different time. Maybe someday they will really get together. Rena wants to wake him and tell him that they have to leave, right now, run away to another place. Greece maybe. The islands are perfect this time of year. He could clean himself up, and they could sun themselves and read every day. Or Morocco. Or Australia. Wherever. She'd pay for it all.

I'm being ridiculous, she thinks. He likes it here. And that's OK. We're together. Things don't have to be the way they are for everyone else. She wants to squeeze him hard, but is afraid of waking him. She compromises by stroking his arm. His skin is smooth like a marble Greek sculpture at the museum.

His limbs are flat and still. Like the way Daddy was. She puts a hand to his forehead, cool as the grapefruit she's just picked out of the grocery bag. She shakes him and liquid seeps out of his mouth. She lifts one of his eyelids and it stays open, staring.

Carefully, Rena dresses. Methodically she checks the apartment for drugs. Under the armchair she finds ten glassine envelopes, five opened, five untouched. She gathers them up and drops them into her purse. Then she calls 911. When she slips out the front door, she leaves it unlocked. There's no reason to stay. Emergency Services will come and they'll know what to do.

THE EMERGENCY ROOM IS SECOND RATE. THE WORK depressing and stressful. The best thing about it is that when you're done for the night, you're done. You never see the patients again. You don't have to think about them. Although you do, you do think about them.

Tonight, Rick is performing jobs he shouldn't be doing, like taking blood pressure and collecting urine and ushering patients to the X-ray room or having to lay out his own suture set. For two hours, he's been the only doctor on duty. In those two hours, three different knife lacerations and four ODs have trundled in the front door. He handles them, even though every time he reaches for something he's found that the nurses have stolen items from his stock. They've run out of sterile surgical drapes. They've almost run out of latex gloves. The place stinks of the sour fluids of the body diluted with pure oxygen. The orderly can't keep up with the dots of blood decorating the floor.

An old jazz trumpeter comes in. Nice guy. Totally demented. Hallucinating. Complaining of diarrhea. Lesions all over his skin. Rick puts it together: the "three Ds"— dermatitis, diarrhea, dementia. The guy's got pellagra, for god's sake! A nineteenth-century vitamin deficiency. Why? Because he's been living on fried white rice. Says it tastes good. Fried rice and black coffee. Now he's completely round the bend. The Medicaid shrinks can't wait to force-feed him Haldol and Klonipin and all he really needs is a square meal.

Like most of 'em, the old trumpeter lives alone, spends his life watching TV, smoking cigarettes and drinking. Of course, the booze doesn't help. The old guy's fondling the cusp of senility to begin with. The alcohol will take that cusp and stab it right through his meek old heart. The guy forgets to eat, becomes malnourished, loses his mind. He'll probably go back to eating the way he likes to eat, fall down a flight of stairs and break his neck.

Clean the guy up and send him home. Stick a couple of cans of chocolate-flavored nutritional drink in the bag for good measure. The oldster has lived his life his own way so his problems are his own fault. It's his own fault he's survived this long.

But not everyone who shows up is geriatric. The immune-compromised appear almost every night, HIV-ers mostly, Hep C. Some hemophiliacs. Half the time it's something simple like a case of oral candidiasis complicated by panic. A can of oxygen and a fistful of tranks and antibiotics usually get 'em through the night until they can see their regular doctor in the morning. They're not bad people, just unlucky.

The kids upset Rick, but fortunately there are pediatric specialists who take care of them. And there are the "normals" who show up like wide-eyed Alices through the looking glass, not sure what the protocol is, more afraid of the place itself than the broken finger or the fever that drove them here. Rick knows them best, members of his own tribe. But their fear stirs up his contempt, so he hides behind his professional mask, and becomes one more impersonal facet of the emergency room.

Finally there are the junkies, not to be confused with the crackheads or coke fiends like the guy who died a while back. The junkies are a hospital-loving society unto themselves with two main subdivisions: heroin addicts (which include methadone addicts) and pill-heads (they lust after a rainbow-colored spectrum of pharmacology: Nembutals, Tuinals, Darvocets, Valiums, Libriums, Biphetamines, Tylenol 4's and Percodans). A pill-head sees a hospital as nothing more than a vast storage facility for pharmaceuticals. Shooters love the place, too. The brand-new syringes alone make the place seem like the promised land. And how 'bout all that Dilaudid, morphine, fentanyl, Demerol, Percoset, oxycodin—gosh almighty, the hospital is Christmas morning every single day. And so junkies are endlessly scamming and scheming, trying to convince the doctors that the Vicodin or the Seconal are essential to their very existence.

This night ends with drama. Two cops show up with a big guy covered in blood. They want him stitched up before they haul him out to Rikers Island. He beat up two Dominican heroin dealers on Avenue A. Put them both in the hospital. Then their friends found the big guy and sliced him up with a straight razor.

Rick insists that the cuffs be taken off the guy, who promises he'll be good. As Rick is stitching him up, he tries to draw him out. "Fortunately, these lacerations are clean-edged. Keeping the wound moist will keep the scarring minimal. Tell you this, though, one more inch to the right and your friends would have hit the jugular and you wouldn't be here, you'd be in the morgue."

"They're not my friends."

"No, I guess not. You from the city originally?"

"Farm upstate. Orchard. No harvest this year."

"No?"

"Van got stole."

"I see."

"My sister's on the cover of British *Vogue*."

"Really?"

"Makes a million bucks a minute. Two million."

"Well, then, I'll send the bill to her."

"You do that, 'cause it's all her fault."

"I will."

Billy squints at Rick. "You Jewish?"

"As I matter of fact I am."

Billy takes this in and decides to clam up.

From their dialogue, Rick concludes the guy is either completely schizophrenic or temporarily out of his tree due to drug use. The cops want the guy to go to Rikers but Rick insists he be sent out for psychiatric observation. Rick has to stay an extra hour just to finish processing the paperwork.

That night, when he gets home, Rick falls asleep so fast, the suddenness wakes him up again. He lies in the dark listening to his heart bumping with fear. Rick gets up and takes a Valium. Is insanity contagious?

THE RINGING WAKES RENA AT ELEVEN. THIS IS A PROFESsional commitment on her part, sleeping as long as possible. Don't get up till the first call of the day. Slumber restores skin, clears eyes, lets the soul find itself. Marissa's assistant calls out to Rena while she hides under the covers. Why doesn't Marissa dial the fucking phone herself? Whatever. Rena stretches in a big yoga arch, her navel aimed at the ceiling, head swimming, legs quivering, before letting herself collapse, leaning out over the bed to find the Marlboro Lights, lighting one, and snatching up the phone.

"Yeah?"

"Rena? Hold for Marissa." Rena pulls the biggest drag she can into her lungs. Some kind of hip Muzak/house music fills the time until Marissa gets on, terse right off the blocks. "Rena? Where are you?"

Sleep recedes, memory cascades into place. "Shit."

"Don't tell me you're still at home."

"Fuck."

Rena flies out of bed, phone in one hand, snatching up clothes with the other.

Marissa is loud. "This doesn't work, kid. This doesn't work at all."

"Don't yell at me, Marissa." She carries the phone into the shower.

"Maybe, just maybe if you had your bookings stacked, I could work this out. But Rena, RENA, here's the deal. They don't hire you not to show up."

"I'll be there in ten minutes."

"No, you won't."

"I will!" Bitch.

"You won't, baby. They already booked your replacement."

"Who?"

"Never mind who."

"A client of yours?"

"Screw you. You fucked this up, kid, don't try to stick it on me." Marissa hangs up.

Rena leaves the shower running, wanders into the kitchen and finds a can of beer in the fridge. Budweiser. Why do I have a Budweiser in my fridge? Was someone here I don't remember? She scans the room. The ashtrays are full of crumpled Lucky Strike butts. Who smokes Lucky Strikes?

Rena sees she's still wearing the bra she had on last night, tugs it off and throws it in the trash, there will be no bra this morning. Did I have sex with my bra on? I'm like a fucking character on that sitcom. Wait a minute, what's her name was at that party last night! How weird is that? Because she's on that show, right? Sarah . . . Jessica . . . No . . . wait a minute, it wasn't her! It was the other Parker . . . Mary Louise Parker! Right. No. Was she? Whoa. Wait, gonna get this straight. Parker Posey! That's who it was! Damn, girl, you're getting brain damage. Gotta slow down.

Fucking book party Marissa insisted I go to. Bunch of leering weird guys. All those boring book party people. Editors making small talk, their pig eyes scouting my boobs. The writers with their bullshit anger. I'm supposed to be impressed. "Oh, I'm just a dumb blonde. I don't even know even how to spell! Please lecture me!" Ivy League assholes who think they're rebels 'cause they can grow a goatee.

Like I give a shit what they do. That dickhead who bragged about how much whiskey he can drink. He didn't last so long. Drink your ass under the table, professor. So wait. Whiskey not martinis. Whiskey not martinis. But I was drinking martinis. Maybe that was later. Or earlier. No wonder I'm hungover.

Mr. Whiskey tried to kiss me in the cab and then passed out. Left him there, right? Jumped out at the corner, found another cab and ended up at Moomba. And then later. What happened later? Later. Later is the problem. Wasn't I drinking bottled water and watching infomercials? The meat was turning and turning on its spit, dripping blood. And I was alone. But what happened before that? Shit. Fuckit. It's OK not to remember what time you go to bed. But it's not OK not to know who you fucked.

Fred is dead. Fred is dead. Fred is dead. Rena lies on the bed and falls asleep with the can of beer in her hand.

She is dreaming about her own apartment. In the dream the apartment has no outer walls and anyone who wants to can wander in at any time. In the dream she's in bed sleeping, unable to open her eyes.

She can feel the people in the room with her, passing through, examining her, watching her breathe. She doesn't mind them looking at her, but she wishes she had walls. Maybe if she moved to a different apartment, changed her address. But for some reason that isn't possible. Yet.

A buzzer sounds and the gaping people disperse like a school of freaked-out fish. And now because they are gone, Rena opens her eyes. She can feel her eyes opening. She can do it. They are open. Except she's still asleep. The buzzer sounds again. She understands she is awake with her eyes closed, dreaming that her eyes are open. The veil of slumber falls away, she can do it, she can open her eyes. Someone is buzzing her apartment.

She opens her eyes, rolls onto her side and checks the blocky numerals of the clock radio. Too early. The buzzer rings one more time. Maybe someone has sent me a huge bouquet of lilies. Paul used to do that. She staggers to the intercom.

"Yes?" Her voice croaky from cigarettes.

"Reba?"

"Excuse me?" Maybe it's one of those garishly packaged invites to a new club. Anything to get your attention.

"Got something for you."

Later she thinks, I should have known. If I had been listening more carefully, I would have figured it out. Maybe I did know and didn't care because I knew this day was coming sooner or later, so it might as well be sooner. Rena pushes the buzzer button, finds a robe, splashes water on her face and waits by the front door.

Without checking the peephole, she lets the door drift open as far as the safety chain will allow. She thinks, I have to move to a doorman building. What if it's some kind of lunatic or stalker asshole? The elevator doors clank open and Rena sees a man enter the hallway, get his bearings, then make his way toward her, checking each door, as if someone had shuffled the alphabetical enumeration, putting the "B" next to the "D" instead of "C." She doesn't recognize Frank until it's too late.

Blindly, he comes directly to the gap and then seeing he is being observed, looks Rena in the eye and says, "I'm here to see Reba Cook."

"Hi, Frank."

"Reba? Cheez Louise. Have you gotten even taller? My god."

"Frank, in New York, we call people before we visit."

"Reba, can I come in, please?"

"No, you cannot fucking come in!"

"It's important."

"Hey, Frank, you're not my boss anymore, OK? You're not anything. You're not even a bad memory. So why don't you just turn around and go back to where you came from and leave me alone? 'Come in'? Fuck you, come in! Go away, go as far away as you can!" She glances over her shoulder. The apartment looks like someone bombed it. Bits of tinfoil crumpled on the rug. A towel shoved into the corner. Coffee cups, beer cans, stacks of magazines. The home of a lunatic.

"Reba, there's no reason to take that tone."

"Uh-huh." He's looking at me different now, isn't he? Now I'm someone special, not some dumb teller. "Frank, stop staring at me like that!"

"You've gotten prettier or something. But I don't like what you've done to your eyebrows."

Rena forces the pressure in her chest back down into her guts. "Frank, you just woke me up and I really really really really don't want to see you." She can feel a tantrum building. Don't give him the satisfaction. She slows down. "In fact, you're probably the last person in the world I want to see. So go away. And don't come back. Ever."

"You don't have to be hurtful, Reba . . . I mean Rena, whatever. And besides, I didn't think you'd want to see me, to tell you the truth you're not the easiest person in the world to find. But I have my ways, I have my ways. There's a certain benefit to being in financial services, despite what you think . . . by the way, the girls at the bank all send their love."

"Oh, jeez." Rena notices her own naked feet, her fingers clamped on the doorknob. It's a metal door, I can shut it, latch it, he won't be able to break it down. I can even call the police.

"Rena."

"I'm closing the door now, Frank. Please don't bother me again." She shuts the door.

Through the peephole she sees him out there staring back, as if his black eyes could burn right through the door. "Rena, it's about Billy."

Frank waits in the hall for twenty minutes while she showers and dries her hair. She applies her makeup precisely. She doesn't want to hear what he's going to say, she wants to put it off as long as possible. Something bad has happened. But why is Frank the one to tell me, and why didn't he just call? Anyway, if he's going to see me, he should see me the way I really am, the new me.

In the end, all her attention to detail doesn't make much difference. When she finally does let him in, he's momentarily rocked by her new look. Then he settles into his formal, lizard-like aloofness.

Frank says, "I saw you in a magazine. In an ad."

Rena says, "Tell me about Billy." She has made coffee without pouring a cup for Frank. Then he asks for some and she serves him while he ogles the apartment, like he's trying to figure out how much everything costs. Good, figure it out, Frank. Add it up, you could never afford it. I can take care of myself. I don't need you or Billy or anybody.

Frank sips with his usual dark grace. "I would drive by the old place about once a week. Sometimes Billy's van was there. Sometimes it wasn't. About four months after you disappeared, I realized I hadn't seen the van or Billy for a while. And being at the bank, I knew the mortgage and taxes and fire insurance were going unpaid. So I stopped up by the house. Must have been around February. Cold. I found a way in and sure enough, house was frozen solid. No pipes had burst, thank goodness, so I got your oil tank filled and refired the burner. Figured it might end up belonging to the bank, better keep it from ruination. Once it warmed up, the place didn't smell so good. Mice had been doing their business. You know. So I thought the best thing would be to clean up a bit. Filled up three garbage bags with stuff."

Rena watches Frank's lips moving. What does he want me to say, "Thank you for keeping my house up so you can steal it from me?" Instead, she says, "Thank you, Frank."

"No, well, it seemed like the right thing to do. Then I opened the fridge. Strange, even though the place was cold, the inside of the fridge was warm. Probably because of the mold and the fungus, I guess. They're living organisms and they more or less give off heat. A milk container had burst open. Not pretty. Not pretty at all. And bad smelling."

"Frank . . ."

"Too much for me to deal with right then. I got Annie to drop over a few days later and she took care of it. Says you have to throw that fridge away now. Once the mildew gets going, you can't save it. She knows a guy who will come pick it up."

"Tell me about Billy."

"Got the electric back on for you, too."

"Thank you."

"I checked for leaks in the roof, and it's tight."

"So you don't know where Billy is?"

"Well, see that's the thing. I asked around and found out about those checks you were sending him. He's been getting them forwarded to a mail drop here in New York. I sent him a letter, he never wrote back. Then the checks started coming back to the town post office. John, you know John, the postmaster? Well, he called me, wanted to know what he should do."

"Frank, just tell me."

"Well, it took me a while to find him. But see, your brother Billy's in something called Creedmore. It's a nuthouse."

"You saw him there."

"Oh, yeah. Got him to sign some papers. That's how we've been getting the checks cashed. I've used some of the money for the house upkeep. Taxes are still in arrears, though. I've been taking care of that."

"I don't care about the fucking house, Frank! So you're telling me Billy is in a hospital?"

"Looney bin. Especially for drug addicts and drunks. Especially those who commit crimes. Violent crimes. The rooms have locks on 'em." Merriment dances in Frank's eyes.

"How far is it from town?" He's enjoying this.

"Oh, it's not upstate. It's right here. In New York City."

"Oh God." Billy came to find me. Got in a fight with a cop. And now I'm supposed to bail him out. "He got in trouble?"

"Something like that. I guess he put a couple of guys in the hospital and got kind of cut up himself. You should visit him, Reba."

"Why?"

"Because he's your brother and for legal reasons. I can cash checks made out to him. But you're co-owner of the house."

"I don't want the house. You said it yourself, it isn't worth diddly."

"It's a little more complicated than that. There's liability, too. Not just ownership. Some kid falls down the old well. You'll get your ass sued."

"How did you find me, Frank?"

"It was easy. The checks. Bankers have access to information regular folks don't have."

"My bank told you where I lived?"

Frank's eyes lie like puddles of dirty engine oil. "I'll drive you out there. It would cheer him up."

"Frank, if I live to be a hundred, I'm never getting in a car with you again. You leave me the address and I'll find Billy on my own."

Frank reveals his yellow teeth and stands. "It's in the phone book, under mental institutions. And I won't bother you no more. But you have to see him. It's important even if you think it isn't."

"Fuck you, Frank."

"Yeah, well, you never were a very grateful person, were you, Rena? Selfish, self-centered, I guess that's the way it is for people like you. Never think of anyone else, because you don't have to. Especially now that you're rich and famous, huh? Don't have to do squat."

"Let me tell you what I don't have to do, Frank. I don't have to work for some hick banker from some hick town because I'm young and I'm dumb and don't know any better. I don't have to run his errands, I don't have to go parking with him and I don't have to put his ugly prick in my mouth. That's what I don't have to do."

Frank slowly takes in the apartment. "Well, I did what I came to do. He's your brother. As far as the house goes, I'll stop fore-stalling the taxes and the town will take it in receivership sooner or later. And I guess that's it."

Rena sits still until she hears the door close. Then she cracks another Budweiser.

THE TURKISH DRIVER FLICKS HIS SAD EYES TO THE rearview every few minutes, as if to check if she is still back there. His clean-shaven face has a blue tint of stubble and his coal black hair stands thick and straight like fur. He is rigid, as if girding for a fight. Rena stares at his muscular neck. What would it be like to touch it? Halfway to the hospital he murmurs into his cell phone and the language is a tattered blend of raw consonants and mewing vowels.

At the hospital, the Turk carefully positions the town car behind an ambulance, leaps from his seat and pops the door for Rena. He smells of mothballs and citrus. Don't they grow pop-pies in Turkey? Aren't Turks bad-asses? Didn't Fred tell me they massacred the Armenians? Rena wonders what his penis looks like. As long and dark as a skinned turkey neck, probably. As she approaches the front of the tan brick building, he grabs a white rag out of the trunk and begins to polish the Lincoln.

Rena checks in through layers of security and a variety of glum personnel, most of whom are in uniform. Everyone is Black or Latino. Everyone looks tired, worn down. The smell of sour cafeteria food hangs in the air like a threat. You get stuck in here, you don't get out.

The scuffed stainless steel elevator rises with sturdy torque, stopping once for a few people in pale green smocks. They all bear name tags and no one gives Rena a second look, which unnerves her. One man clutches a thick knot of latex hosing. She sees no patients.

When Rena gets to Billy's wing, she finds herself in an empty corridor dead-ended by a locked steel door. Beside the door is a large button. She pushes it and waits. Eventually a nurse comes through and Rena, ignored, slips in.

The ward features a smaller glass-walled room built into its center. In the room, three black women in white are filling in reports. Outside, a dozen chairs face a television set. A half dozen patients watch the set. One stands alone by a fruit juice dispenser, fumbling with a cup. A male patient next to Rena says, "Hey baby. How we doin' today?"

Rena thinks, maybe I should just try to find Billy's room without help.

"I said hey, baby, how's the weather out there? I heard on the news that it's 'sposed to be a nice day. I wouldn't know. They keep the air under control at all times. All kinds of infectious germs floating around. They float right in the door, attack the brain cells directly. So your best bet while you're in here is don't breathe. If you don't want to catch nothin'."

A woman wearing a kerchief on her head is slumped in a chair scribbling in an "easy" crossword book. She says, "Shut-tup, D."

"Suck my big black cock."

"I seen it. It ain't so big."

"You never seen my cock. You wish you did."

"What's a five-letter word for happiness?"

"Joy."

"That ain't five letters."

"Yes, it is. You jus' don't know how to spell."

A female patient in pajamas, white socks and flip-flops trudges by, glances at Rena, enters the glass-walled room, picks up a piece of ruled paper, scratches her ass and leaves.

Rena enters the sanctuary. "Excuse me?"

One of the women, as if noticing her for the first time, says, "Uh-huh? How can I help you, sweetheart?"

"Uh. My brother? Billy Cook?"

"Billy? Should be in his room."

"Where . . . ?"

"Number 222. Just down that way. I think he's resting."

"Can I just go in?"

"Oh, sure. Knock first, though, don't want to scare him. Has a reputation, but he's a pussycat."

A thin window has been punched into the blond wood door. From the outside, it looks like any hospital room. Not a prison. Not an asylum. "Billy?" She steps into the gloom, leaving the door open behind her, letting light seep in from outside. The room is empty. A vacant impersonal space for madness. And then she sees the shape. The hospital bed has been pulled into the middle of the room. No sheets, no blanket, and on the bare waterproof surface a long thin body is laid out like a corpse.

"Oh, I'm sorry, I thought this was my brother's room." The man moves, very slowly, as if arthritic, and leans over to touch something beside him. Recessed luminescent lighting flickers on, green yellow. The man sits up. A croak: "Reba? Is that you?"

Blue eyes, made all the bluer by the russet skin, the scruffy beard, the gray pajamas. Sibling.

"Oh, hi." If I run, will he run after me? Does he have the strength?

"I've been waiting for you." An old voice, whistling like wind through a forgotten canyon.

"Uh-huh. Well, here I am, Billy." She wants him to see how good she looks. Her armor against his anger. But when he raises his face the orbs are bleached with pain. In them is a flicker of Billy.

"I've been waiting a long time, Reba." He coughs.

"Billy, what happened to you?" She has to pee badly.

"I've been sick, Reba."

He is Billy and he isn't Billy and the territory between what she sees and what she knows stretches out like a war zone. Almost a year has passed, but he is so much older, tens of pounds thinner, and since when has Billy been able to grow a beard? And my god that scar reaches almost down to his neck.

His eyes are dull blue fire. The fury has been replaced by wincing fear, cushioned in flesh creased by a hundred sleepless nights. Her whole life, she has known one fact, that Billy is big and Billy is strong. He has always been her rock. And now, here he is, skinny and fragile.

Holding his hand up to his face, he begins to quiver. Is he crying? God. And how did he get so damn thin? Hands like claws, fingernails yellow and thick. Reba keeps her distance while he sits on his bed, hand to face, tears running. On the wall, someone has Scotch-taped a kid's stick figure of a boy standing on a hill. In the corner of the drawing is a scrawled signature: "Billy."

"OK. Now. Listen. Stop. Stop that or I'll have to go." Did my brother draw that picture?

"It's just . . . Jesus, Reba."

"How did you end up here, Billy?"

"I went looking for you. When you didn't come home."

"I called, you were never there. I called you for months."

"When?" He gazes at her with wet uncomprehending eyes. Like a kid, she thinks. "You know, I've been trying to get back home. But they took the van away."

"Who took the van?"

"You know."

"You should have called me."

"How?" He lies back on his bed and stares at the ceiling. When he moves to scratch his nose, he's like a man sculpted from lead. The syllable hangs in the air.

Rena thinks, he wants me to feel sorry for him and I'm not going to. She says, "When did you decide to grow a beard?"

Billy doesn't answer.

"Listen, Billy, I don't have to be here. And to be honest, neither do you. You've got a home. That's where you should be."

"I can't leave. I'm mandated."

"I'll talk to them."

"Yeah. You do that."

"I'll talk to them right now."

Billy addresses the ceiling. "You think you're so smart. Think you're so special. Rolling in dough. I've seen the pictures. I had a collection, but they took it away from me."

"I'm going to go talk to them, Billy." My bladder is going to burst.

"Reba. Stop pretending you don't know. It just makes me angry when you pretend. You know why I'm here. Trying to teach me a lesson, trying to punish me. Does saying I'm sorry change anything? The Chinese girl, she didn't mean any harm. And I've talked to the therapist here and he said masturbation is not incest. Not. But this is what you wanted, right? And you know, Reba, if it makes you feel any better, I'm so ashamed of what I did. And I wish, I wish I could make it up to you. But I don't see why I have to be penalized like this. All these Negroes and Spanish, you know how they feel about me. They cut me to pieces. Do you know, that they spit on me? Talk about me behind my back. They want to fight me. All the time. All the time. Especially the blacks. They all want to fight me. And why? Because you told 'em to. How's that supposed to work? Explain that to me! I sit here and try to figure it out and I can't. Can not. And you know, a little forgiveness wouldn't be such a bad thing. I can't help it. It's just something out of my control . . ."

"What is?"

"I don't want to say it again."

"Billy, stop talking crazy. I know this is some kind of act to make me pity you, and I'm not going to do it."

Silence.

She tries again. "Why on earth would I want to punish you, Billy?"

"You watch me from the pictures and I know you know, because you can see what I'm doing. And God I don't mean to. Shit, I'd cut it off if I could. I even asked if they could give me an operation. They do that here. Just leave me a little stub to pee with. But they won't even give me the electroshock."

"Billy, you're scaring me. Stop it."

"I'm the one locked up and you're scared. Hah, that's a funny one." Billy coughs.

"What do you want me to do?"

"I'm tired. I need to sleep." He closes his eyes. Rena waits and he keeps them shut, still as stone. He doesn't look angry at all. Rena counts to one hundred, then walks out of the room. It's only after she is back in the locked corridor that she thinks to look for a bathroom. But it's too late.

THEY HAVE SET THEMSELVES UP FOR THE BEST VIEW, glasses of Chardonnay perched upon the railing. Cape Cod Bay stretches before them, an undulating canvas of shifting flecks of black, violet and orange. An American flag lies slack against its pole. The sunset diffuses through the reed beds on the headland. Below, children dig the last hole of the day and straggling beach-walkers stroll. Somewhere, someone is playing a bagpipe. The outgoing tide laps against the barnacled two-tone jetty, each retreat a little weaker as sandpipers scurry through the slick piles of gulfweed.

Rick points to the shrubs embedded in the sea grass. "See the red orange things on those thorny bushes? Those are rose hips.

Like the stuff you get in health food stores. A natural source of vitamin C."

Laura says, "It's getting cool down there. Does Henry need a T-shirt?"

Rick thinks, the sea is the biggest thing in the world. Bigger than mountain ranges. I can see it, but I can't imagine it. How long would it take for that surf to roll me into its stony bottom and shred me to pieces? How long before there was no trace left of me?

The evening breeze kicks up and lifts Rick's mood. The flag stirs and a massive flock of gulls returns to wherever they come from each morning. Rick thinks, this is good. His next thought is, I wish I had a cigarette.

The original plan was that Rick would commute to Cape Cod every other weekend. Long weekends. But they hadn't stuck to the plan, so in a kind of compromise, he had come up for a full week. Arrived around three this afternoon.

Laura says, "You want to get fried clams for dinner? Put the kids to bed early?"

"Yeah. Sure."

"Don't sound too enthusiastic."

"I'm always enthusiastic. Lemme unpack. I'll shave if we're going out."

"Don't shave. Well. I mean, yeah, shave. For later."

Rick enters the rented shore house and the smell of knotty pine and sea sand embraces him. Shaving as foreplay, thinks Rick. Like drying the dishes. Are we as pitiful as Ed and Jane when we have sex? A puff of ocean air lifts the white lace curtains. Rick pops his suitcase and grabs up a mass of socks and underwear, proud that he's brought clean clothes. Clothes he has laundered on his own.

At a picnic table outside the roadside diner the family calmly digs into their food. The children are too worn out for frenzy. When they get back to the dark house the meal sits heavy in their guts. Everyone piles onto the Scotch-plaid couch to watch a video on the old VCR. Trina falls asleep almost immediately, Henry fights it, but he's a goner, too. Rick and Laura transfer the limp bodies to the bedroom, tucking them in beside a lit night-light and an assortment of collected shells.

Rick loves the volume of Laura's body, her large full breasts, her wide butt. He likes that she isn't fragile, that she has a heft. Is she gaining weight or am I getting smaller? It doesn't matter. Her body is my home.

After fifteen years of marriage, he knows how she wants to be touched. It all happens without much thought. Once they're past the preliminaries and the small talk, Laura eases herself into her pools of pleasure and Rick muscles his way into his. He's no longer Rick the doctor, the husband, the dad, instead, he's a stiff-legged and shaggy satyr, forcing his hard red prick into the wood nymph he's snared. She urges him on to the nasty thing. He's corrupting the nice midwestern wood nymph and she likes it. Loves it! Everything connects to everything else, he isn't a man any-more but the person he has always been, the bad, bad boy, and he's having his way.

She transforms again and she becomes all the women he has burned for, stared at on all those long, long school days, his brand-new pubescent hard-on trapped under his tight jeans. Laura becomes the teacher, the school nurse, the crosswalk lady, all of those women of his youth whose breasts were so carefully shielded beneath layers of blue gabardine and underwire brassieres. These women knew he wanted them and that's why they leaned so close, why they smiled at him, why they drove him crazy with their intoxicating perfume of hair spray and antiperspirant.

Well, here is one of those ladies now, one that is letting me touch her breasts, her back, her ass. I can do all the bad things. I can fuck the teacher, the lady behind the counter in the candy store, the next-door neighbor in her pink terry-cloth bathrobe bending over the flower bed in the morning, flashing the white-ness of her bosom. Here is the college babe on the subway glanc-ing up from her novel, the firm-assed Latino chick in tight stone-washed jeans standing in line at the deli, the bitch flashing tan marks and thong-strap, every last one of them.

They all want him and he is ready for them all, ready to break them into a million fragments like a suicide bomber of love. The women, not Laura, the women, the bellies, the spread pussies, the hard-nippled tits, the belly buttons, the mouths open, suck-ing on him, wanting him, needing him.

Rick figures Laura is out there somewhere twisting and twirling weightless in her own dimension of lust. Romantic love is too limited to accommodate the carnal moment. Look, her eyes are shut tight, she's focusing on something inner. That's all right, we couldn't be more together on this familiar ride through unfamiliar terrain. Whip the horse harder, lean forward and spur. Faster, straight down the mountainside. All of us, me, Laura, everybody, flags waving, trumpets squawking, in a roar of dust and hooves, like Custer's cavalry, into oblivion.

Rick watches Rick. He has to think about himself as he cums, think about the stupid antique bed squeaking out its annoying rhythm, think about the sheet tangled around a toe, about the fact that he's cumming. I'm no libertine or sex machine, I'm a man handcuffed to my own self-consciousness and insecurity and so I have to obsess about myself even now, even in this most unconscious moment. Why can't I shout, bite, punch? But I can't. Mustn't wake the kids.

Rick bucks a few more times, then holds on tightly to his wife, like a life raft. A wave of tremendous well-being fills him. I love this woman. The world begins and ends with her. We are happy and warm together. We are husband and wife as com-pletely as any husband and wife ever were. Sex is the best thing ever invented. I love you, Laura!

Laura groans, "You're heavy" and Rick rolls off. As he lies

next to this "wife," this stranger, someone named Laura, he thinks, OK. Here we are. At rest, happy with each other. This is something I cannot be with anyone else in the world. This is serenity. I love her. I love what she is and how she is. We've done this, we've gotten this far. I hope nothing ever happens to her, even though I don't really know who she is and she doesn't really know who I am. This is as good as it gets.

Rick can tell by her soft even breathing that she is probably not thinking about anything in particular and he is happy that she is happy. She falls asleep with an arm draped over his chest.

Thirty minutes later, he extricates himself and gropes his way down the stairs into the unfamiliar blackness of the kitchen. He slips out through the creaky screen and finds his old friends, the stars. Cool, humid air wafts over the roar of the restoring tide. The warbly laughter of an invisible young couple rises from the warm sand below. In the dark deep sea stretched out to an invisible horizon fish are swimming. Lovers, fish, a man smoking. The right feeling of a half hour ago has already melted into the outlines of a concept. Not enough.

The remainder of Rick's vacation time is a loosely organized string of meals, day-trips and shopping. Almost everything involves driving. Children fester in the backseat, the local radio station plays "oldies but goodies" and they retrace the same two-lane highway, pass the same antiques shops and gas stations again and again. The traffic inevitably clogs and Rick focuses on the bumper of the car in front of him as Laura chatters happily. When she spies a collectibles shop or a farmstand they pull over and park. As they examine the bruised furniture, the chipped pottery and wicker-ware, Rick thinks to himself, I'm being a good husband.

In the late afternoons, Rick tries some athletic swimming, making a straight line parallel to shore, back and forth. He likes to swim, but not this much, and as he pushes himself along, he considers all the good it's doing his heart. He goes for long walks by himself, another good thing. That's what vacations are for,

for doing all the good things you never do. Rick gathers up the kids, drags them into the water, pulls them out over their heads and they churn like drowning kittens. On the beach Laura reads her novel under a beach umbrella.

Rick has brought along his old fielder's glove and prods Henry into a game of catch. After a while they both get tired of the charade and sit in the sand. Henry asks his father, "Will you and mommy ever get divorced?" Rick says "No, of course not!"—knowing that Henry is curious because one of his first-grade buddies has parents who've just separated. Henry wanders off to find his Game Boy and Rick takes his place next to Laura. He gets high on Mount Gay Rum and his eyelids droop under the slanting sun.

Although the plan is to bliss out on white wine and grilled fish and make love on top of the quilt at least every other night, it doesn't work out that way. By the end of each day, Rick and Laura are too relieved to have the kids in bed to attempt anything more than shelling roasted peanuts in front of the TV.

The evening before Rick heads back to the city, they bicker, then end up watching the local news on cable while holding hands. At a quarter to midnight, Laura checks on the children and announces she's getting her cramps, so she's going to bed. Two commercials in, Rick gives up on the TV, feeling guilty that they have ended the week without a final seal of affection. He creeps up the steps and finds Laura asleep or pretending to be asleep. He thinks, I should lie next to her and hold her.

Rick strips off his bathing trunks and polo shirt, flosses in front of the large bathroom mirror. Too many lights in this bathroom. His flesh, which early in the week was bright with sun, now sags from the fried fish meals and butter-dipped lobster. The first four days he had jogged on the beach as the sun rose and got tanned for the first time since the middle of winter when they had taken that trip to Orlando. He was liking the way he looked and felt. But by halfway through the week, he was sleeping in every morning. No wonder Laura doesn't want to fuck me.

His body is padded with fat, his shoulders slump and instead of his father's black Astroturf Rick has nothing but swirls of fuzz on his chest and back. His eyes are bleary. Tufts of wire sprout from his nose and ears. His crown is thinning. And his limbs ache even when he's done nothing more than push a cart around the huge vacationland supermarket. He flosses and spits pink.

The next day, on the five-hour drive back to the city, Rick misses Laura and the kids. On the other hand, he's relieved to be on his way. He dials the cruise-control to seventy, chain-smokes and sings along to sad songs on the radio. He lets himself cry amid the Corollas and the minivans.

THIS ONE IS SPECIAL, RENA IS WAY WOUND UP. WAY. They have asked specifically for her. She went in and met the agency people in New York and everybody loved her. This is it.

It distracts her from the headache Billy has become. She visits him once a week, but he either lies there mute or goes on long rants begging her for forgiveness or cursing her out. His trembling and finger-tapping has gotten worse. The nurses say it's a side effect of the meds. They throw words at Rena: Thorazine, Stelazine, Haldol, Xanax. They say Billy is bipolar. They say he spits out his Lithium. They mention electroshock therapy.

Marissa is back in the picture, plans to fly out with her, they're best friends again. To celebrate, Rena stops by to see Barry and cops a bundle. She doesn't plan on doing the whole thing, but it seems stupid to buy three bags. Besides, there might be a situation.

At the airport, Rena snorts two tiny lines of heroin in a stall in the terminal bathroom. When she gets back to the first-class lounge where Marissa is sitting, the dope hasn't kicked in. She can't go back to the restroom, Marissa might get suspicious, so Rena waits until they are onboard to slip into the head and finish the bag.

Marissa blabs about the menu and the movie. Rena nods out and misses the whole three-course meal. Marissa has the sundae, wraps a blanket around herself and takes in the movie like she's never seen one before. She ignores Rena's beauty sleep. Party girls are like that.

When they land, the limo drives them straight up to Shutters. Rena is strangely clearheaded. So when Marissa says she wants to hang out in the lobby people-watching, Rena retreats to her room and snorts more heroin. She'd been in L.A. for an hour and has already knocked off three bags and is barely high. She hits the speed-dial on her cell phone.

"Yeah?"

"Hey, this shit is no good."

"Untrue, sweetness."

"Barry, I've done three bags already."

"You're building up a tolerance. It happens."

"That's crazy."

"Oh, yeah, crazy. Best thing to do is lay off for a couple of weeks. Don't want to get a habit."

"Don't say that, Barry."

"Hey . . ."

"Whatever." Rena hangs up on him. She ends up drinking three little bottles of Johnnie Walker Black and puking in the bathroom. After the booze wears off, she figures the best thing to do is to sniff one more bag, order a pot of coffee and take a shower. An hour later, caffeinated and finally sedated on dope, Rena stares at the TV, mummified in her Shutters robe.

Talking to Barry has put her in a pissy mood. Plus she doesn't like Los Angeles anymore. All anyone does is go to bars and hang out, or go to parties and hang out. A city of pavement and attitude.

Last time out, she'd let an actor pick her up at a small party at a producer's house in Bel Air. She'd seen the guy in a movie, he was Latino and sexy, so why not? It wasn't going to lead to anything, and she didn't expect it to. He was so handsome there was no point in falling in love with him. And he had a gentle way of talking. Very sure of himself, nice cologne. He steered her out behind the pool house and kissed her gently up against a palm tree. Said that was all he wanted from her. One kiss. It was like starring in a movie with him. But then the kissing kept going. And then he didn't even ask. He unzipped his pants and what else could she do?

With his thing in her mouth, she thought of Frank. Which spoiled it a little bit. But he smelled good. And in the cool night air beside the pool his cock was blood warm and felt right. He lost it a little bit when he was coming and she could feel that, feel him losing his control, exposing himself totally, his soul. She was thrilled to be so intimate with a real movie star. As he came he barked a few words in Spanish. She swallowed his cum, rose up before him and he kissed her again and then they held each other in the night air. He whispered, "Our secret, right? My girlfriend would be very upset with me if she knew."

When they went back inside, the people in the house were oblivious. Later the beautiful movie star zoomed off in his Testarossa. He never asked her name. Didn't even say good night, just glanced at her as he was going out the door and gave her a knowing look, but that was OK, too.

The morning after the flight, Marissa wakes Rena at six AM and miraculously, she feels rested. The opiate residues pinging around her metabolism blend with anticipation and put her in a good mood. She and Marissa drive up to the shoot in Malibu together.

The beach is cluttered with tables of food, equipment vans, people addressing little headsets. A friendly girl in a baseball cap runs up to Rena, checks her name off on a clipboard and escorts her to the makeup trailer. In the overlit box the hair and makeup folks are full of caffeine and good cheer, sharing dirty jokes and dropping names of supermodels they've worked with. They all have tattoos. One hair girl has a pierced tongue. If they aren't making someone up, they're working on themselves. All eyes are on the mirrors. Coffee brews, music beats on the sound system and Rena's gay hairdresser shimmies and hums while he brushes her out.

Rena is one of three girls on the hair conditioner gig. A blonde, a brunette and a redhead. Everyone has great hair, of course, and the hair people are thrilled to blow and chemicalize it to the max. The cold spitting ocean is only yards away, and that's a problem. But these are experts, they aren't defeated by saline humidity.

The other two girls live on the West Coast, so Rena doesn't know them. They seem a bit younger, a bit fresher. Don't talk much. Are they frightened? Rena isn't frightened. She's saved a bag of dope in her knapsack if she needs it. Marissa has told her it's going to be just like a photo call, probably easier.

The trailer door opens and a burly guy with a full black beard flings himself in. Like the others he is teeming with energy and optimism and greets everyone with tremendous animation. The director, obviously. He knows the other two girls, but he's especially gracious to Rena and she likes him right away. He's as wired as a squirrel in a cage and Rena is relieved when he goes. Marissa pops her head in, but when she sees the director has left, she slips away. Rena is in makeup for three hours.

The shooting begins and the director isn't happy, endlessly adjusting the light, playing with filters and giant fans and reflectors. He seems perpetually unsatisfied, and all the friendliness he displayed at first evaporates. Now he doesn't smile at all. Rena thinks, when this is over, I'm going to sleep with that guy.

The director finally gets the lighting the way he wants it, but the performances don't make him happy. He asks Rena to say her seven words over and over again, patronizing her like a four-year-old. Eventually he's done with the other girls, but keeps working Rena. At one point he whispers in her ear, "Do you need something? We can get you whatever you need." Take follows take. Every time Rena looks up at the camera crew, they're smirking or cracking jokes. It's as if they're waiting for her to screw up.

Lunch is called and Rena sits with Marissa, who says she thinks it's going very well. The director walks by and makes a show of checking his watch. He says nothing to Rena.

After lunch the assistant director releases the other two girls. They continue to shoot Rena. The director chews out his assistant. At one point he leaves Rena in the middle of the beach and speaks very emphatically on his cell phone for fifteen minutes. When he returns a bloom of sweat stains his linen shirt.

Finally, the director leaves and doesn't return. A half hour later, the first AD tells Rena she's done for the day and can go get cleaned up. Rena asks if she's supposed to work tomorrow. The AD says he doesn't know.

Back in her room, Rena is snorting her last bag of dope when Marissa calls to tell her she has been fired from the hair conditioner shoot. The client has decided they'd rather feature only two girls. They say it creates a "better dynamic." Marissa assures Rena that it's not her fault. Then she tells Rena that she isn't feeling well and won't be making the movie premiere tonight. When the concierge calls Rena to tell her that her car has arrived, Rena decides to go to the party alone.

On the Avenue of the Stars a dozen limos queue up before the theater. The red carpet runs two hundred feet, lined with roped-off paparazzi. Women in fancy gowns and pantsuits accompany men in suit jackets and tieless white silk shirts. The lobby is packed with overdressed people vying for free popcorn and Pepsi.

Rena has never seen so many beautiful women in one place. It's as if every blonde in West L.A. has shown up. Trophy wives, ex-model girlfriends, starlets, wannabe starlets, even professional athletes have arrived to show off. And these are only a fraction, a mere fraction of a fraction of the total—all stunning, or almost stunning—of the babe population of L.A. basin.

Cameras pop, actors smile and wave. The starlets are taller than Rena thinks they'd be, the men shorter. Agents and managers hug their clients. Producers and studio execs kiss and hug one another. Everyone is happy to see one another.

Men run their eyes over Rena like the professional appraisers they are. She knows she's looking good. But no one approaches, no one makes a move. Tonight is not for picking up the odd piece of ass. Tonight's too important to waste time with hobbies. There's money to be made, a pecking order to climb.

In Paris, in New York, backstage behind the runway, the dressers and the stylists and the hair and makeup guys, they all know me, they are my family. Here, who am I? A no-name, a body. A nobody. Paul was right about me. Bones. With money. What do I do? Nothing. Exist. It's like I'm carrying a giant shell on my back, like a hermit crab, the place where I live, where I hide and stay safe. My face.

In the bathroom, Rena snorts the remainder of the dope. During the movie, she nods off. After the applause everyone rises and she's straight again. People flow out of the theater toward a huge chunk of the Fox lot, only a few hundred yards away, where the party will take place. Rena joins the crowd as it migrates into the Fox lot and suddenly feels trapped.

Rena finds the fringe of the party where a chain-link fence has been erected. Security men lead Alsatians along the perimeter.

Rena aims herself toward an exit gate where three beefy black guys in tuxedos and earsets stand guard. One, a guy with big brown eyes, says sweetly, "Can I help you, miss?"

"Do you know where I can find some coke?"

The sentinel throws a look to his colleagues and says, "The bar's that way, miss." As he points, Rena sees the holstered gun. Then her eyes meet his. Who is this guy? Ex-cop? Veteran? DEA agent? Dangerous. What am I doing?

Back at the bar Rena finds herself jammed up against a tall guy wearing a Prada tux asking the bartender for seltzer water. His eyes don't linger on Rena. In that fraction of a second, she knows. She follows him as he steps away from the bar.

"Hi." She says it flatly. No flirt.

He continues to scan the crowd. The guy's dapper, cool. He lets his eyes flicker over her. He says, "You in the film?"

"No. Just visiting. From New York." Rena knows she's right about him. She can feel his immunity to her charm. But he isn't gay. It's something else.

"Used to live in New York." His tone is even and smooth. Cool. A little like Barry. A little like Fred.

"Uh-huh. I figured. You remind me of an old friend of mine."

He exhales and says, "Well, it was nice meeting you. Say hi to New York for me." He walks away.

Rena takes a step with him. "I'm sick. I have to get straight."

He grins a wise grin and says, "Say hi to everyone in Tribeca for me."

"Please?" She bites her lip.

" 'Get straight.' I'm not sure what that means."

"I don't have a connection out here. I just burned through a bundle in twenty-four hours. I'm strung out."

He pauses. "You have cash?"

"Yes."

"I'm supposed to meet the producer of this piece-of-shit movie. We're supposed to discuss a writing assignment but he's off getting drunk with the director. Everyone knows this thing is a bomb. He's not going to show his fat ugly face tonight. OK. We'll take my car."

They drive down to the Santa Monica freeway and head eastward, hip-hop chugging on the radio. On the black leather of the backseat lie piles of glossy red bound scripts, emblazoned with the CAA logo. They exit downtown, then backtrack along Wilshire westward. Near MacArthur Park, he pulls into a doughnut shop parking lot. A dark guy wearing an unbuttoned flannel shirt saunters out to the car. Rena tries not to listen. The window powers up and they are back in the flow of the midnight traffic.

They're smoking the tar before they've hit the highway. By the time they enter the lobby of Shutters, they are stuporous. In her room, not much is said while they work on another black pea. Rena feels her shoulders unlock with relief.

Her companion stands. "Well, it's about that time." Even though he's high, she can feel his uneasiness.

Rena says, "I owe you."

He says, "You took care of it."

Rena pulls him to her. "But I want to do something for you." Don't lose this guy. You never know when you might need him again. Maybe tomorrow.

Rena drops to her knees and fumbles with his pants. She thinks, the sooner he comes the sooner he goes and I can get good and fucked up. After five minutes he nudges her head away.

"It's OK. I appreciate it." He zips his fly. "Can I give you some advice? You seem like a nice girl. You should clean up and go back to Minnesota or wherever you really come from."

"I know. I'm going to." Rena is so high she can't stand up.

"They have rehabs and things like that." His eyes have the pinned determination of someone who will never set foot in a rehab.

Rena tries a smile but her facial muscles aren't working. "It's been a stressful weekend."

"Yeah, well, it's been a stressful couple of centuries." He opens the door. "Be good."

He leaves Rena on her knees.

RICK'S HEAD WEIGHS NINE THOUSAND POUNDS, IMPOS-sible to lift. The room is filling with the lava of the morning's sun. What do you do with a nine-thousand-pound head? Open your eyes, Rick! He does and he's blinded by the brilliance. He closes his eyes again, rolls off the lip of the bed and crawls to the bathroom, blind. He rappels up and over the edge of the tub, only to find he's still got his pants on. Shrugging them off, he digs a mangled pack of cigarettes out of the pocket. Lights. Inhales, head swimming, flips the taps and lays under the flow like a corpse, arm extended out past the fake rain like Marat.

Don't fall asleep here, big fella, you'll burn the house down. Trembling, he stands, head hung low, keeping the butt dry, piss-ing saffron onto black wet ashes. Gooseflesh embroiders his nakedness. I wonder how my liver is doing these days? Kidneys? Lungs? Prostate? Does jerking off prevent prostate cancer?

Weak-kneed, Rick extricates himself from the streaming jets and shaves without bothering to towel off. Eye bags and wrin-kles have appeared overnight. "Ladies and gentlemen, the ugli-est man in the world!" he announces to the mirror, shaving cuts bleeding pinkly into the white lather. "Why does Laura stay with me? Shitty bod. Ugly face. Must be my breath." Rick flosses his wooly teeth, doesn't brush, gets dressed, pants sticking to damp legs. In the kitchen he chews six Advils, flushes them down with half a can of Miller Lite and forces movement out into the world.

The car drives itself to the ferry, parks itself. Rick finds the men's room in the terminal and throws up. Onboard he buys coffee and chugs two more Advils. As the ferry cuts into the Hudson, he drapes himself over the rail and lets the rushing wake hypnotize him. Bringing the hot coffee to his lips, he loses his grip and the cup tumbles down into the green froth.

Making land, he propels himself through the dead streets to the clinic, irritated by the heaps of trash, the broken bottles, sodden bits of clothing and dry lumps of dog turd. The baking sun glazes the exhausted streets, evaporating the bodily fluids and leftover alcohols into a miasma.

Too early, he creeps around the empty office suite of the clinic like an intruder. I need Zoe to revive me with her flirting. I should have paid more attention to her, appreciated her. Why couldn't I have an average screwed-up life, like all the other doctors, married, fucking my assistant? Doesn't that solve things? Don't the small problems distract you from the larger ones?

Zoe appears eventually but it does no good. Rick fumbles his way through his appointments until lunchtime when he surrenders to the hangover and stretches out onto the cool skin of the examination table. He closes his eyes. Everything stops and Rick drops into a chasm of black, thinking, this must be what death is like. Out of the void, Zoe knocks gently, her face at the crack of the door whispering that the waiting room is full. Rick wakes unrefreshed, stale and angry. He splashes rubbing alcohol on his face, rinses with cold water and swallows two ten-milligram tablets of dextroamphetamine sulphate, stuff left over in an unlabeled vial from his intern days. Doubtful of the potency, he forgets he's taken the dexies until a half hour later, when he starts feeling human. An hour later he's obsessing on how he's never told his dad how much he loves him. He considers making a call and decides to postpone the emotional moment.

Just before four o'clock, Rick notices a new face in the waiting room while guiding a middle-aged patient to the front desk. Rick knows who the new face is. It's the girl who called about her brother. The crazy guy from the ER. The girl flips idly through a magazine, her body almost too long for the leather-clad Knoll couch. Her hair is pulled back, revealing an amazing facial symmetry. Ankle to wrist Dolce & Gabbana, no jewelry. Like a visitor from another universe, nothing like the stylishly shabby downtown patients Rick is used to seeing in his waiting room.

Rick ushers Rena into his office. On the phone she'd been hesitant and careful in her description of the situation. In person she seems weirdly calm. Now they sit, facing each other.

"So is your brother doing better?"

"I don't think so."

"Uh-huh. He was in pretty bad shape when I saw him."

"Yeah."

"I wasn't sure if he was only momentarily disoriented or if it was something chronic. That's why I suggested he get examined."

"Yes. You did the right thing."

"It didn't seem Rikers was the right place for him."

"No."

"So."

"So, they're not being very helpful. Since you're the doctor who signed him in I guess that gives you some kind of authority . . ."

Zoe knocks and pops the door. "Dr. Levine is on line one. He says it's important."

Rick picks up the phone with a tight smile to Rena. "Robbie?" Rick fiddles with a paperweight on his desk. On it are the words "Viagra" and in parentheses, "Sildenafil Citrate"—he can feel Rena's eyes on him. "Yeah. Yeah. I got you. No problem. Have fun out there." Rick hangs up. Zoe knocks again. She appears, but before she can speak, Rick interrupts her.

"Zoe? No calls till I'm finished here."

Zoe's eyes register a kind of panic. "Yes, Doctor." She leaves without relaying her message.

"Listen. Ummm. You want to get a cup of coffee? It's been a long day. I gotta get some fresh air."

"Oh, sure."

The diet pills have immersed Rick in a snap-crackle-pop reality. The last thing he needs is coffee. But he doesn't want to talk to this woman in here. He's not sure why that is, but he doesn't. He says good night to Zoe and walks out the door with Rena.

At the patisserie, a place Rick usually avoids, Rick and Rena order skim cappuccinos, since they don't make soy lattes, Rena's favorite. All around them are tables of women dressed in linen and silk, clinking and gossiping. Large glossy shopping bags lie by their feet like sleeping dogs.

Rena pours three packets of raw sugar onto her coffee, letting the crystals float on top of the foam before folding them down into the liquid. She nibbles the sugary lather off the miniature teaspoon. When she catches Rick staring, she smiles. Rick sips from his own cup, burning his tongue.

"First of all, you should know that my degree isn't in psychiatry. In med school, I took a few courses in psychology. I'm not a specialist. I'm just a GP." Rick avoids her eyes, plays with the sugar. "My name's on his file because I'm the doctor who signed the paperwork. The razor cut was very bad. He took about fifty stitches. And he was obviously not mentally stable. I figured someone should talk to him."

"My brother isn't a criminal. He drinks too much sometimes. See, we're not from the city. We both grew up on a farm. Being here freaks him out. He needs to go home."

"Uh-huh. But the institution where he has been, uh, mandated, is a lockup. He can't leave now. It's for, uh, patients who have committed crimes. That's a separate issue. You need a lawyer for that."

"He beat up some drug dealers. Believe me, they're not going to press charges." This guy thinks I'm some dumb blonde. Good. OK. Doesn't mean he isn't going to try to make me happy. Charm him.

"At the ER I see psychotics every night. Most of them are very nice people. But they don't know what's real and what isn't. There's only so much I can do and I don't want to be blamed if something happens because I get him signed out."

"Billy just wants to go home."

"OK, look. I'll talk to the people in charge." Of course I will. You're a babe. I'm a schmuck. You know it. I know it.

"I believe you." Rena gazes into his eyes. She smiles. "Thank you."

"When I have some info, I'll call you and give you feedback." Truly amazing eyes. And skin. What would it be like to touch that face? Just for a night. One night? One night in my whole life.

The waitress clears their empty cups. Rena squints at him and says, "It must be nice to heal people." Why isn't this guy hitting on me? Maybe he's married. Maybe he's a good guy.

"Sure." Rick coughs. A cigarette would be nice right now. "I'm a regular Mother Teresa."

"Who?"

"Medicine's a business. But yeah, I like taking care of people. Sure."

"Does the clinic belong to you?"

"Uh-huh." This girl's very existence is killing me. That someone this beautiful exists. Someone from another dimension, one I could never go to. How depressing is that?

"Does it bother you to be around sick people?"

"Most of them come in with colds. No matter how many times I tell my smart-ass patients that the common cold is caused by viruses unaffected by antibiotics, they insist on unnecessary scrips for amoxycillin and tetracyclin. These people are used to getting what they want. So I write the scrips." What am I talking about?

"You sound like you don't like your patients."

"It's a living."

"But what if someone is really sick?"

"I refer 'em. It's not my job to deliver the bad news, just to bird-dog it. Two years ago this old geezer came in who'd been a patient of mine since I started the practice. I detected a heart murmur, so I shipped him off to the cardiologist. Things got busy at work and I lost track of the guy. Last spring I heard he'd passed away. We stamped his chart "deceased" and dropped it into storage. Fucked up, huh?"

"My parents are dead."

"Oh, I'm sorry." Yeah. You asshole. Foot-in-mouth asshole. Trying to sound cool, end up sounding like an asshole.

"No. I mean. I don't know what I mean."

"Mine are alive. But I don't see them much."

"Well, you should try to see them, because when a person dies, that's it. You don't get any second chances. Whichever way you leave things, it's kind of locked in like that forever. Besides my brother, I don't really have a family. It's just me."

Her brother's a psycho, tried to murder people. On the other hand, she's so fucking beautiful. Makes me nervous just talking to her. Like a kid. Fuck. Say something, Rick. "When I was an undergraduate and decided to be a doctor, I thought, I'll learn how to heal people and I'll make lots of money. And people will respect me."

The waitress appears. "Anything else?"

"The check."

"Yes, sir."

"What was I talking about? Oh, so I'm a med student. Gotta take all these verkocteh courses, stuff I'm never going to use. One day the professor takes a bunch of us down to a basement where some archeologists are sorting out a dig. So there's this long wooden table and on it are like three hundred skulls lined up in neat rows. And in the center of each frontal bone, fore-head, crown, whatever you call it, is a carefully inked numeral. The skulls of an entire extinct village. The scientists had dug them up, brushed off the dirt and brought them to this basement. They belonged to people who had lived five hundred years ago and now, here they were lying on a table." Why am I talking so much? Fucking dexies. And the point is . . . ?

"So I'm in this gloomy basement and I'm looking at what's left of dozens and dozens of people. People who had been alive, just like you and I are right now. People who had smiled, laughed, cried, loved each other. People who had known each other by their faces, by their personalities. But now, without the skin and the eyes, they're virtually identical. Because skulls don't have faces, only sockets and exposed worn-down teeth. No skin. No hair. Just bare bone." God, you are boring this poor girl into the ground. Just pay the bill and let her go. "Stick John Lennon's cranium next to Princess Di's and most people can't tell them apart. All the personality we associate with someone, the faces we greet at the cocktail party, the smiles, the beautiful eyes, all that is beautiful or admirable, it all rots away. Everything we think of as a person is just a few bits of sculpted flesh and gristle, or in the case of the eyes, fragile globes of fluid."

Rick's voice echoes in the near-empty restaurant. Longest pause yet. Rena fiddles with a forgotten spoon. "And you're married?"

"Fifteen years. My wife decorated the clinic." She got a lot out of that speech. What did I expect? She's a babe. A bimbo. She's not even listening.

"Children?"

"Oh, yeah. Sweet, sweet kids. Two. Boy and girl. They're away right now with their mom. On vacation, that's why . . ." Why am I saying this? What am I telling her? She's smiling at me? Laughing at me. "I'm sorry. I'm kind of burned out. I overdid it last night. Partied. Or whatever you call it. I'm getting too old for that shit."

"Too old?"

"You know what I mean." She's probably into some Italian ski bum or rock star or bond trader. She's thinking, OK, I got what I want, time to go.

"I don't. What do you mean?" See the veins on the backs of his hands. He's not young. He's married with kids. Supersmart. Good guy. Why can't I ever find someone like this guy?

What do I mean? I mean, I'm an old guy and can't flirt with you because you'd laugh at me. "Well, anyway. Tell you what, I'll make some calls and see what I can do for your brother."

"Thank you, um, Doctor. I feel funny asking a stranger to help, but I don't know what else I can do."

"No, no. It's my pleasure."

No more coffee to drink, what happens now? Nothing. Rick shoves his chair back and it screeches on the floor. He rises. Rena looks at him, surprised? This is the kind of girl who hangs out all day in places like this, smoking cigarettes, looking beautiful. Sorry, sister, I'm in a big rush, I have to get home to my couch and my beer and my remote control.

Outside, the sun dims through a red gold aerosol as it loosens its grip on this side of the planet. The tunnel traffic stands choked and growling. They awkwardly shake hands and turn in separate directions.

The same trash, dog shit and broken bottles of the morning lie in Rick's path. The same but different. Rick thinks, my headache's gone.

RENA SLIPS THROUGH THE LATE AFTERNOON SWELL OF shoppers, workers, street people. This guy, this doctor, what's up with him? Never really looking at me. Telling me all that stuff. How old? Over forty? Like Paul. But not like Paul. Paul's fucked up. This guy is a nice guy. Helps out, doesn't want anything back. Pretty straight. Shy. A brain. Afraid to look at me. Peeking at my tits like a little boy. What would he have done if I'd reached out and touched his cheek?

This guy is a good guy. He cares about people no matter what he says, I can see it. He has a heart. A real heart. He's smart and he can get things done. He put that whole clinic together, he can do anything. He'll do what has to be done. Don't worry, Billy, lil' sister is going get you out of there. One thing at a time. Get Billy settled down, then clean up off the dope. Steer clear of Barry. This could be a turning point. Get some money together. And then what?

This doctor, this guy, he must have such a nice life. A simple good life. Wife and kids. Plus he's smart, always been smart. Jewish. Takes care of people. That's what I want. Can't be running around all the time. I never wanted this insanity. I only wanted to get away from Stupidville. Would've dried up like Maureen if I stayed there.

This doctor knows things. He could tell me things. Not for Billy. For myself. I could ask him: What's the secret? How do I get to be happy the way you're happy? Help me find the way. Fix me. I want to get clean. Really, really clean, like from inside out. Get me away from all these monsters and garbage. Too many monsters. There's got to be a world without monsters. I know it's out there.

STONED AGAIN. WASTED. CHUCKLING TO MYSELF LIKE a loonie. Pot. I'm turning into a fucking pothead. Rick takes a big pull off the fat doobie he's rolled, sitting like a backyard Buddha. Nothing wrong with having time to think.

That girl, the model, had the most amazing voice. Like raw silk. How old can she be? Twenty-two? But a woman. Did you see that neck? Long, muscular. Didn't she say something about being from a farm? Probably milked cows since she was five. What would it be like to kiss that neck? To press my cheek against it? Just a kid. Still.

Beauty, that's the deal. True beauty, like art. Eyes like bits of colored glass, skin like a baby's. Said she was a fashion model. Wonder if I've ever seen her in anything? Probably. Yes. Must have seen her. That's why she looks so familiar. Like I've always known her. Lips the faintest shade of pink, pearly. Is that right? Can lips be pearly?

What's that sound? Crickets? Tree frogs. Like some kind of Tibetan monk chant. Katydids, that's what that sound is. Droning. Humming. Scratching, that's it, rubbing their legs together. Trying to get laid, right? And that background sound, like wind chimes, or a harmonica. Do Tibetan monks get laid? Probably. Not hung up like the West. Probably chant to attract the lady monks. Something about harmonic overtones, isn't that what that sound is? There's the fundamental that makes the pitch and then there's the overtone, like a bell. Or like a chime, or a phone ringing, deep inside my head.

The phone ringing. Laura. She's going to know I'm stoned. So what? I have a right to get stoned.

Rick enters the kitchen, picks up a piece of fruit and bites into it as he lifts the phone. "Hey," he mumbles. The juice dribbling down his chin. God, that's good, he thinks.

The voice on the other end says, "Hi."

"Kinda late, isn't it? You guys been out?" Nectarine all over Rick's fingers. He snatches a leaf of paper towel and wipes his mouth.

"I'm always up this late."

"Hello?! Who is this?"

"Guess."

"Oh. Hi. How . . ."

"You gave me your numbers, remember? Is it too late?"

"No. No. I was just, uh, watching TV."

"Is this a bad time?"

"No. No. This is a good time." Rick tosses the half-eaten fruit into the sink and misses. The pit skids across the counter, onto the floor, leaving a snail track of sweet slime. "How are you?"

"Fine."

"Good. I was going to call you tomorrow. I, uh, spoke with someone on the ward. Seems that they think Billy's not being very cooperative." God I am so stoned.

"Yeah. I know."

"I explored the idea of transferring him to a private institution. Could you afford that? It's not a simple thing. Requires a huge amount of paperwork, hiring a lawyer to make an appeal." I'm too stoned to be having this conversation. Tell her you'll call her tomorrow.

"Thanks, it's nice of you to do that."

"No, it's nothing. It would be your headache if you want to go through with it."

"That's wonderful, Doctor."

"Doesn't mean he'd be released. They see him as kind of a menace. Guess he beat those guys up pretty bad. And Billy doesn't get along with other, uh, inmates. Especially those of color."

"Of color?"

"You know. Black. Minorities."

"Yeah, he was always prejudiced, but he was never, you know, violent."

"Could be a lot of things."

"Yeah."

"So." God. This is better than a 900 number.

"Well, thank you, Doctor."

"Call me Rick, please. And listen, I'll let you know what they tell me. I'll look into places he can go. And I'll find a lawyer who does this kind of thing."

"That's so . . . wow. I mean." Pause. Rick hears a sob. "I'm sorry."

"Hello?"

"No. I. I've been going through some stuff lately. And it's nice to talk to someone who is, you know, a good guy. For a change."

"I'm only pretending to be a good guy. It requires a great deal of effort on my part." Why did I say that?

"What?!"

Is she wiping away tears? Fuck. "You sure you're OK?" She doesn't understand irony, asshole. Why don't you make some more dead parents jokes?

"No." Rena giggles. Relief all around.

"Oh, because I was a little worried." More irony.

Rena laughs again. "Um. Rick? Would you ever have time to have another cup of coffee? Just to talk. All this has been pretty overwhelming and the stress of my job and everything. Do you have time for that? Oh, I know you don't have time for that, you've got your kids and everything, the clinic, you've already done so much, I'm sorry, I'm being a pain in the ass."

"No. You're not. I'm pretty free until my family gets back."

"How about the day after tomorrow? Same place as before?"

"Around six? I'll see if I can get some more information. About alternatives."

"Good." Long exhalation. "I feel so much better that you're helping me. Thank you." Silence.

"Stop thanking me already." This is surreal.

"Sorry."

"Well, don't start apologizing, that's worse."

"OK."

"I'll see you in a couple of days." My god, I'm flirting with her. That's nuts. Don't flirt with her, Rick. Don't be a jackass.

"OK."

Rick hangs up the phone, half expecting Laura to walk in from the living room. Laura and the kids. Laura and the kids. Just keep saying it out loud to yourself. Like a mantra. Laura and the kids.

You're stoned, you're delusional. This is a young woman who wants help for her brother. But we're having coffee again. OK. So what's that about? She needs somebody to talk to. I'm playing uncle to her little girl. Those model types are "high maintenance." Like a kitten that's been weaned from its mother too soon. She needs me to focus on her. But Rick, Rick, Rick!!!! Hey asshole! Don't get confused! This is a kid, a fucking model for god's sake. She hangs out in L.A. with movie stars and all that. Wears a thong. Makes piles of money. She knows what she is and she knows what you are. She needs something so she turns on the charm. Right now she needs some hand-holding. That's it. End of story.

What it is, see, is she needs someone to get her through. Nothing better than a nice doctor, minus balls and dick. Nice sweet sexless avuncular doctor who will listen to her problems. Normally you charge $175 for a twenty-minute consultation. She's gonna get it for free.

After she's gotten all the attention she needs, she can wander off and suck off some NBA superstar. Wait a minute. Stop. She's a nice kid. Do you really think she's that trashy? With those eyes? Those lips? Not possible. It would be a travesty against nature. On the other hand, maybe. Probably. She probably has tattoos. A belly button ring. Drinks Stoli and smokes Ecstasy. Who the fuck knows?

Besides, what's the difference between sucking off a jock and sucking off a doctor? Because if you would just be honest with yourself, for two minutes, you'd admit if she snapped her fingers tomorrow, you'd follow. Right? Well, it's not just the sex. She's . . . she's more than that. She's sweet. Oh, Jesus. How did

184 • ERIC BOGOSIAN

we get to this? This girl is taking up space in your head, my friend. You are actually *thinking* about her.

Rick relights the joint and wanders back out and contemplates the astral canopy. Not just stars up there but satellites and spaceships. The blinking red bits are jets filled with people crossing the night sky. Hundreds of people on their way to the next big moment in their lives. People full of expectations and desires and hopes and movement. Moving toward the big moment. Life is either the big moments or the filler. All the stuff in between the big moments you forget. In the end, what you call "your life" is the big moments, right? Speaking of which, when was the last time I had a big moment? Cape Cod. Sex with Laura. Watching the kids play on the sand. You know what? The big moments don't feel so big anymore.

No lights next door. Do Ed and Jane know what I did on their cedar deck? Have they found my little present? Doubtful. There's not enough cum in me to get noticed. Besides, they're probably on vacation. As I should be. The suburbs are launch pads, way stations. You're not actually supposed to spend this much time here. The point is to get away, it's summer, go. Go to your loved ones. Ed and Jane are with each other. Just as I should be with Laura. But I'm not. I'm in my backyard smoking dope, dreaming about a teenager. I'm a fucking cliché.

The sad truth is that I'd love it if this girl snapped her fingers. Just once. Just snap those beautiful long fingers once. Just for the hell of it. Snap, snap. So I can come running. Like a little dog. Like a frisky little dog.

RICK AND RENA SIT IN A STARBUCKS, EYES LOCKED, talking about everything and nothing. Their fourth meeting.

They've been making the rounds, getting good at having coffee together. Oblivious to the hustle and bustle. Recounting life stories and traumas, the words themselves as insignificant as clouds over an empty sea. It's supposed to be about Billy but they don't talk about Billy.

Rena laughs. "Your life is so different from mine," she says.

"This isn't my life. This is a break from my life. I never do this. Take a breather." Rick feels his own face. Stubble. Forgot to shave again.

"No?"

"My life is very structured. Always has been. There's always another thing I have on my to-do list. My life is a list and when I've checked everything off there will be no reason to live. Except I forgot to shave this morning."

"That's unhealthy."

"Not shaving or keeping an existential to-do list?"

"The list! Existential! Listen to you! It's unhealthy because you're not living inside your own life! And you have a good life, you should enjoy it! You love your wife. You love your kids. You have a nice job."

"You sound like my therapist."

"Maybe I am your therapist."

"No. Definitely not." Rick wants to say, I don't want to schtup my therapist. Probably not a good idea to say that. Instead he says, "You also have a nice job. Make piles of money . . ."

"All I do is stand around and look pretty."

"Your work is work. From what I've heard." What do I know? I don't know anything. I don't know her. I don't know me.

"But what you do has dignity. Taking care of people. Showing up at that ER once a week, that's so great. We would never have met if you weren't doing that."

"I do it to mitigate my guilty conscience. I'm a quack, a pill pusher. A representative of pharmaceutical corporate America."

"OK, we won't talk about it."

"I was just going to say."

"What?" Rena laughs again.

Rick gets an anxious look on his face.

"What?"

"Stop saying 'what'!"

"Why?"

They laugh in unison and Rick is in the stratosphere, soaring.

Rena says, "I don't like my work. I don't want to deal with those people anymore. I want to sit in coffee shops forever."

Rick says, "You'd die of espresso poisoning, I think."

Rena reaches into her bag. "I got you something. A thank you for helping Billy."

"I haven't done anything for Billy." She's buying me things. A rich girl is buying me things.

"But you will. You're going to." Just don't go away. Stay with me. Talk to me. Help me.

Three long days have passed since they'd last done this. She can't tell him that it's because she'd been withdrawing from a mild case of heroin addiction. She thought she had the flu. Then she figured it out. Didn't leave the bathroom for twenty-four hours. Nerves are on edge, but it's been worth it. Because now I'm with Rick. Clean. Happy. I don't think of using when we're talking like this.

"This better be something my wife would understand. Like a book about gardening." Rick unwraps the little package.

"Why wouldn't Laura understand that you have a friend who happens to be a woman?"

"Oh, gee, I don't know." My wife's name on this girl's lips. Like an invasion of privacy. But she knows Laura's name because I talk about Laura. About the kids. I talk about them because of fear. I'm afraid if I stop talking about them, I'll forget they exist. But it only brings her closer to me. When I tell her about my life at home, she lights up, like I'm a genius spouting a new theory of quantum mechanics.

A small carved piece of wood drops out of the package. "What is it? A bird?"

"It's a lion. Very old, from ancient China. See? Its tongue moves. Carved from some kind of rare wood. I think the samurai hung things like this on tassels off their swords. You could hang it off your sword."

"I don't have a sword." Should I tell her that the samurai were Japanese? Nah.

"No?" Coy.

She's fucking with me. She's way ahead of me. Way, way ahead. "You know, Rena, you're a big flirt."

"Am I?"

"Yes. But I don't mind. It's harmless. I guess." Make a big show of checking my watch. "Shit! I've already got appointments in the waiting room."

"It's a waiting room, right? Let them wait."

"They're sick people." A few blocks away a car alarm wails.

"No, they're not. You told me so. They're just a bunch of whiners."

"Whiners who pay me the big bucks to listen to them."

"And feel them up."

"Actually, I have three-way sex with them on the examination table."

"Who's the third person?"

"My assistant, Zoe. Very hot babe."

"Really?"

"Listen." Rick finishes his coffee. "It's so boring, it's beyond boring. Gotta go."

"Why do you stay there if it's so boring?"

"It's my clinic."

"But every day you go there, time is passing. Your life is passing." Rena furrows her brow as if angry at the world for harming Rick.

"And how would I make a living?"

"You don't have to make a living. I'll take care of you. I have plenty of money. Just hang out with me."

"I gotta go."

Rena's hand shoots out and grips Rick's wrist. "No." Her eyes are steely.

"I don't want to. I have to. You know I love sitting here with you. Talking with you."

"Do you? Do you love it?"

"Yes." Get up and leave. Now. You're on a slippery slope, pal.

"So if you love it . . . I mean, Rick, why isn't this time, right now, the time we spend together as good as any other time? Do you have to be making money to have time count? Why can't you just be with someone?" She releases his wrist. "Look, never mind. Go. But call me later. Please?"

"OK." Rick feels the beat of his blood. High from her touch. From her need. "Are you going to be OK?"

"Sure." But all of a sudden she doesn't look OK. She looks like the little kid who's gotten lost at the mall.

"I'll call you." Rick makes for the door. When he turns to wave, she smiles a brilliant smile, the blues dispersed into the late summer air. She mimes "Phone me."

Walking back to the clinic, Rick grins to himself. Oh yeah. Here we go. Insanity. OK. This is what you do, Rick. You help her with her brother and then clear the fuck out, asshole. But I don't want to clear out. I like it here. The funny thing is, I don't think she realizes the power she has over me. Isn't that strange? I spend my life in the clinic, with Laura, with the kids. All so predictable, so good in its way. It is good. But boring. And here's this girl, that's all she is, is a girl, who lives on another planet. Sending me signals, beaming me across space. And I would fly to her world in a heartbeat. What would that be like? To feel her breath on my ear? Not even all that. Forget the sex. Just to be with her. To sit with her like that, forever, like she says?

Look, she's just lonely. She's playing with my head. Probably goes home to her boyfriend and they make fun of her new best friend the pathetic old doctor. She probably does this all the time, collecting old farts who are thrilled just to sit and bask in her glow. She recharges her batteries with the attention. It's just something she does.

Besides, she's a ditz. A model. A kid. You don't care about her. You just want to "do" her. And you better watch out, pal. What if you do manage to get her in bed and it doesn't work out? What if she laughs at you? What then? Write yourself a scrip for Viagra and run back to Laura? OK. First of all, this isn't really happening. You're delusional. Second of all, she's a bimbo and you're pretending she's something more. Third of all, don't be a schmuck. Oh, and fourth of all, you are married with two kids. Fourth of all. Listen to me.

Suddenly missing Laura, Rick speed-dials the Cape. When he gets dropped into Laura's voice mail, he hangs up, doesn't leave a message. As he crosses the street toward the clinic, Zoe's anxious expression radiates through the plate glass. The waiting room is packed. I don't care. I don't care if they're in there puking blood. Turn around. Rena's back in the coffee place, she's still sitting at the table and she's waiting for me to come back.

When Rick walks in, Zoe tries to pass the phone to him. A woman is on the phone and insists it's very important that she speak with him. An emergency. Rick strides into his office and picks up the phone.

"Yes?"

"Listen, what are you doing tomorrow?"

"I . . . uh . . ."

"Because I forgot to tell you, um, that someone at Details gave me tickets to the McCartney concert. Right up front."

"Wow, that's great but um, I . . . I'm driving up to the Cape."

"Oh."

"I only get a day or two to see the kids."

"Uh-huh. No. That's cool. I was just thinking, because I didn't want to waste the tickets . . ."

You're not driving anywhere. Go to the McCartney concert, even though you can't stand his music. Rick wills himself to say the words: "No, listen, I appreciate it."

"And um, anyway. Whatever."

"What?" No laughter on either end.

"Yeah. So. OK. Listen. Could you call me when you get back? From being with your family?"

"Of course."

"To talk about Billy."

"Right."

"OK. Well, um, have a nice time this weekend."

"Thanks."

"With Laura."

"Yeah. Thanks."

"OK. Bye." Beat. "I'll miss you."

She hangs up. Rick is holding his breath.

A LONG ORANGE TONGUE SLIDES FROM THE MOUTH OF the bottle and swirls into the gushing bathwater. Naked and spent, Rick tracks the creep of the burgeoning foam, frowning as the water rises. He places himself on the edge of the tub and considers the liquid heat. Cecilia Bartoli's "Chant D'Amour" echoes through the cottage.

Disengaged from the usual bone-gnawing worry Rick's mind floats freely and aimlessly. Usually, his thoughts crunch into each

other like subway cars at rush hour. Usually, his thoughts live
inside of one another, like those nested Russian dolls, each more
intensely painted with anxiety than the last. Now yawning gaps
have grown between them, and in those gaps is nothing. Simply
a feeling. And the feeling is all about Rena. A kind of high. It's a
place he can settle himself with, return to again and again, savor.

The night before, he had driven up to the Cape and neglected
to eat. In the morning he had one egg, no lunch, and salad for
dinner. Swam all day. Now he checks out his reflection in the mirror. Looking very tan and thin. Face uncharacteristically lean,
eyes crystalline. In the two weeks since I've met her, I've changed.

Does Laura notice? The sex was great this morning, under the
covers while the kids watched cartoons, but she didn't seem to
notice. Spending all this time with Rena is making me miss Laura
more. Obviously the girl is getting me wound up. I'm becoming
a love junkie. My heart hurts. My heart is an itch I can't scratch.

Rick spins the roaring taps shut and the only sound is the
crackle of bubbles expiring. He carefully lowers himself into the
water, letting the heat cook his ass, his balls, his thighs. He dips
his shoulders and the tension flares through his muscles. Why am
I so tense?

The bubbles caress his face and the heat flows into his limbs,
healing him but making him a bit jumpy, too. The water's too hot.
I'm a cored apple baking in the oven. I'm dead. No. Not dead at
all. I'm alive. I haven't been this alive in a long time, have I?

"Rick, what are you doing in there?" Laura senses a vacuum,
Rick is here, but not here. Where is he?

"Taking a bath."

"Is that tub clean?"

"I was feeling sore from the workout, so I thought I'd take a
bath. I'm happy, leave me alone."

"Did you scrub it out first?"

"Don't worry about the tub."

"You don't know who's been in that tub."

"It's not dirty! It's fine. I'm fine." She has a sixth sense and a seventh sense and an eighth sense. She knows when I'm thinking about another woman.

After a silence: "Are you going to be in there long?"

"It's a bath, I'm not going to jump right out. I'm bathing."

"But I wanted to wash my hair."

Maybe if I turned off the lights, I could conjure Rena. Hey kid, what are you doing right now? Are you thinking about me?

"Rick!"

"What?!"

"Did you use some bubble bath or something?"

"Yes, go away."

Rick floats in the hot water weightless, no thoughts, nothing to tie him down to earth. Everything has dissolved. Life has dissolved. Everything is gone, except for Rena's spirit, infusing him.

"Because you'll get a ring if you don't."

"I used the bubble bath!"

"Which bubble bath?"

"I don't know. The bubble bath that was in here."

"That's not bubble bath."

"Whatever. There's bubbles."

"That's bath gel, Rick!"

"Laura, I have a headache."

"What?"

"I don't want to talk right now, I'm trying to relax in here for god's sake!"

Silence. Rick listens. Is she outside the door? The bubbles clear and a submarine landscape becomes visible. Penis and scrotum float pale and lifeless, like the pickled fetuses back in med school. Slightly buoyant, a little cooked.

Rick pinches his penis. Wags it. The ur–bath toy, the dick. Something I used to do when I was little. Let the little guy's helmet come up from under the water. The submarine conning tower breaking up through the foam. All sorts of games you can play with your dick when you're small. Of course at six you have no idea what kind of trouble playing with this little monster is going to cause. The little popgun. The little soldier. Fucking troublemaker.

Still quiet outside. Rick wags his penis again. Kicks up a little wave. Flip-flop. Deceptively playful. Enjoys all the attention. "You like that, fella?" Never talked to my dick before. Never named it, either. Don't really think of it as part of me or not a part of me. One thing for sure, you and I are in this together, pal. And let's face it, if I didn't have you, my whole life wouldn't have happened. A person can be missing a finger, a leg, an eye, a person can still fuck around. But if you don't have a dick you can't fall in love, can't have kids, can't cheat on your wife. Well, maybe you can fall in love. Hopefully I'll never find out the answer to that one.

"It's just you and me, guy." And of course Rena's pussy and Rena. That's what this is all about, isn't it? Pussy on the radar screen. Going on a mission. Playing the sensitive helpful uncle, the good listener, get her interested, then reel her in. Right? As if I know what I'm doing.

Rena's like someone I knew long ago, an old friend who's returned. And it's like we have that and we know we have it, that old memory. We can feel it. It flows between us. With Laura, there's always that separateness, that invisible borderline between us. And borders are where wars take place. That's the problem, war can break out at any time. Laura and I don't trust each other. That's the way it is with being married, there's always the threat of going our separate ways. But that isn't how it is with Rena. Is it? With Rena, even if I never saw her again, she'd still be part of me. Because she was part of me before we met.

Wait a minute, Laura's a part of me, too, what am I saying? And no one's a part of anyone. That's just an illusion. We're alone. I'm alone.

Rick massages his penis. Firmer now, just thinking about Rena makes me hard. It's a different kind of erection, isn't it? I don't consciously think of being horny, it just shows up. Like something straight from my viscera. No, not viscera. Soul. I don't even have to visualize Rena. Just open my heart and I go hard.

The heat is making me sleepy. There she is. There are her eyes. I'm nuzzling her neck, touching her soft breasts. Pushing into her. She's digging her heels into my back, pulling me into her, harder and harder. Her mouth . . .

"Rick?"

God!!!

"Rick, what are you doing in there? Are you all right? Rick?"

"Yes." Too weak. "I said, yes, I'm all right. I'm fine. I was, uh, meditating."

"I want to rinse some underwear, are you going to be in there much longer? I can do it in the kids' sink, do you want me to do it in the kids' sink?"

What is she going on about? "What?" Silence again. Still hard. Conjure Rena back again. Smell her. That perfume she wears. She's here with me right now. She's in the room, she's squatting down on top of me, her gentle hands, bringing my face up to hers, she's kissing me. Kissing me . . .

"Oh *shit*!" Rick clutches himself and curls into a fetal position, the hot water filling his mouth, his ears. When he opens his eyes everything is defused, shimmering with orgasm. The twisted white worms of his cum float in the hot water. He can't help but think: denatured protein. He moans, "God."

"Rick?"

Rick recalls seeing a building once that had been set with hundreds of dynamite charges so that when they exploded the building collapsed in on itself. That's me. Imploded. There are no words, now, only sensation and color and Rena. Rick lets himself slip down into the foam. I could drown this way. Boiled alive. Why not? I've lost my mind, it makes no difference.

"Rick?"

Don't move. Just die.

"Rick? Answer me! Are you OK?"

Rick yanks himself up, clutching a towel which falls the wrong way into the water, instantly heavy with wet. He brings the sopping cloth up and smothers his face.

"God," he murmurs. "God."

"Rick, are you all right?"

"God." He whispers to a cluster of bubble foam, to the tiles on the wall.

"Answer me, Rick."

"No. I'm not fine."

"What?"

"Go away. I'll be out in a minute."

Rick carefully places the soaking towel on the edge of the tub, presses his face down onto it and listens to his heart beating.

RENA WOULD TUG ON THE BRANCHES UNTIL THE WHOLE tree shook and the apples fell like summer hail. It was the only way to get at the ones too high up to pick. Pull and shake until the vibration ran up through the applewood into the twigs, and the fruit, swinging like mad pendulums, would have no choice but to fall.

That would be around this time of year. End of the summer. The apples wouldn't be quite ready, but I wouldn't mind. The sweet cider running over my teeth and tongue. One minute the fruit's on the tree, then it's in my stomach. As simple as that.

From where Rena sits at this moment, it would be impossible to know the season, let alone the time of day because she's sitting in the pale olive waiting room at Billy's hospital. There's been an "incident." This time the nurse doesn't seem so friendly.

She has Billy's folder on her desk. She scans it, and without looking up, announces, "I understand you want to transfer your
brother out of here." She jots something down, pockets her pen
and closes the folder.

"I was looking into that option." What opiate is this nurse
on? Vicodin? Percodan? Thai white?

The impassive black woman glances up at Rena, brown eyes
impenetrable. "Well, you can look into whatever you like. But
right now, Billy isn't going anywhere."

"What do you mean, 'right now'?"

"Last night, he decided to act out. He smashed the TV with a
folding chair. Threw an inmate into a wall. Did a lot of screaming. Screamed his head off. Fortunately no one was hurt. If
someone gets hurt, Miss Cook, there will be consequences, no
matter what his status."

"I understand." Get me out of here.

"Do you? I think you had better inform your brother that he
can't afford these tantrums. I don't care who his sister is. Billy
may not like our ward, but take my word for it, Miss Cook, soli-
tary lockdown is an even more difficult place. Some people go in
and never come out. Mental health is not a precise science."

"That sounds threatening."

"We took the straitjacket off him this morning. Increased his
meds, so he's sedated but aware of what's going on. If we have
to, we will continue balancing the medication to prevent any
more outbursts. That's for the benefit of the other inmates, as
well as for Billy's. Most of the people in here want to get better."

"Let me see him."

"You'll see him." The woman stands and and walks out of
the room. In the ward, the nurse turns to Rena before leaving
her. "You say he's a good guy. It's not my concern whether he is
or isn't. My concern is his mental health in the context of this
institution. You're his sister. Tell him he's got to get with the pro-
gram. If he isn't getting better, he's getting worse. That's just the

way it is, Miss Cook. He listens to you. He likes you." Rena turns to go as the woman keeps talking. "You can have all the money and connections in the world. It's still my job to approve a transfer. And I will only do that when he's showing improvement, I don't care how many lawyers call me."

The nurse walks off and Rena thinks, how does someone like that decide to be a caregiver? So she can be a patronizing asshole? So she can have power over all these poor fuckers? If you control the crazies, does that prove you're sane?

Billy's door is ajar, dark inside, as usual. "Billy?" Nothing. She steps inside. He's moved his bed to the diagonal. Sheets and pillows are scattered on the floor. He lies on his back, palms upward, eyes open, facing the ceiling. The mattress is bare. He lies here, like the radiant core of a nuclear power plant.

"Billy? It's me, Rena."

Nothing. His eyes are open.

"Billy? Hi?" He doesn't blink. The eyes examine the ceiling. He taps the mattress with an index finger, jaw in flux as if chewing cud.

"I brought you some cookies." She places the tin of cookies on the table next to the teal blue water bottle and cup. Box of tissues. Lotion. The smells. Any energy Rena possessed as she entered drains away. "Billy? Can you at least say hello to me?" No, he's not going to say hi or move or sit up or do anything. His eyes rotate in their sockets. He glances at her, looks away.

"If you're going to be like that, I'm gonna go." But this is stupid. To come all the way out here and then just leave. It's not his fault. He's sick. I have to have patience. She pulls a heavy armchair out from the wall. "Why don't I sit for a minute. See if you want to talk."

He's staring at the ceiling again, his lips no longer chewing an invisible stick of gum. Instead he's forming inaudible words with his lips. Tapping his finger like a machine part. Robotic. A song in his head, maybe?

"Billy, I know you can hear me, they told me you can hear."

He shuts his eyes and opens them again. As if in assent. Or to signal absolute fatigue. Or as a sign of dismissal.

"Hey, Bill. Guess what happened? I got a renewal on the bebe contract? Cool, huh? It's been so much harder to get work lately. Marissa says the business is in a slowdown, so I was pretty amped about getting this job. We shoot next week, so I won't be able to come when I usually do. But I know you'll understand."

Billy turns his eyes on her. Doesn't blink. Doesn't tap. Doesn't chew. "Billy. I know you're on special medication, so you're probably not up for conversation. But . . . but, listen, I'm trying to get you out of here and throwing shit around isn't helping, you know? I mean, I'm doing my part and I know it isn't easy, but you have to try. I know you're frustrated. We're all frustrated. That head nurse is a bitch. Still, you've got to control yourself. Even now what you're doing and I know you're doing it, is not easy to deal with. You can talk to me, at least."

Billy begins to chew and tap at the same time.

"OK. OK. Don't get all agitated. You're in a bad mood. Listen, I'd hate it too if I had to stay here. But why don't you just hang in, don't do anything bad for a week or so and then you can go to a much nicer place. OK?"

The tapping stops. Resumes.

"I've been working with this very nice doctor, the one who admitted you? Do you remember him? The night you were in the fight? Well, he's going to help me get you out of here."

Billy closes his eyes. This time they remain shut.

"I guess that means yes. OK. OK." Now she knows why the tissues are on the table. She takes one and wipes her eyes. "Hey, you know what I was thinking about before I came in here? I was thinking about the orchard. There must be apples on the trees right now. It's almost September. I can smell them. Can't you? So why don't you think about that, OK? Think about getting out of here and getting back up to the farm. OK? I will drive you up myself. I can't stay there, of course, but I'll visit. It'll be fun. OK? Think of the orchard. Whenever you get upset, think of the orchard."

Billy begins to snore. His breath is labored. He looks so much like Daddy. It's like watching Daddy coming back to life. And dying all over again.

WHEN RICK WAKES, HIS FIRST THOUGHT IS: AGAIN. DOWN-stairs, Slavic voices growl at one another and the sour aroma of latex paint wafts up to him. They're down there. What day is it? Before Rick can think about the clinic, he thinks, Rena. His cell phone rings.

It could be Laura. It could be Rena. Seven forty-five AM. Laura is not calling me. Don't answer. But I want to. Rick clicks on his cell phone.

She speaks before he can say anything. "Hi."

"Hi." Fuzzy voice. Cough. Try again. "Good morning."

"Were you sleeping?" Her voice is low, soothing.

"No. I was listening to the painters working downstairs."

"What painters?"

"Bunch of Polish guys who are here to paint my house. Sup-posed to be finished weeks ago." I'm lying in bed, talking to Rena, and I have to get to the clinic. And I don't care.

"How's Billy?"

"Not so good. They're real bastards over there."

"I'll see what I can do to give it a push."

"Thank you." A pause. "Are you still in bed?"

"Yes. No. I just got up. I'm moving."

"Does the house look nice? All freshly painted?"

"Terrific."

"Can I see your house? I want to see your house."

"That wouldn't be a good idea, Rena." He thinks, come see my house, come see my bedroom, get in my bed with me and never leave. That's what we both want.

"Why wouldn't it be a good idea?"

"Umm. It's a residential neighborhood. Filled with residents, i.e., neighbors. They do neighborly things like watch one another's houses and gossip."

"That's stupid."

"Actually, it's not. It's protective."

"You know what, Rick? You worry too much about what other people think. What other people think about what you're thinking. Basically, you think too much."

"It's a bad habit of mine. I'm gonna join a twelve-step group. Thinkers Anonymous." Did I get fucked up again last night?

"Don't you ever do just what you feel?"

"No." In the bathroom Rick tries to piss along the inside of the bowl so Rena won't hear the gurgle over the phone.

"Never?"

"If I did whatever I felt like I'd get arrested." He weighs himself. Fat. Right. Last night, pizza with extra cheese and seven hundred beers. I can't shave and talk to her at the same time. Make coffee. He wanders downstairs, cell phone, lifeline, in hand.

"How do you know?"

"I know." The painters ignore him. When Rick catches the eye of one, the man nods. Do these guys speak enough English to know I'm talking to my girlfriend? Rick finds himself in the kitchen. No milk.

"Are you in bed?"

"I'm getting ready for work. It's this funny thing I do every day. Don't ask me why."

"Why?"

"Because my patients have this odd codependent relationship with me."

"You sound weird."

Rick feels himself getting hard. How does she do this to me? "I'm hungover."

"You get wasted because you're lonely."

"That might be true. Wait. Yes. That's true. Where are you, anyway?"

"Me?"

"Yeah, you."

"In the bathtub. We were working late. Then we all went out. I just got in now."

"Wow."

"How was the Cape?"

"Good. I took a bath up there. Bubble bath. You're not the only one who knows how to bathe."

"By yourself?"

"Yes, of course." With you, actually.

"Well, that's a good sign. You should do that more often. Take care of yourself."

"Yeah." Tell her what else you did in the bath, asshole.

Rena's voice drops. "You should see me right now. I look pretty good. Little bits of suds floating around my nipples. Nice warm water all around my . . . you know . . . my thing. Oh, look! Time to shave my bikini line!"

"Rena."

"What."

"This isn't fair."

"How long will those Polish painters be there?"

"They leave at three."

"I have an idea. Don't go to work. Go back to bed. Doctors can call in sick, can't they?"

"Easy for you to say."

"What's that supposed to mean?"

"You know. You're a jet-setter. All you do is party."

"Hey. Fuck you." She hangs up.

Dreamy, Rick stands before the coffeemaker as the last drops of black liquid plop concentrically into the pot. We're having spats now. Great. He finds the cell phone again but before he can dial the Cape the phone rings in his hand. He says, "I'm sorry."

Silence.

"Rena?" And what if it isn't? What's if it's Laura?

"Yeah?"

I can't say it. I can't tell her to go away. "Come by around four. I'll make coffee." The walls close in. So easy to say, to hit the first domino. And then what happens?

Just do it. Go in, make it a short day. See the people you have to see, move a few appointments around. Be back by three, beat the rush hour. Let go. Live. See what happens. Look at it this way: what would Dad do?

From the time he gets off the phone until he gets home at two thirty, the day's life assembles itself in jump cuts. Rick's consciousness barely touches down. He's on his way back to the house before he realizes that he hasn't checked in with Laura.

"Hey."

"Hey."

"How's the sand and surf?"

"Rainy. The kids are stuck in the house. We're cutting up construction paper. They're making surprise cards to send to you."

"Oh."

"How's the office?"

"Good. I actually, uh, knocked off early today. Some stuff I want to do around the house, so I thought I'd make a short day of it."

"What stuff?"

"Well, the painters moved some things around. I want to clear up a bit." She knows. How does she know?

"Oh. Cool. You deserve a short day. You've been working hard."

"Yeah. Whatever."

"Are you driving right now?"

"Yeah."

"I don't want you calling me when you're driving. I'm gonna get off."

"OK."

"We can talk tonight."

"OK. Have fun with the construction paper."

"Thanks. Have fun with the painters."

"Bye. Love you."

"Love you."

Back home, Rick bangs around the house like an eager kid, cleaning. Sorting. Throwing out the newspapers and OJ cartons and cereal boxes stacked by the back door. He takes a shower, dresses and sees that the painters are taking their sweet time wrapping up for the day. They lounge in the front yard, smoking and spitting flecks of tobacco on the Japanese yews. What are they blabbing about? Probably cussing out the dirty Jew they're working for. When Rena shows up, I know what they're gonna be talking about. If she shows up.

Quiet. Rick sneaks a peek out the front window and sees the workers' gray commuter van finally arriving. A Lincoln Town Car passes the van and wheels into Rick's driveway. Rick jumps back as if the windowpanes are on fire. He waits.

The doorbell rings. What am I doing? Why is this girl coming to my house? Don't open the door. She doesn't know you're here. You're not here, a madman is here. Wait. Don't appear too anxious. Take your time. Smile. Open the door.

He opens the door and is overwhelmed. An angel stands before him, tall, perfect, her hair glossy and curling over her square shoulders. She waits a beat, letting him take her in, then says, "Hi." This is what she does, makes an impression.

Looking past the girl in the doorway Rick sees the painters loading into the van. In the driveway next to the town car a

204 • ERIC BOGOSIAN

dark-complexioned man stands gazing up at the maples as if trying to appraise their height.

"Come in." Rena enters the house. She stands in the foyer,
unsure. Rick closes the door, cutting off the view of the arbor-
phile. "You have a driver."

"Are you kidding? I never would have found this place.
He's Turkish. We don't talk. I used to think it was fun to talk
to drivers. Now I just say 'get me there.'"

"Good. I mean, I'm glad you found the house. Come in, come
in." The world tips. Colors pour in and out of one another.
Logic unlocks. Rick thinks, she's in my home. Laura's home. The
door closes behind her and the deed is done. How could he ever
explain her presence from this point onward?

Rick leads Rena back toward the kitchen. "We installed these
bookcases after we moved in. Built the mudroom when the kids
were little. The original owners installed wall-to-wall carpeting
everywhere. Had to rip it all out. Sanded the floors, dust everywhere."

"It's a pretty big house."

"We got it for a song. At the time we didn't think so, but in
hindsight, it's amazing. Appraisal doubled. Actually, I wasn't
really into the place, but Laura saw the value right away." Why
am I explaining my life to this girl?

"Did Laura decorate it?"

"Uh yeah. Yeah. She did. Before we were married she was an
interior decorator. Do you want something cold or coffee? Or . . ."

"It has good vibes."

"Well, my kids were born here. I mean, they weren't born in
this house, but you know . . ." Rick opens the fridge and stares
at the contents.

Rena steps up to Rick. "Hey, relax, it's just me, Rena. Your pal."

"Uh-huh. My pal."

"What?" She touches his shoulder.

"I'm happy you could stop by." My mouth is dry. If I kiss her she'll think I'm disgusting. Besides, she doesn't want to kiss me. She thinks we're friends. Pals. That's what we are. She just came by to visit her buddy the doctor.

"That's what pals are for. To visit each other when they're down." Touch him. Keep touching him.

"Yes, that's true." I can't breathe. What should I do? Nothing. Do nothing.

"Just me and you. We've never been alone before."

"Can I say something here?" Rick removes a carton of OJ, shuts the fridge door and steps away from Rena.

"I love it when you talk."

"First of all, I keep thinking you're a kid and you're not a kid. You're a woman, a beautiful woman. Secondly, you know I like you. I mean, as a person and . . . this sounds idiotic, as a woman. It's obvious. I'm not going to try to hide it. And, stop me if I'm hallucinating, but I think you like me. And I have to assume that part of the reason you like me is that you think you know me. But Rena, you don't know me. You think because I've got a wife and kids and live in the suburbs that I'm a nice guy. But I'm not a nice guy. I'm not. And uh, wait, uh, see, lately, I've been trying very hard to be a good husband and a good father and, in short be a good guy . . ."

"A good guy who isn't happy."

"Wait. Wait. Let me finish. I don't know if I'm happy or not. I don't even think that's the point. Happiness is, I don't know what happiness is."

Rena says, "Happiness is when you don't want anything in your life to change. That's what happiness is. Unhappiness is when you want everything to change."

"Yeah." This is the problem. She knows me. She's not a bimbo. She's smart. "But, let me finish, that's true, but let me finish. I'm working hard at making my life work. It's just the way it is. I mean, I'm twenty years older than you, different times of your life have a different rhythm . . ."

"But Rick, you're always you. Deep down. Don't you feel that? You know who you are, deep down. And you know who I am, deep down. And besides, why does life have to be such hard work? That's depressing. I'm so sick of this therapy attitude to life, like we're climbing some kind of mountain we're never gonna get to the top of. I've worked hard enough." Don't be afraid of me.

"Yes, but listen, like I said. I like you. But I want to like you in a way that's innocent. I don't, how can I say this, I don't want to make this . . . uh, friendship, into something physical. I guess that's what I wanted to say. OK? I mean, I don't mean to presume what your intentions are, but whatever, are you OK with that?"

"That's what you want? Really want?"

"Well, I do. But I mean I'm trying not to think about it, us, in that other way."

"But is that true, you don't think about it that way?"

"Rena! Stop! Let me finish. I love spending time with you. More than anything. It's crazy. But I do. Just standing here next to you is exhilarating for me. And uh, you know, just something as simple as holding your hand would probably drive me nuts. And that's wrong. You know it's wrong. That's why it won't happen."

"Even though it's what you want."

"It's wrong."

Rena holds out her hand. "You can hold it if you want."

Rick stares at her hand as if it's a weapon pointed at his heart. A hand. That's all it is. Touch it. Touch her hand. He reaches out and takes it in his. It's warm and relief flows into him, like a drug. She carries his hand up to her cheek and caresses it. She says, "I like your hand."

Rick steps forward and kisses her. He's ten years old and jumping onto a sled on top of the highest hill in town. He's flying downward with appalling speed toward an unknown destination, and he's lost the ability to steer. Her lips are soft and her scent enveloping. She's stronger than he expected. Farm girl. Cover girl. Everything surges. Just kissing her is more intense than sex.

A knocking. Rick opens his eyes. Someone is knocking on the front door. Laura has come home early! She's lost her keys. No, Laura wouldn't knock. Rick pulls away, Rena holds on to him. Her eyes are vague and hungry, dilated.

"Rena. I, we. You gotta go." My god, I have an erection. And I'm still holding the goddamn carton of orange juice.

"I know. I know." Two people in limbo.

"Yeah. We both know. I . . . wow. Here we are, making out like schoolkids."

Rena says, "Is that what we're doing?" The sadness has entered her voice. The wisdom is gone.

"I don't know what we're doing." I don't want her to be sad.

"Don't think about it so much, Rick! When God gives you a gift, just take it." Another knock.

Rena turns and walks to the front door. Opens it. If Laura is standing there, my marriage is over. Rena says, "Hi. What?" No, not Laura and the kids. The driver, saying something. Rena calls back to him, "Fuck! I have to get into the city. They need me."

She runs back into the room where Rick stands, frozen. She gives him a quick kiss. "I love you. You know that? Call me later."

And she's gone.

SHE LEANS ACROSS THE TABLE AND SLIDES HER HAND into his. "Come here," she says. She tilts her face up, the warmth of her skin pulsing. "We're being watched," she says. Could we be any more obvious?

The Greek counterman tracks the couple in the corner. Rick thinks, You want to know how I ended up with her, don't you? You want to know if I'm fucking her. Well, I'm not. But I will be. Or might be. If I can. If she lets me. If I can get it up. But see, that's not important, but you wouldn't understand. Because you can't understand my feelings. This is bigger than your fantasies, that's why you can't get near my Rena.

It isn't just the guy at the counter, it's everyone in the diner. Everyone is watching us, because we have what everyone wants. The myths about the gods falling in love were created because people feel like gods when they fall in love. Pure emotion is a reflection of the forces of heaven. Who gets to possess pure emotion? Very few. So here it is, everybody. Take a good look. It's not something to hide, it's something to proclaim to the skies. I am alive! I am obsessed! She touches his face, her lips inches from his. Her touch is the gentlest touch he's ever known. "Kiss me," she says.

I'm doing it. I'm kissing a woman who is not my wife in a diner off the West Side Highway. Where is Laura right now? Standing by a window in the cottage, watching the kids playing? Wringing out swimsuits? Shucking corn on the cob for dinner? Is she thinking of me? I'm thinking of her. I'm thinking of you, Laura, while I'm kissing a girl in a diner on 57th Street. I am occupying a space I should not be occupying and I'm gonna burn in hell someday but I can't help myself. How can something be bad that feels this good?

She tries to kiss him again. "I'm married, Rena, for god's sake."

"OK. Let's go where no one can see us."

"I can't."

"I have an idea. Tell Laura you have to go to a medical conference. And we can fly down to Saint Bart's for a couple of days. It would be so nice. I know the best places. I'll pay for it. It won't show up on your credit card. We can hang out on the beach. We can swim. We can do a lot of things."

"You're nuts."

"And you're not?"

"With you I am."

"You look angry."

"I'm not angry. I'm confused. Rena, you're just a kid."

"Please stop saying that, Rick. That has nothing to do with what's happening between us. Look into my eyes. We know each other. You know me and I know you. It's so obvious. I know you know it. I'm here for you, just accept it. You've been out there my whole life, I've been out here your whole life. Well, almost your whole life. Look at me. Every night since I was a little girl I thought of you before I fell asleep. Because I knew you'd be in my life someday. And here you are, sitting right in front of me."

"Yeah? And what if I'm sitting here for the wrong reason?"

"And what would that be?"

"That you're physically beautiful, that you're more beautiful than any woman I've ever been near."

"Gee, that's such a terrible reason! Don't you understand, I want to be beautiful for you. For no one but you. I want that. You're beautiful to me, too. Inside and out. Why is that so bad?"

"It just is."

"You're crazy." Rena beams at him with total joy. "I don't care if it's wrong. Tell me to go away. It won't change anything. I love you. I love you for all of you. Even the fucked-up parts. I see you, Rick, isn't that obvious?"

They leave the diner and idle down 57th Street, going nowhere, content to be walking beside each other. Not even walking in a straight line, Rena leaning her hip into him as they stroll, her arm slung over his shoulder. Passersby check them out, a middle-aged doctor and his trophy babe. A fucking cliché. Sure, Rick, leave your wife, be one more statistic. And what will everyone say? They'll laugh at you, that's what they'll do. They'll hate you for hurting Laura. You'll be a joke. You'll have no real friends. Your kids will despise you. But you'll have something you've always wanted. And what is that? What is that, Rick? He feels her beside him, emanating warmth, love, whatever it is, pure intoxication. And you know what the punch line is, pal? You leave your wife for this, and then this girl gets tired of the game the minute you give in to her. Anyway, no one's leaving anybody. You're just fucking around, as always. Asshole that you are. Lying to yourself. Lying to her. Because there is no truth.

Rick pulls Rena into the courtyard of a skyscraper. He leads her behind a pay phone. The world swims about them. Bits of litter blow by their feet. The stream of humanity proceeds only a few feet away, like cattle lumbering to slaughter. But here, in the epicenter of the universe, love. Do it. Kiss her as hard and as much as you want. Touch her, squeeze her. You can do what you want with her. Everyone else wants to touch her, only you can.

Kiss her. Taste her. Feel the heat under her clothing. Go now, find a bed, an alley, any place, and be with her. Never leave her.

Rick pulls away and says, "I gotta go, Rena. I gotta." Coward.

Rena's eyes are brimming—with tears? With lust? Does she lust for me? Is that possible? Her smile, crooked, a sad smile. All the sunshine in her drained away, replaced with this awesome melancholy. How unhappy is this girl? How unhappy are we both?

Rick leaves her propped against the side of the phone kiosk like a wasted mannequin. Within moments he is on the subway, roaring downtown. The swaying humanity around him clueless. There's a hurricane in my heart, can't you see it? Sleepwalkers, all. Zombies. None of you has ever had this. Never have had a smidgen of what I've got. Rick makes his way through the car to the end, wrenches open the door and steps out into the clamor of the flashing darkness. Roaring surrounds him. Through the Plexiglas he looks back at the illuminated blank-faced people as they rock to and fro, heads bowed over books or lolling in fake sleep. Just normal people, people in between dramas. The din of the train as massive as his heartache. This is crazy, this is crazy, this is crazy. The surface of the tunnel rushes past, pocked with hundreds of nooks and crannies where rats and maybe homeless people hide, like my heart, dark, unseen, unvisited. When something's hidden, does that automatically make it sad?

RICK'S PULSE TAPS AT HIS WRISTS LIKE A MAD WOOD-pecker, in his temples, in his legs. Mouth dry. Dry mouth causes bad breath. What am I doing? What if someone I know sees me? But who would know me here? A Midtown tourist hotel? Isn't this how history is made, by bad coincidence? Except this isn't history, this is my life.

Rena turns and smiles at him. "Hi." She takes his hand, moves to kiss him. He draws back. "Not here."

"Don't be nervous."

"I'm either going to faint or throw up."

"Me, too. I'll go get the key." Rena strides toward the front desk. That's the way she moves, she strides. Because she's a model, asshole. I'm in the lobby of a Midtown hotel with a twenty-one-year-old model. Why don't I just take out a display ad in the *Times*? I'm driving the car off the cliff. Let's go. Fuckit. It's time. I can't spend another minute looking into her eyes. We've been holding hands, we've been making out. What difference does this make? It's time.

Rick observes Rena from across the lobby. The front desk people fawn over her. This is her life. She lives in a world of obsequiousness. She lives in a world where every door is open. No, better, opened for her. With a fucking bow. Yes, all of you pricks out there, you can show your teeth all you want, she's getting in that elevator with me.

Drifting into a kind of inebriation, he memorizes her body language. Every male eye is on her and she is happy to take advantage of that fact, but she doesn't want their eyes. She's doing this for me. She walks for me, struts for me. Her power is terrifying. Rena gets the keys and returns to Rick. She says, "Follow me." And he does.

They step into an elevator lined with polished wood veneer and carved froufrou. Rick catches a glimpse of his freaked-out grinning self in a chunk of decorative mirror. I am a dork. I am a lunatic. Her breath stains my lungs, my heart. I am wild. I'm a bag of snakes. A box of rabid squirrels. We're madhouse newlyweds.

Rena takes his hand and squeezes it as the elevator door opens on their floor. A man shuffles on as they get out. His hair is wet, he needs a shave. Is he here for misconduct, too? The tired-looking guy runs his eyes over Rena in a mechanical way, as if he's expected to give her the once-over. But Rena slips past him and moves confidently toward the door of their suite. Rick follows, dizzy with anxiety and lust.

With the door shut and locked behind them, it's as if they have entered an amazing chamber outside the normal space-time continuum. The room itself is lifeless, fitted out in tans and yellows, the nearby skyscrapers block the sun. The bed takes up most of the space, an out-of-date TV stands in the corner. It's an old-fashioned room, generic, cleaned a million times. Rena and Rick leave the lights off and move through the gloom like ghosts.

There are so many ways this could go wrong. There is so much pain waiting on the other side of this moment. Rick thinks, I should probably rinse out my mouth. And pee. "I have to use the bathroom," he says.

She nods, like a kindergarten teacher. "OK."

He leaves her standing by the end of the bed and enters the compact bathroom. The setting sun has found a chink in the skyline and warms the white tiles orange and pink.

Rick unwraps the little bar of soap and washes his hands, then wipes them on the brittle plush of the hotel towel. There I am again in the reflection over the sink. A man possessed. Happy? Is this being happy?

And now Rena is behind him, pulling him into a fierce embrace, launching into him, pressing her mouth to his, pinning him against the wall. Rick thinks, I've never been here before. They take a breather and he leans back, the room even darker now, her eyes mere bits of glitter floating in the perfect geometry of her face. She kisses him again, and again, her strength surprising him. There isn't much to her, but she can pin me to the wall. Farmgirl.

I want her. Why prolong the torture any longer? He leads her back to the room and eases her onto the bed, wrapping himself into her. As they hug, he shivers. Rena whimpers. He draws himself back again and tries to look into her eyes. Tries to see the chasm he's about to throw himself into.

But he's blind. He stands and flicks on a lamp by the bed. She lies there watching him, expectant. He undresses, and she observes his movements as if she has no idea what he's doing. And so, naked, and oddly vulnerable in spite of, or because of, his cantilevered prick, he comes to her and opens her blouse. The heat of her body surprises him, the perfect smoothness of her skin. I know how wonderful she is, but in fact, I can't find any imperfection. Everything about her, her aroma, her heat, her every tactile aspect, is flawless. Must be an illusion, right? Am I so much "in love" that I've lost any judgment? What is judgment? An illusion.

Rena draws away, stretches across the bed and finds the clock radio. Touches it. Pop music. TLC, as if by a miracle, singing "All Night Long." She rolls off the bed and watching him, she dances, rolling her hips slowly, drawing her jeans down off her ass like a fantasy girl, letting them bunch over her knees. She steps out of the crumpled pants. Rick thinks, see, she is wearing a thong. She unsnaps and releases her bra, lets it drop, still dancing, her full breasts animate, her ribs, belly, everything exposed as if for the first time, just for Rick. She lies down next to him. Touches him.

Nude, Rena twists her body so Rick can't get between her legs and he embraces her awkwardly that way. Like a high school date. They kiss. They stop kissing.

"This is going very fast," Rena says.

"Is it?" Rick says. The demon has risen. I can't come this far only to turn back . . . When did I cross the line? A long time ago.

"I don't know. This is so weird, us being naked like this. I feel funny. It's so different."

"Don't you want to make love?" Wasn't it going to be the other way around? I was going to be the one incapacitated. I still don't know her.

"I . . ."

"We'll do whatever you feel comfortable doing." I'm an idiot. This has been my idea all along. She doesn't want this. You saw it coming, pal.

"Just hold me."

Rick holds her, skin pressing skin, electric with nerves and lust, and his head fills with Laura and the children. This situation is something I better get away from as quickly as I can. Should. Should do that. Right now. Should. Fuck should. Look what she's making me do! She's testing me. And I can't help myself. She is a naked angel. How can a man turn away from a naked angel? How is that possible? But I'm not hard anymore. Why? I don't care. I don't care about sex.

Rick thinks, we're not fucking. We're doing something else here.

"Look at me. Look into my eyes." And he does. Cornflowers. The blue of the sky on the most wonderful day of the year. This girl's beauty is not like any beauty I've ever known. I've slept with beautiful women. This is some kind of endless, infinitely transforming beauty. She's different every time I look at her. Today, like a little girl, innocent. She's letting me look at her. Like a surrender.

"What are you doing, Rena . . ."

"Just hold me. Shhhhh."

And she falls asleep in his arms.

RICK SENSES HER BEFORE HE SEES HER WALKING A FEW feet in front of him on the crowded sidewalk. Her scent has become the trigger of the hypnotic mechanism. It's part of her and it is her. It sets things in motion. Rick hurries forward and touches her neck and she turns with a smile, knowing it's him. She knows because she knows.

Rena thinks, I've come this far, why not throw everything I have into it? He's married. So what, he was unhappy, everyone is unhappy in this world. A person has the right to get as happy as they can get. I love him, I feel it from my heart down to my toes. Because he's not trying to prove anything. Because he'll take care of me. Because I can see in his eyes how he adores me. Because he knows how to touch me. Because he isn't coming at me like a dog, like a con man, like a stud. He's just who he is. Lovable Rick. Beautiful Rick. Sweet Rick.

They are meeting for the third time this week. The night before he'd gone to her apartment for the first time. Agitated, because he had lied to Laura, told her he was working at the clinic. How could she know, she's three hundred miles away. Whatever he tells Laura, once Rena and Rick are in each other's proximity, thoughts of others leave their minds.

Rena has surprised Rick. She's passionate and her skin tastes like dark heaven. He gets drunk on her sublimity. And he doesn't hold back, he comes into her like he's hemorrhaging his soul and heart. As he does, he thinks of Laura. He is ecstatic and horrified at the same time.

They lie next to each other, still and connected, and she gazes at him. My god, he thinks, has anyone ever looked at me like this? He grows hard again within minutes. This is the dominion of the impossible, passion with no boundaries.

The second time they make love she whispers in his ear, "Fuck me" and he moans when he comes. They pass out, dream for a while, wake up and begin again.

Exhausted from the anxious expectation he slides in and out of her for what seems like hours, watching her perfect face morph into a million faces—all hers. He pins her arms over her head, cleaving her, flattening her breasts. Her mascara smudges around her eyes and they kiss slowly and longingly as if they have gone beyond fucking.

They fall in and out of sleep, still fucking. Finally, Rick comes to and finds himself asleep in her arms. There's blood on the sheets.

He tries to sneak away at dawn, but when he kisses her she wakes and without a word watches him get dressed.

Rick phones Rena on his cell phone as he drives home. Once he gets there he sits in his driveway murmuring to her, engine idling, for twenty minutes. What if a neighbor saw me from a window? Would someone report this to Laura when she got back? "Your husband sits in the driveway at six in the morning, talking on the phone." "Who were you talking to, Rick?"

The house is still when he enters the back door. It smells of fresh paint and absent children. He flips on the bathroom light, and sees a lunatic staring back at him. An incredibly handsome lunatic. He goes to bed as the sun tints the bedroom walls rose, stinking of his lover, and he falls away, dreaming of her.

When he wakes a surge of excitement wells in his chest and his first thought is, I did it. I did it. I wasn't a coward. I did it. I am alive.

Does it make any difference I was with Rena and not at the ER? Does any of it make a difference? In a hundred years all this will be the forgotten random acts of some dead, forgotten people. All that counts is what I'm feeling right now. She said, "Fuck me." She did.

She had said more. Before they finally fell asleep, Rena told Rick she loved him again. Isn't it obvious? I said I loved her, too, but that statement means nothing if I'm not going to leave Laura. Right? Rena didn't ask me to do that. She simply said that she loved me.

So now, here they are again, in the city, going for coffee again, swimming in the current again. Forgetting everything else, letting everything else drop away. There are only two states of being now—with Rena or away from Rena. She puts her arm around me and I let her. Let the world see. I'm in love.

NOW I UNDERSTAND WHY HAVING A BABY BOY WOULDN'T be so bad. Always thought little boys were a curse. Mom always said so. But a little boy, a boy before he becomes a man, a boy who belongs to you in every way, predictable, dependent, that would be so sweet. I could comb his hair, give him a bath, dress him in short pants, teach him how to tie his shoe. A boy before the man. A boy just like Rick.

Rick never stays the night. Every time we're together the whole next day he's jumpy and full of guilt. I don't mind his mood swings even though he's made me cry more than once. I don't mind because it's honest. I would be more suspicious if he were all easy about it, because that would mean that he wasn't really in love with me or that he's the kind of man who can just walk away from his family. And what kind of man is that? We're falling in love more and more every day and our love is a lifeline for both of us. So it's understandable that with such a huge thing as love entering his life, Rick is overwhelmed. I understand. I'm overwhelmed, too.

He's always so chatty right after sex, like he's so happy. Blabbing about a dozen things at once, like it all has to be said right now. His voice so soothing. I don't even have to listen to what he's saying, just let it flow over me like music. The sweetest music. And I love to watch the way his lips move, the way the darkness shades just under his eyes like he's never really gotten enough sleep. I love the curve of his chest, the fullness of his arms. Rick isn't just any man, he is my man and I'm going to see him every morning for the rest of my life.

And that night when he had trouble. Has there ever been a man so vulnerable? So afraid! I whispered in his ear and licked his belly and sang him a lullaby and when he fell asleep I made it all right and then he was finally inside of me, what did he say? "Please don't kill me." That's when I knew how much he loves me.

It's like we're all covered in scars and when we touch each other, we have to be so careful not to touch the scars. So gentle. I told him I want to have a baby with him and he smiled and said, "Only one?" And I said, "No. Dozens."

We confess to each other. He's always so guilty. Like he's done a million wrong things. Told me when he was little that he played doctor with the girl from across the street. Said he wanted to kiss her bare pussy. And I said, "So what?" He told me that he had cheated on an exam in med school and that he was on pep pills the first day we had coffee. I didn't tell him about the drugs. About Barry. He doesn't need to know that.

I'm going to do whatever it takes. Stay away from Barry and the drugs. Simplify my life, drink gallons of water and go to work. Even stop smoking eventually. I count the hours until we can be together again, see him, touch him, feel him inside me.

RICK FLIES TO HYANNIS AND PICKS UP LAURA AND THE kids. During the ride back to the city, while he and Laura discuss Henry's need for new sneakers and the paint job in the house, Rick daydreams about Rena.

Rena and I have had sex seven times. What does that mean? Does that mean we're lovers? Having an affair? Do I even want to see her again? Can I afford to? Can I afford not to? Vacation's over, big guy.

Laura doesn't notice. She's in her domestic zone of mentality, plotting timetables in her head for the piles of laundry she'll have to do when we get home, shopping, setting up play dates. She's hoping the painters haven't splattered paint all over her things. She's wondering if the cleaning girl has been able to keep up with me. Thinking how nice it will be to be in her own bed, with me, her husband, tonight.

They arrive like homeless bag people, struggling with sacks of gear and damp clothing, luggage crammed with half-empty bottles of sunblock and bits of seashell. With the turn of a front door key, Rick's bachelor lifestyle is expelled like a grain of sand from a bivalve. No more joint smoking on the back lawn. No more undisturbed, somnolent TV baseball while stretched out on the couch. No more gorging on onion-slathered meat sandwiches over the sink while the blood and hot fat drip down onto piles of encrusted dishes.

But how do I end the all-night chats with Rena? The late afternoon leisure in the city parks and coffee shops with my new girlfriend? The flirting. The sex. How do I go back to being a married man?

It takes a few days to get into a normal cycle, to cook a meal at home, to get all the clothes washed. Laura and the kids are a multifarious mechanism, noisy and time-consuming, retaking the house like an occupying army of three. Armies have to be fed and clothed, armies will not be denied.

First day of school looms. The family takes a trip to Old Navy. Rick posts himself outside and smokes, checking out trampy-looking high school girls. They notice him, give him the eye, because somehow they know he's with Rena. Rick isn't sure how they know it, but he knows that they know. At the sneaker store, the Israeli cash register girl flirts with Rick while Laura deals with Henry's cargo pants. The Israeli girl knows, too. They all know.

Back home, everything gets sorted out and the kids, exhausted by the newness of their familiar toys and furnishings, finally go to bed on time. Rick and Laura lie stretched out on the couch, passing a half carton of Ben & Jerry's between them. They watch *Sex and the City*. Rick swallows the last dollop, licks the spoon, and adjusts himself into Laura's bulky warmth. He tells her how tanned and rested she looks. "You look great, babe."

"So do you. We should spend more time away from each other."

"I don't look good. I've been drinking too much, smoking, eating shit."

"I thought I smelled cigarettes."

"Only one or two a day."

"I started running in the morning. About two weeks before we were going to come back, I thought, if I don't do this, I'll never do this. Ran most mornings on the beach."

"Wow."

"Hey, if I don't do it, I'm just gonna get fatter and fatter."

"You're not fat."

"Yes, I am."

"I like you just the way you are."

"Well, you're just going to have to get used to the new me. Tan and skinny. I lost seven pounds."

"Yeah?" Rick slides a hand under her. She may be lighter but compared to Rena Laura feels as heavy as a small pony. It doesn't matter. I want to touch my wife. I want to be with her. If for no reason than to think she might forgive me. I love her. That's the problem. If I didn't love Laura, I'd just walk out the door. It happens. But I do love her. Rick nuzzles his wife's shoulder. She turns and gives him a matter-of-fact sideways glance. "Are we turning off the TV?"

"Depends on whether you want to watch Chris Noth while we fuck."

"Can you take the competition?" Laura gets up, gathers the quilt and heads upstairs. Listening to the water running, Rick flips channels before flicking off the TV. The dead screen presents him with a witness. What am I doing? What do I want? I don't know what I want. If I love Laura, how can I be doing this?

He follows Laura up. As usual she takes forever in the bathroom. Making herself nice for me. Because she loves me. Because she's devoted to me. And how do I pay her back?

"Do you like it?" Laura appears in a new nightgown.

"It's great. Now take it off." She picked that out for me. To look good for me. This is my wife, thinks Rick.

The sex is edgy and eager. Laura grabs at Rick like someone in a hurry. Rick feels unusually robust and they howl and shout in unison before collapsing onto the bed like prizefighters after fifteen rounds. Rick thinks, When a man has nothing else, at least he has this.

Afterward, he lies on his back with eyes open and contentment rolls in like spring fog. He thinks, we're in such different worlds, and she doesn't know it. She's asleep because she feels so secure with me.

For a moment Rick imagines Laura in coma. Imagines her dead. How would you like that, Rick? That would solve things, wouldn't it? But it wouldn't. Because then I would wake up from this daydream. If I could do what I want, really do what I want, would I want to?

He sniffs the air. It's diffused with their respiration and pheromones. The stink of our living selves, nothing more than biology. Except when the excretions belong to us they become us. Become what we are. This is how I know Laura. If I couldn't see her, couldn't smell her, how would I know it was her? All of this is us, isn't it? So delicate, a so-called "relationship." Bump into it too roughly and it breaks. This is ours, only ours. Our children. Our life. Rick thinks, you got what you wanted. Here it is. Now choose.

That morning over breakfast, Laura had told Rick that the neighbors, Ed and June, were divorcing and had gone their separate ways. It's like death, thinks Rick, isn't it? Inevitable. Laura and I are not going to survive as a couple forever. The cards are stacked against us. We can try, but it's futile. I'm all hung up on this girl, why? Because I'm a fucking asshole, crazy asshole. But if this thing with Rena weren't happening, where would Laura and I be? In a way, don't I love Laura more now that Rena's in the picture? How fucking sick is that?

Laura breathes softly. She and I have everything together. We struggled. We did this, despite the obstacles, we made this life. Here it is. It is real. Unless I make it not real. Unless I say, I'm walking out. Then, from that moment on, it's like it never happened. All that we have will become nothing, mortally wounded. Not even a pleasant memory. Except that all the people will still be here.

THINGS ARE NEVER GOING TO RETURN TO NORMAL. That's just the way it is. What doesn't kill you doesn't make you stronger, it makes you weaker. Chop a tree down, split the wood, toss it in a fireplace, that's it, it's ashes. No way those ashes are ever gonna be wood again. Never going to get "better" because you have to be good to begin with and there never was a good. Never was a good. If you got nothing to grab hold of, well then, you fall, that's all, you just fall. It's just a question of how hard you want to hit the ground.

She's talking with that Jew doctor. Figures. Think they'll get me out and then who knows what trouble is up their sleeve? I should never have brought her to the city. That was my first mistake. Well, it's too late to save her, but I can save myself.

Billy charted his course and executed it. First of all, he got the staff to like him. After upgrading his status through persistent good behavior, he began to participate in group activities and share in the group therapy and show real improvement. As the paperwork that Rick and Rena had initiated slowly percolated through the system, a kind of stalking horse, Billy methodically effected his plan. Because he had made headway, he was given more and more opportunities to show progress. The staff was pleased and proud that their work had paid off. Billy had been a hard nut to crack, his improvement reflected well on all of them. So he was invited to join a group on a day-trip. And while the meds-saturated gaggle of loonies wandered over smooth lawns, Billy walked away.

He has money in his pocket. Fifty-three dollars in coins and bills accumulated through minor pilfering and petty loans. With the money he takes a cab into the city. At Port Authority he grabs the bus at gate 303 and rides it back upstate. When he arrives in town, no one recognizes him. He shuffles along the two-lane to the farmhouse and arrives with the long shadow of early evening.

A water-stained notice of repossession greets him at the kitchen door. Billy balls and tosses it into the profusion of honeysuckle and bee balm that has flourished by the foundation since his departure. A galvanized hasp and a sheathed padlock bar the door. Peering through the glass Billy sees that someone has swept the kitchen. With the weather so warm, even if the heat is out, the pipes aren't gonna burst for another six months. The place has been stabilized, dropped into suspended animation. Billy fondles the padlock. Stainless steel. Assholes. The world is populated by assholes.

Billy trudges down the back steps and finds the bulkhead around back. The hatch lifts with a squeal. A garter snake slithers into a crevice as Billy descends into the clotted spiderwebs. A stack of moldy wood lies where he left it two winters ago. In that stack, bigger snakes maybe, careful. Billy twists the overhead bulb, but the juice is out. Figures. At the bottom of the steps he finds the cellar door firmly shut, puts a shoulder to it and with a thump rips the hinges off the frame. Strength isn't what it was, but I can still kick a door down. Stupid fuckers. Any kid could get into this place.

Billy pats his way through the dusty murk, pills rattling in his pants pocket as he climbs the basement steps. More pills, different pills. Pink, blue, white. Official pills. Pills to fix me. To make me feel like a moron. Life is stupid enough, why do I have to take pills to make it any dumber? Can't throw them away. As shitty as they make me feel, what's the choice? Unlimited mind-speed, overheated engine block, rods shooting through the hood, cams burning, no detour around the spiny chasm of pure fear. Can't do it anymore. Too tired.

When Billy makes it up to the first floor he finds the kitchen dry and spotless. No mouse droppings. No bottles. Nothing. Like a room you see when you visit those historic buildings. Swept and still. A fork lies on the counter. Ate meals with that fork. So did Mom and Dad and Reba. It's something we knew. But we don't know it anymore and it doesn't know us.

Upstairs, things are different. Someone has baited the house with warfarin and the musky scent of decaying mouse flesh hangs in the corners of the empty rooms. A squirrel has found a way in and didn't find a way out. The mullions on every window have been gnawed flush to the panes and the dessicated body of the rodent lies flopped over Mom's favorite armchair. Its flat dead eye is black and accusative. Yeah? Well, it's your own fault. Fuck you, too.

In Billy's old room, things have been neatened up by someone, but it's all pretty much as he had left it. Good. On the floor of his closet, wrapped in a faded beach towel, Billy finds the Ruger 10/22. In the back of the shelf, a box of long-rifle shells. There aren't many things you can count on. A firearm is one.

Since leaving the hospital this morning, since escaping the day-trip, Billy has been carrying a small knapsack. In it are two bologna sandwiches, an apple, and a small carton of Hi-C with a sipping straw. Back downstairs, he places all these items carefully on the kitchen table. He eats half a sandwich while keeping an eye on the rifle.

He also has his newly created archive. The orderlies took the old one. Probably burned it along with his clothes. Billy has patiently assembled a new one. Sorting and examining the torn bits of magazine every single day while he had been in the ward. Stupefied with medication, that was all he was up for. The scent of moldy magazine pages rises up from the scraps and in sympathy Billy flows up out of himself, unmedicated, uncorrupted, a phoenix rising up and out of the ashes. It is a bristling weird feeling, probably what the butterfly feels when it's breaking out of its cocoon, but Billy wants it to happen. It's time.

His tired eyes absorb her image in all its convolutions. Here's Reba sitting by some large rocks on a beach. Here's Reba walking a runway under a tent in Bryant Park. Here's Reba applying face cream. Here's Reba in jeans. In a vast parka, in an absurd boa, in an evening gown, in strips of colored tinfoil, covered in jewels.

Billy returns to the beach photo. In it Rena is wearing a homely bikini, gazing straight into the camera. Her legs are tucked under her, resting on the sand. Her manicured right hand rests lightly on her right thigh. The left is invisible, off the edge of the page, and her body is bowed just enough to form a small crease six inches to the left of her navel. Very little material covers her crotch, her smallish breasts. Her lips part slightly, only the tips of her teeth show. A breeze has caught her hair, which looks like it's been washed in saltwater and left to dry. The sun rises behind her and lemony light caresses her shoulder and upper arm, illuminating the sweet fuzz there. Her eyes pour into Billy, fixed, eternal. They tell him how much she loves him and wants his forgiveness.

And now she adjusts herself, reaching behind her back, undoing the strings of her top. It falls forward and Billy thinks, I can see your breasts, Reba. I'm looking at you, Reba. I'm looking at all of you, Reba. And you want me too, don't you? You do, I know you do. Show me.

She undoes a tie at her hip. The bottom falls away. She kicks it off. Now she's completely bare-assed, in the sand. The grit is wet and cool under her bum. Her eyes limpid as she lies back, legs splayed gently. Billy brings his arms around her waist, feels his erection dip into her heat. She never breaks her gaze, beaming into him. He says, "I love you, Reba." And she says, "I know, Billy. Shhhh. It's OK." And then he realizes, that this isn't about him forgiving her, it's about her forgiving him. And she does.

When he comes to, he wipes his hand on his shirt. Outside the sun is setting again. Can't stop it. The apples are out there. Could check on the apples. No. No more apples.

Billy pops the magazine, presses three bullets into the clip and snaps it back into the stock. He thumbs the bolt, setting the shell into the breech. He flips the safety. Frozen in time, Felix the Cat says clearly, "Better hurry up."

Reba beams at him from the beach as Billy clamps the barrel under his jaw, just above his Adam's apple. Precision is important. His last thought is, I love you, Reba.

RICK FINDS A PAY PHONE OUTSIDE THE SUPERMARKET.
A kid who could be Eminem's twin brother is smashing shopping
carts into the queue beside a man-high pile of watermelons.
Every time the kid passes the electric-eye door, it swings open.
Rick figures he's doing it on purpose. The phone rings on the
other end. Rick prays for a live voice.

"Hi?"

"It's me." Rick always begins with as few words as possible.
Ready to cut and run.

"Hey."

"Can you talk?"

"Rick, I can always talk. You're the one who can't talk."

"What are you doing?"

"Right now?"

"Yeah." Eminem passes Rick and spits.

"I'm in Calypso. I'm buying a pullover. Wait. Yes, these two,
not that one. OK, I'm back. Hi."

"Maybe you should finish what you're doing and call me."

"Where are you?"

"Pay phone in front of a supermarket. I don't have my cell
phone, I . . . whatever." He gives her the number. "I'll wait."

An old couple, clutching each other, almost staggering, enter
the supermarket. Eminem collects the carts. The sun bakes the
parked SUVs. Rick thinks, what if this is the love of my life and
I can't see it? The love I've been waiting for forever? Edith said,
"Maybe you're afraid to take what you want?" The phone rings.

"Hello?"

"You sound tense. Are you angry about something?"

"No. I'm in a good mood, I think. I wanted to hear your voice."

Rena says, "Yeah. I'm glad you called."

"I feel a little nuts when I'm not talking to you. Though to be
honest, I feel nuts when I'm talking to you, too."

Rena says, "I was thinking about you last night. Thinking about being with you. Thinking about how you feel inside me."

"Well, that's nice. I think about you almost every second of the day. Even when I floss my teeth I'm thinking of you."

"That's gross."

(silence)

"Sorry. Let's start over: Hi."

"Don't apologize, there's nothing to apologize about, Rick. Can I say something? I love you."

"Rena?" If we ran far enough away, I could love her forever. It happens. Things like that happen all the time. The kids could handle it, right?

"Yeah?"

"I . . ." I don't trust her. That's the snag. I don't trust her to stay. If you're going to burn your whole life down, she's gotta stick. It's a gamble. Balls. It's all about balls. Do I have the balls to take the gamble?

"Yeah?"

"Nothing."

"Just say what you were going to say. Why do you stop yourself like that? What were you going to say?"

"I want to say, 'I love you, too' but I feel crazy when I say that kind of thing."

"It's not a 'kind of thing.' It's a statement. It's either true or it isn't. And only you know, Rick."

"You don't have kids."

"You're avoiding the issue. You can love me and love your kids at the same time."

"It has something to do with guilt."

"I'm not inhuman. I know. The question is, do you love Laura? Really love her, with all of your heart?"

"Of course I love her. I can't say I don't love her. It's just different with you and me."

"Better?"

"I've never felt like this in my life. I feel like I'm drunk all the time. Like I'm losing my mind."

"And what about me, Rick? If you love me, don't you care about the pain I'm in?"

"Rena, you're twenty years younger than me. More than twenty years younger."

"I love you. It has nothing to do with age or anything like that. You. I love you. You. You. You. And that love is everything to me. I'm not going to treat it like some bullshit thing I can just ignore or walk away from. And being guilty about something as pure as love, what is that, Rick? That's being guilty for being yourself. Not saying what you want, what is that, Rick? You have one life, here it is, happening right now. How can you deny the love in your life?"

"Yeah. I guess."

"Don't you know? Don't you know how you feel? I know how I feel."

"I just love hearing your voice. I love being with you. I want to touch you. I want to hold your hand. But there's always all this other stuff going on. My life." Eminem rolls by.

"I can come by the clinic."

"No. Don't do that."

"I can make an appointment. You can examine me."

The electric-eye door opens and Laura emerges maneuvering a laden cart. She blinks into the sunshine, searching the lot for Rick. She doesn't see him standing at the phone. Because he sees her and she doesn't see him, he feels a surge of pity. What am I doing to her. I am a monster. "I gotta go."

"Don't go. I want to tell you something."

"I want to tell you something, too. I'll call you in one hour. Can I call you in one hour?"

"One hour." Rena's gone.

Laura rolls the cart past Rick as he hangs up the phone. "Any emergencies at the clinic?"

"Uh, no. No, everything's fine. I should check back in though, go over the schedule for next week."

"I bought swordfish."

"Great."

"There's still some corn on the cob. It looks pretty good."

"Cool."

"Did you get the wine?"

"No. Shit. I'll get it."

"That's OK. I think we still have half a bottle of that Australian white from last night. No biggie. Come on, help me with this." They sling the shopping bags into the back of the SUV. Laura lets her body touch Rick's. "Hey there, big guy."

"Hey there."

"It's pretty great about the play date. I didn't think we'd have five minutes alone this weekend."

"No, yeah. It's nice. It's weird but it's nice."

"Why's it weird?"

"Because it feels funny to have the kids off somewhere. Doing something, but I don't know what. Out of sight. It's strange."

"I've been with them all summer, Rick. Nothing wrong with them being out of sight. I need some serious non-kid time. Besides, you didn't mind them not being around when you were here alone."

"That's different. You were with them."

"Oh, I get it, me and the kids are a package, is that it?"

"No."

"I hope not."

"Hey. I just miss all of you, is all."

"Let's get home before the ice cream melts. Then we can fuck before the kids become visible again. Followed by a nice grilled swordfish, a glass of wine, some mindless cable. I have a serious cable jones. The TV at the Cape sucked."

"It all sounds good. Very good."

"The fish or me?"

"Shuttup." She wouldn't be joking with me if she knew. If she knew, she would never speak to me again, except through an attorney.

Rick and Laura stow the groceries. Rick wanders off and dials his cell phone. Rena picks up after one ring. "What do you want to tell me?"

"Actually this turns out not to be the best time. I'm . . ."

"What? Rick, don't say you're going to tell me something and then don't tell me."

"I'll tell you when I see you in the city." Why did I call her?

"Tell me now!"

"It would be better—"

"Rick, tell me. What?"

"It's just that I've been thinking . . ." Say it.

"Did you start thinking again? That's not good."

"No. It is good. It's important. It's . . . Rena, look, I'm married."

"That's a stupid thing to say, Rick. Why are you saying that? You're pissing me off."

"I mean. I'm married. I have kids. I love my wife."

"Jesus, Rick, what are you saying???"

"I think we should take a break. From each other."

A beat. Then, "Oh. OK."

"Rena?"

"No. That's cool. I understand. You're married. And you have kids."

"No, you don't understand. I don't want to say this. I want to see you."

"I understand."

"You're angry."

"Angry? No. That's not the word for how I feel. Sad. I feel very sad. But I understand. I gotta go." A pause, no click.

"Rena? Are you there?" Rick can hear sounds. Sobs.

"I've never loved anyone the way I love you."

"Yeah. I know, baby."

Laura calls down the stairs. "Rick, are you coming up or what? We have an hour at most."

He calls out "OK!" No answer. "Rena, we'll have to finish this conversation later. Hello?" Rick holds the dead phone in his hand. That's it. Fallen away, like a stone down a well. Never. Never say never. But it is never, because that's what women do. They go away.

AGAIN FRANK. OF ALL THE PEOPLE TO GIVE ME THE NEWS, why does it have to be Frank? He says, "Rena, you're gonna have to come up here."

"No, Frank. I have a lawyer now. He said he can deal with everything from the city."

"This isn't about the house. This is about Billy. He showed up."

"Showed up?" Is Frank saying Billy is up in the country? After the hospital said that Billy ran away, Rena assumed that he was in the city. She figured he would call her apartment or she'd hear from the police. She never thought he'd head for the farm.

"Some kids found Billy in the house."

"Billy's living in the house?"

"No, Rena. Not living."

She breaks the phone when she hurls it and cries for fifteen minutes. She calls Frank back, thinking he's at the bank but he's not. Instead, she gets Annie, who tells her most of it. It's easier getting the news from Annie.

Kids had been pitching rocks at the windows and had discovered the open bulkhead. They found Billy at the kitchen table with his rifle. He had died instantly. The body had been in the house for at least a week.

Annie gives Rena a number and she calls the funeral home.

They treat her like an old friend. For the third time in four years I'm talking to these folks. Rena mumbles a credit card number to pay for the embalming, the casket and the plot. She pays extra to have Billy buried in the section of the cemetery where Mom and Dad are.

After she gets off the phone, Rena calls the car service. Forces herself not to call Rick. She has to think about clothes for Billy. He has lost so much weight, none of his old stuff will fit him. She has the Turk buy her a bottle of Stoli and drinks her way to the farm. She comes to as the car rolls up the gravel drive. Weirdly sober, she holds her breath as she rushes upstairs where she finds some things for Billy. She and the Turk take the clothes over to the funeral home. She sees Billy's body and he looks a lot like how he looked at Creedmore. It's not a shock.

The wake and the funeral are a blurry two days. It's easy to find alcohol everywhere and just in case she can't find a drink, Rena keeps refilling airplane bottles that clink together in her purse. Vodka gets her through the afternoon and evening of the wake. She sits as straight as she can on the folding chair, Billy lying before her. There aren't many flowers and she doesn't know most of Billy's friends who come by to say they're sorry. Everyone remarks on how the funeral home did a terrific job. Folks treat Rena like a celebrity. Even when she dresses down, her glamour clings to her like haute couture. But her new career is an indictment as well. What happened to Billy is her fault. She left him behind, didn't she?

After the wake, the Turk drives Rena to the Ramada Inn out on the interstate. She doesn't know or care where he goes afterward, maybe he sleeps in his car. No one calls her at the hotel. She leaves a message for Marissa telling her what happened. She drinks until she passes out.

At the funeral, Rena sits numbly under the eyes of the same Jesus who had gotten her through so much. She tries to conjure his love the way she used to, but it doesn't work. She tries to think about all the things that have happened, but her mind won't settle. So she stares at the casket and no one speaks to her, which is fine with her. After the short service, the old buddies of Billy's lift the coffin and walk it out of the church.

On their way to the cemetery, she gives in and calls Rick from her car in the funeral cortege. He's guarded until she tells him what has happened. Then he confesses that he has missed her, that he was hoping she'd call.

Rena says she can't talk much right now, but when she gets back to the city, they should see each other, to discuss the situation. Rick agrees. Then for about thirty seconds neither Rick nor Rena speaks. They don't hang up, either. They listen to the breath on the other end of the line. Finally, Rick says, "OK." And Rena says, "OK" and she gets out of the car and buries her brother.

IN THE COFFEE SHOP, THERE IS NO HAND-HOLDING. NO kissing. No deep gazing or shy smiles. Rick tells Rena he's sorry about Billy. It's his fault in a way. Rena says, "It's not your fault." A fine line bisects her brow.

"If I had gotten him out of there."

"Rick, everything isn't about you."

Rick thinks, she's being critical of me. This is new. "I'm still sorry."

"How's Laura?"

"She's good. Kids are back in school."

"Yeah?"

"Yup. Everything's back to normal."

"Not everything."

"Are you working?"

"I'm not going to work for a while. I can't."

"OK."

"Rick, I want to see you. As a friend."

"Yeah. See, I don't know if I can do that. I don't know if I can handle that."

"Oh."

"You think this is easy for me? Being near you this way?"

"Someone said to me once, if you want to know what's important in your life, make a list of what you do every day. That's what's important in your life."

He says, "You're not being fair."

"Life isn't fair."

Rick thinks, I can't be friends with her. What is that? Defeat? No, realism. "I just wish I could hold you right now."

"No one's stopping you." A trance descends over them.

He takes her hand. "Jesus, Rena."

Rena says, "You wanna come over to my place?"

Rick says, "Yes."

In the cab, they don't speak. They enter the apartment like condemned prisoners climbing the gallows steps. Rick touches her back and she slips away into the bathroom. He's left standing in the midst of her life. A vodka bottle sits unopened on the kitchen table. If I walk out the door right now, thinks Rick, she can have her vodka and it ends.

In the bedroom, Rena pulls the drapes shut and lights a dozen candles. Wax and magnolia scent the air. She smiles a weary smile and opens her arms. "Come here." Rick moves toward her and they hold each other, absorbing the blood warmth, the smell of each other. "You think I'm angry at you. I'll never be angry at you."

Later, as he's leaving, Rick says, "I can't hurt my children. I can't hurt my wife."

Rena says, "It's what you want."

They don't kiss good-bye.

BUZZ THE BUZZER. THE GOOD OL' BUZZER, HASN'T changed in all this time. Talk into the box. "It's me." Pause. The longest pause in the world. Maybe he's not up there. Maybe he's up there with someone else. Maybe he said come over just to mess with my head. Sure. Torture me. I deserve it. I fucked with you now it's my turn. Come on. Just open up. You fuck-head. Stop! Don't think that or he'll read your mind. Doesn't matter. He already knows what I think of him, that I think he's slime. Because he knows he's slime. And what does that make you, little girl? Lower than slime. But I'm not slime. I'm not. This all really happened. Like an avalanche. Rick knew what he was doing. And now look. Now look. Don't cry. Get your shit together.

The door clicks open. As Rena ascends the stairs, she can hear the locks sliding and scratching on the other side of the portal of hell. And here he is. "Rena!"

"Am I interrupting? 'Cause if I am, you know, it would be okay with me if you just, you know, sell me some shit and I'll get out of your hair."

"You're not in my hair, baby. I don't have enough hair to get into. Come in, sit down. Make yourself comfortable."

"Why are you in such a good mood?"

"Because you came by."

"Barry."

"What, honey?"

"Cut the shit, OK?"

"What do you need? A bag? A bundle?"

"How good is it?"

"I was just about to find out."

On the table lies a pile of tan powder. Sets of syringes. A tiny scale, some glassine bags.

"Can I have some?"

"You can be my official tester. Here." Barry flicks out his

pinkie, shovels a tiny heap of heroin onto the tip of his long fingernail and holds it under Rena's eager nostril. "Go for it. But careful." She sniffs. He makes another tiny dip. She sniffs again.

"Oh God."

"Yes?"

"Yeah. Yeah, that's it. Thank you, Barry. You are such a great guy. You're the only person in the world I can depend on."

"I know. That's why I knew you'd be back, sooner or later."

"You don't know shit. Mmmmmm. Really needed that. I've been so wound up."

"Let me guess. You fell in love?"

"My brother shot himself in the head with a hunting rifle. Do you have a cigarette?"

"Whatever you need, Uncle Barry's here."

"Maybe I can lie down."

"You can lie down. Sorry about your brother."

She rises at ten in the evening and knows exactly where she is. A very hungry badger is clawing its way through her guts. In the meager light, she reels into Barry's squalid bathroom. Her stomach clenches and spasms, wringing itself out like a wet sheet in a washerwoman's hands. Her bowels erupt as soon as she gets her jeans down.

Barry finds her doubled over, unable to get off the bowl.

"Hey, you OK?"

"No, I'm not fucking OK!"

"I'll fix you up."

"Get out of here, Barry! I'm sick. I have no pants on. Get out of here!"

"I'll get you something."

It has never been like this before. She cleans up and pulls her clothes on while her stomach flips and flops. She finds Barry in the kitchen. He holds the tinfoil up to her and she inhales the smoke.

Instantly she is well. Better than well, good. She takes another

238 · ERIC BOGOSIAN

hit. Her belly calms and relief flows through her shoulders, down through her torso into her legs. She dissolves into a chair as Barry fills a syringe. He meticulously cleans the back of his hand with alcohol, then inserts the needle with surgical precision. He leaves it stuck in his hand, poised to shoot. "You see, kid, all that shit about tracks and all that, that's because people are sloppy. Not hygienic. You think diabetics have tracks? No way. You always use alcohol, sharp needles. Then you're cool. And never shoot in the same place twice."

"Why am I so sick?"

"You know what they say in NA? Your disease has been doing pushups. You come back to it and it's stronger than ever."

"I want to smoke some more."

"You hold on for a sec. My turn." He presses the plunger and his lids lower. He licks his lips. "Uh-huh."

"I'm still sick, Barry."

"Something you gotta understand, sweetness. Your body has adjusted itself to the presence of opiates. And now you gotta do a little more just to get straight." Barry sinks back, uncoils.

"No. I'm going to quit. But I need some more now."

"See, that's what I'm saying. You need more. And if you want to get high, you need a lot more."

"I don't want to get high."

"Oh. OK. Well then, you just sit there for a minute."

"I'm fucking sick, Barry. And I'm in a bad mood."

"Baby, you're bringing me down. Give me some space here."

Rena gets up and opens the fridge. She scans its rank insides. Orange bottles of methadone are tossed in with foil-wrapped burritos and lemons shriveled into brown balls.

"See, I'm trying to explain something here and you're not listening. If you want to be efficient, you have to let every molecule of the drug into your beautiful body. You have to let it have its way."

"I'm not shooting up. I promised myself."

"Who said anything about shooting up? You can skin-pop."

"What's that?"

"Try it once and tell me you don't love it. Here, I'll set you up." Barry tears open a B-D envelope, taps out a fresh needle, cooks a spoon of heroin and fills the syringe. "See this? Nice hot junk, ready for you. Now come here."

"Barry."

"One time. You don't like it, it's the last time." He swabs her shoulder with alcohol. "Look at the wall for a sec." He spears the needle into her deltoid. "That's it, a little mosquito bite. You're all set."

She thinks, what's the big deal? Then the high hits like a Louisville slugger. The kiss of God. But not like smoking it, not like "here it comes, there it goes." No, it keeps coming and coming. Her chin droops to her chest.

Barry talks through her nod: "Did I ever tell you you are an angel? You are the most beautiful angel I have ever seen. You are. My whole life I have pestered and pondered the female race, and I have had my share. Remember old Gina? In the day, in the fuckin' day, she was a veritable Mona Lisa. But you, Rena, you are the angel of mercy herself. You redefine the word beauty."

She slurs, "Shuttup."

"I can't, baby, I can't. Because you are the thing itself. You are the thing. Itself. The thing itself."

"God."

"Feel that hit? How nice is that? You like that, right? I made you a good one."

"How come you won't shuttup?"

" 'Cause I'm doin' speedballs, beautiful. You want one?"

"What?"

"I just lay a little coke in there with the dope? Get you right like you never been right.'Cept you gotta take the mainline."

"I feel, uh, pretty good right now, Barry. Thank you. Thank you . . ."

"Any time, sugar."

They lie on Barry's bed and watch TV until Rena falls asleep. This time when she wakes up jonesing, she reaches out to Barry. He's still awake. A rerun of *Hawaii 5-O* is on the tube. "Barry, I don't feel good."

He stubs out his cigarette. "You gotta sleep, baby." He makes up another shot, gives it to her and she falls away.

In the late morning, they manage to head out for breakfast. For some reason the claws of the badger retract for most of the morning. But by noon, she's in withdrawal again. Baby animals grow fast when they're fed.

It takes two days for Rena to try hitting up in the vein. It only takes Barry one day to get her to beg him for more. He says he doesn't want things to be this way, but after all she rang his buzzer. And the way the world works, a girl like Rena would never do that unless a guy like Barry had something she wanted.

Barry confesses to Rena that he's loved her since she first walked in his door. He tells her he wishes she would come to see him because she wants to, not because she wants to get high. Barry weeps in front of her. Finally, Rena gives in and lets him have sex with her.

There's no point in thinking about it too hard. She needs the drugs, he has the drugs and as far as Rena is concerned, the rest of the world doesn't exist.

Later Barry explains what he calls "the Philosophy of Barry." With girls who are like Rena, it's always a trade. Sometimes it's junk, sometimes it's money, sometimes it's attention. But it's still a trade. This for that. Junk for sex, attention for sex, money for sex. And in any trade, there's always some bad feelings. Resentments. Resentments cause resistance. If there's enough resistance, well, this creates pain. But pain can go both ways. Barry's in pain, Rena's in pain. They both want the pain to go away. That's what life is, making pain go away. The thing about pain is, pain always beats thought. Ask any torturer. Rena thinks she can walk out the door, but she can't. She thinks she's free to do what she wants, but she can't. But see, neither can Barry, because he's in pain, too. That's why he does what he does. And so everything has to happen the way it happens. Simple physics.

RICK STANDS POISED IN THE MIDDLE OF HIS KITCHEN, a Williams-Sonoma stainless steel sauce pan in his hand. He has been staring at it with incomprehension for a full minute, not really sure what it is. Not really sure what anything is. Laura is out getting her hair cut and he has forgotten that, too. The children are enmeshed in their video games and Barbies elsewhere in the house, but he's not sure where they are.

He can't move. Every cell in his body is infected with Rena. He thinks, it's not over just because I say it is. A fling, an "extramarital affair" and I've ended it because it's wrong. Except that it doesn't want to be ended. Because I'm in love.

Rick has never starved or caught his leg in a bear trap or murdered someone. All these things have real meaning to someone somewhere, and he can imagine them, but he doesn't really know them. Now he knows the true meaning of the words "hopelessly in love." The situation with Rena lives outside the bounds of the rational. It has no future. It has no past. It's just *now now now,* like a psychic car alarm overwhelming every waking thought. I'm lovelorn, no, lovesick. Why did this have to happen? I liked my life before. Sort of liked it. It was OK. I never said I wanted to fall in love. Did I? First of all, I don't believe in falling in love. I'm already in love with my wife, still in love with my wife, in fact. Things were fine as they were.

And this girl, because that's all she is, a girl, isn't even somebody I like that much. She's uneducated. Never really thinks about anything but the world in which she lives. It isn't like we could have a conversation about politics or art. She's from a different generation. She's a kid. She doesn't like the music I like, doesn't like the movies I like, doesn't even like the food I like.

I trained and busted my hump for eight years to get to where I am. And Laura helped me. Together we busted our humps. Something we did together. This girl, she fell down a rabbit hole and became a model. She makes more money than she knows what to do with. We have nothing in common. And I'm willing to throw everything away. Don't I respect my own life? Don't I respect Laura? What we made?

I'd trade it all just to be in Rena's arms. Or would I? Or did I? Have I already made the deal with the devil?

Is it because she adores me? And does she adore me because she can't have me without wrecking my life? Isn't she just a spoiled little jet-setter, who has everything she wants and now she's decided she wants this married guy and is using every wile she possesses to clobber my poor defenseless middle-class ass into submission? What kind of love is that? That's not love, that's greed.

Maybe she's a siren, maybe she's a witch. But does it matter, Ricky-boy? Never felt like this in my whole life. And this thing, this love affair, whatever the fuck it is, diminishes everything else. I thought I knew everything, but I don't. I'm like some hillbilly who finally leaves his backwoods home for the city. I can't go back, can I? To a life without her?

I can't hurt the children. Right? It's logical that love cannot come out of hurt. She wants to have children with me. But I already have children! And the children are innocent. I'm not going to hurt them. Like Dad, with his lady in the closet. Only concerned with his own fucking life and his own fucking needs. Fuck him. Fuck her. Fuck everybody.

And besides, I don't want to leave Laura. I love Laura. Can't live without Laura. And do I actually think that I could make a life with Rena? What would that be like? Chaos on a stick. Anarchy. And how could I ever trust her? That's the real question, isn't it? Or is it? Fuck, I want to touch her one more time. What's wrong with that? Everything. And so I've done the right thing because lust is no excuse to ruin a life. Except that I did just see her a week ago. And even though we say we're not going to see each other, that's impossible isn't it? It's a maze and I'm lost and everything leads back to her.

Clutching the pan, Rick begins to cry. It starts as a trickling pain, stabbing his heart, then with a rush, it floods up from his belly, into his lungs, his throat, his face hot and moist and then the tears. Wracking, sobbing. Why am I crying? Because I feel sorry for myself. Because I have never been adored like this. And don't want to let go of it. Why can't I have it? Why can't I have what I want? It's not fair.

He steadies himself by reaching out to the polished granite countertop. Laura's countertop. With care he puts the pot down, wipes his eyes as a few more tears seep out. This is crazy. This is crazy. I've lost my mind. I don't know who I am.

He holds a crumpled wad of paper towel to his swollen eyes. OK. OK. It will be OK.

"Daddy?" Henry and Trina are standing in the kitchen doorway, watching their father. Henry is holding his Game Boy and the bright figures dance on its screen.

"Huh?" He blows his nose.

"Are you crying, Daddy?"

"Where's your mommy?"

"We don't know. There are no lights on in the house."

Helpful Trina. "Oh, is that why you're crying? Because you miss Mommy?"

"No, uh. Yeah. No. I just, I was just thinking a sad thought and it made me cry a little. Listen, go back to the TV. I'm all right. Everything's all right."

"Can I have some juice?"

"I want some juice, too."

"Yeah, yeah. Sure. Henry, you get it for you and your sister."

"You should have some juice, too, Dad."

"Yeah. Yeah. I should. Thanks."

"No problem, Dad."

They finally leave and Rick dials her number on the cell phone. He gets her voice mail. He can't help himself. "Rena. It's me. Call me."

He sits in the backyard, cradling the phone. Five minutes later, it rings.

"Rick?"

"I just wanted to see if you were OK. I have to know."

"I'm not OK, Rick. I'm not OK. I've been having a hard time."

"Me, too."

"No, with me, it's different."

On the ferry Rick thinks, I am blowing up my life. I'm breaking laws here and if Laura finds out, there is no explanation for what I'm doing. Is this going to be the system from now on? Sneaking around? Claiming I have a patient in New York I have to see? How many times will Laura buy that? But this is only going to be this one time. This is a special circumstance. If this starts up again, Laura will figure it out. And then she will hate me. The kids will hate me, too. Everyone will hate me.

When Rena opens the door, Rick doesn't see her. Her skin is the greenish yellow of spoiled chicken, her hair, dense with oil and grime, lies flat against her skull. She doesn't raise her eyes to his, turns back into the room.

Is it a sign of love that I can see her like this? That she lets me see her like this? Or doesn't she care if I see her like this because she doesn't love me anymore? Because I've pushed the thing past love? What is there after love? And when did we ever have love?

Rick steps into the wretched atmosphere of the apartment. Rena has sealed the windows with packing tape. I am walking through her breath, Rick thinks. I am inside her. Rena crosses to the couch and slumps onto it. She lights a cigarette, finally looks up at him and flashes him the briefest of guilty smiles. "Hi."

Rick finds an armchair, sits. "How are you doing?"

"It hurts. A lot. To be really honest with you right now, Rick, I'm just in incredible pain. I've been puking and shitting and last night I thought maybe I was going to die, which probably wouldn't be such a bad thing."

"It would be a very bad thing."

"Really? You think so?"

"I brought the stuff."

An expression crosses Rena's face, something like the scrunch of her features when she has an orgasm, but also something like disappointment. The one place Rick has never entered. "Well, that's good. Should we uh, get to it?"

"Of course." Rick opens the little black bag that he never carries and removes alcohol swabs, a sterile syringe and an ampoule of Dilaudid. "It's not the same as heroin, Rena."

"I don't care."

Her nose is running. Didn't notice that when I came in. Rick takes her arm. The first time I've touched her in what, six days? "God, Rena."

Rena snatches the swab from him and scrubs her own arm. "Come on, Doctor. I'm sick."

Rick stabs the syringe into the neck of the tiny bottle, retrieving one dose. Her inner arm is covered with purple splotches. Rick wants to say, "What have you been doing to yourself?" and thinks, I don't know her.

Rena says, "You want me to do it?"

"No. Just grab your bicep hard with your other hand and make a fist with this one." Her veins are as fine as silk. He misses and a fresh discoloration appears under her translucent skin. Finally, he gets it in. He retracts the plunger and the blood blooms into the barrel of drug.

Rena falls into his eyes with something indistinguishable from love. "OK. Do me." He urges the syringe forward and the drug flows into her. She closes her eyes. "Hmmmm. Yeah."

I'm still holding her arm. I'm touching her. "Rena?"

A long pause. Eyes closed. "Yeah."

Rick thinks, where are we now? How far from earth? "You OK? Is it too much?"

"Never." She opens her eyes. "You broke my heart, you know?"

"You broke mine."

"Just don't go away." She shifts her weight into him. "I love you, Rick."

"I love you."

"Kiss me."

She's a ruined version of Rena, but I don't care. Kiss her. And his mouth finds hers, spoiled with tobacco, her limbs loose and weak. Under her unwashed rattiness, she wears her old scent like a ruined aristocrat wears jewelry.

"You can fuck me if you want."

"God, Rena. I just want you to get better."

"Rick." Don't tell him about Barry. Don't tell him why you couldn't go back there. That you'd kill yourself first. "Rick, please."

He's pulling at her clothes, finding himself, instantly hard, finding her, in her. He puts his lips to her shoulder, amazed by her frailty. She tastes like almonds. It's her. It's my love. It's my love. He comes in seconds and falls away spent. My god. It's all I want in the world.

She smiles at him and touches his hair. "Wham bam thank you ma'am."

"Yeah. I'm sorry."

"Baby, don't ever be sorry. Every time you touch me, I'm in heaven."

"Did the Dilaudid get you high?"

"It fixed me for a few minutes. But what would be really great is if you could make a double of what you did before. You don't have to shoot me up, I can do that."

"You'll overdose."

"No, I won't. And if I do, there's a doctor in the house, right? And there's ice in the freezer. Just shove a cube up my ass. That's what Barry says you have to do."

"Barry?"

"A guy I know."

Rick maintains a vigil over Rena's wasted sleep, tracking her shallow breath. He thinks, Me and Rena, we are innocent. She's a little girl. She's my little girl and I will take care of her.

DOGS COME TO MIND. HUNGRY, FORCED INTO WIRE cages, shivering with fear, sniffing the shit and slobber of the other canine presences, biting their own tails. Or folded into themselves, lying still, with ears pricked up, alert, waiting. Then how does it go? The men in white lab coats arrive and slap down the cool, freshly hacked hunks of beef, filling the hard plastic bowls. Then what? The placards. The placards thrust before the dripping muzzles. Placards inked with bold geometrics, a binary choice: outline of a rectangle or a circle. Yes-No. On-Off. Rectangle equals meat. Rectangle means satisfaction. See a rectangle, get meat. But the circle. The evil circle! When the electric current passes through the metal floor, the dogs dance in pain, whining, and then the circle placard is revealed. The horrible circle of agony. And so the dogs learn all about circles and rectangles, rectangles and circles. The dogs come to understand what is good and what is bad in a universe where men with lab coats reign. Everything becomes very clear.

All clear, until the researcher-gods show up with new placards. And on these new improved placards, the rectangles have
rounded corners and the sides of the circles are flattened. These
symbols are further improved, the circles becoming more and
more rectangular. The rectangles more and more circular. Soon
the dogs are eyeballing shapes that are neither circular nor
square, a twilight zone of symbology, of ultimate truth. They
can't know what's coming next. Nonetheless, the shocks and
feedings continue. Satisfaction and pain, but now no longer connected to any placard logic. And the dogs go mad. Totally fucking mad.

When did I learn all that? Third year? Fourth? Kleinman?
Phipps? Piercy? What the fuck difference does it make now?
Those dogs are long gone, incinerated, memorialized as a long
footnote in a behaviorism textbook.

We're seeing each other again. I've gone insane.

His eyes like slit-open gray prunes, Rick traces the contours
of his immaculate living room, the flawless eggshell finish, tran-
quil in the early morning light. He drags on his cigarette and lets
the smoke trail upward. I could cash it all out right now, cash
out the IRA, take the money, run away, run to Alaska, buy a
cabin, never see another human being again or if I felt like it,
take a running jump into polar ice water and die. Fuck me. I'm
like one of those existential philosophers you see on the back of
the book jackets. So full of thoughtful thoughts I'm giving myself
a headache.

I'm falling like an apple from a tree. Hey, you can't fight gravity, right? It's a law of nature. Anyway, it feels good to be on the
move, a nice change of pace, exciting to see my life flying past,
all the things and people and events kind of equal. All the parts
unfettered and pointless. I'm like Alice down the rabbit hole,
there's all my stuff floating in midair right before my eyes: my
penis, my asshole, my teeth. My mother, my father, my car, my
house. My children, my money, my gallons of semen, rivers of

piss, mountains of fingernail clippings, oceans of shit. Everything I am or have ever been.

The ground is coming up pretty fast. Could hit any second now. That's going to be interesting. Really interesting. It's like that dream where I'm alone in a car but my hands aren't touching the steering wheel. Except it's not a dream.

Why can't I figure this out? For forty-five years I've figured it all out. Found my way out of every life-maze. Hurdled every hurdle. Broken the code and deconstructed every incomprehensible passage. And now, here I am, a man of means and status, flummoxed by pussy. Of course it's worse than that. More pathetic. It's love. Love has arrived like a disease and I'm sick.

I'm almost fifty and instead it's like I'm fifteen again and I'm running home after school, stumbling up to my room, bruised and broken, sobbing into the bedspread, pounding with heartache. The heartache never went away, did it? Every time I look into a girl's eyes, every time I come, every time I wake up in the morning I'm thinking, Wait a sec, who am I again? This has been the light I've wanted. It was this that I've needed all along.

But if I reach out for it, I burn down my whole life and how can I do that? Easy, Rena said, it happens all the time. The world won't stop spinning and five billion people will keep breathing. This is just one more infinitesimal event. She says, if there is an infinity, it is in your heart. And your heart is the only heart, only you know what you know and only you have what you have. Follow your heart. Your heart will tell you. Burn your house down. Run from your wife and kids. It happens all the time.

Rick lies on the couch and plans scenarios of escape, of divorce, of suicide, of murder. He embezzles his own money and runs away to anonymous midwestern cities. Or to a houseboat in Amsterdam. He prays. He considers a proposal of bigamy. He does all this, but he doesn't sleep.

Three times tonight, he has gone to the kitchen and standing in the gloom, cell phone in hand, checked his voice mail to see if

250 • ERIC BOGOSIAN

she's called in. That's what she does, calls in the middle of the night and leaves messages like "I love you, I miss you. I wish you were here." And when Laura finds me standing here, in the night, in the lonely, lonely night, cell phone like a dick in my hand, how will I explain?

Knowing I'm a fool doesn't make me less of a fool. Where's a confessor when I need one? And who can I turn to for advice? What elder? What sage? All alone now. There is no one. This is what it means to be a grown-up, finally. Marriage didn't do it. Kids didn't do it. Ultimate peril is required to see how alone I am. Maybe there is no answer? Eventually time will provide one. Or accident. And how stupid will I be then, explaining it all, not only to my wife, but to my children?

If Laura caught me she wouldn't understand. Fuck wouldn't, couldn't. A woman says she understands desire, but she only understands feminine desire. Not the kind that makes you get up in the middle of the night and prowl. Not the kind that makes every female a piece of anatomical acreage, good for one thing, needed. And when a man feels that way, every man is the same, tortured, blue-balled, stumbling for it, willing to ruin himself for it, put everything at stake, be condemned for it. Any man who says he's above that, has never been tempted. No woman can understand that. And the rules of the game are set by the women, aren't they?

I'm just one more aging asshole, doing pushups, rediscovering my dick, thinking, this never happened before. But it has, hasn't it? A million million times. And never.

Was it too much to ask to be happy? As things are, I'm not happy now. Would I be happy if I followed my heart? Why not? Why the fuck not, let it all come down. Let myself be swallowed whole by the anarchy of her beauty. Be immolated by it. Be burnt to dust and blown away by the first stiff breeze. Why not? Why the fuck not?

And what about my other heart? The heart that lives here

within these freshly painted walls? My unconscious heart, the one that beats when I'm asleep, surrounded by my loving family. Because it works both ways, I don't just protect them, it is their love that lets me rest peacefully every night. They are the glue of my life, their love holds everything together.

Rick makes a final round of the quiet house. His heart rattles inside his chest like an old seed in a gourd. He touches his chest. Do I have a heart anymore? Can love kill a person?

In Trina's room he takes in her sweet scent. Her slim chest expands in its even, shallow course. She says her prayers every night because she believes in God. I'm God to you, aren't I? I'm what stands between you and all the bad stuff.

Rick pulls the sheets up to her chin and kisses her. She dreams in safety. He whispers, "I will not leave you, sweetness. No pain can make me do that. Don't worry. Daddy's going fix it."

RICK IS AT RENA'S. HE'S TOLD LAURA THAT HE'S COVERING for someone at the ER tonight. They've ordered in sushi. They make love, Rick holds her in his arms. Rena's clean again. She's been working. They've seen each other once a week for the past month.

"Rena, I have to tell you something."

"No. Don't tell me anything, Rick."

"It's not about us."

"No?"

"It's about something you should know about. Something I did."

"You can tell me anything, you know that."

"Maybe not this."

"Did you kill somebody?"

"I fucked my assistant."

"You fired your assistant?"

"Zoe. The girl who works for me. I slept with her."

"When?"

"When you were . . . gone."

"Oh."

"I missed you. I was horny. She's always teasing me. Things happen."

"I don't believe you."

"Why not?"

"I know you."

"I told you I'm not a nice guy."

"Are you still seeing her?"

"I don't know. Maybe. It's hard to say."

"I don't understand. Rick, why are you lying to me?"

"I sleep with Laura and you don't mind."

"She's your wife."

"I'd understand if you slept with someone else. Barry, for instance. Whoever he is."

"You're making this up."

"I can call Zoe right now if you don't believe me." Rick takes out his cell phone.

"No. Stop."

"I love you, Rena."

"Yeah? You love Zoe, too?"

"Look, I'm a man. I have needs."

"Wow."

"I told you you wouldn't like it. I'm just being honest. That's our deal, right? Honesty?" Rena stares at him. "You're not going to start using drugs again, are you?"

"I don't think I can have this conversation right now. I don't think . . . I think . . . I think you have to go, Rick."

"Go?"

"I don't feel well. I'm tired. Let's talk about it tomorrow."

"Tomorrow?"

"Yeah. OK?"

"Rena. I'm sorry. Things happen."

"No. I understand, I do. And I'm not angry. You slept with her. No big deal. We're all grown-ups. But I gotta get some sleep."

Rick leaves. Later he stands outside her building and watches until he sees her lights go out. Like a scalpel in my heart, he thinks.

THAT ENDED IT. SHE CALLED ME THE NEXT DAY AND suggested we take a break. I didn't give in to temptation. I didn't call her. Of course I pored over every one of Laura's magazines for pictures of her. But except for an old print ad she'd had running for months, she disappeared from sight.

About two months later, in a moment of weakness, I called her cell phone. It was disconnected. So was her apartment. I went by. Her name was no longer over the buzzer. I called the agency and they informed me that they no longer represented her.

I thought about hiring a detective, but to what end? I let the days pass. I was making a decision by doing nothing. She wasn't going to call me, wherever she was. And I was pretty much back in the fold with Laura. Ironically, Zoe gave notice as if our fictional affair weighed on her mind.

Every day, a sliver of memory would prickle like an unexpected spine on a thistle. I wished I could talk to her one more time and relive those nights we spent together.

I had begun to see old friends. I'd get together with a bunch of guys from school and we'd play dollar ante poker and smoke cigars. Bunch of assholes. I thought, this is my life now. Better to have loved and lost than never to have loved at all. I thought I had forgotten about her, but in fact, I was always thinking of her.

The kids were growing fast. Henry and I developed this habit of taking long walks together. He was almost ten and he wanted to talk about life. He said some kids at school had "girlfriends" and wanted to know what I thought about that.

A kind of normalcy reigned and I didn't mind it.

Then one early spring night, I was driving down the West Side toward the tunnel. I had lost about eighty bucks in the poker game, I'd had three drinks and knew I'd get to bed too late. I was low. But in this post-Rena state of mind, it didn't bother me. Nothing bothered me.

The cold rain fell in sheets, slashing my windshield, whipping the pavement. I tried to focus through the blur into the oncoming headlights of traffic. Didn't want to fishtail and broadside the furious cab flying next to me.

Up ahead a melted red dot of a traffic light floated in the black. On the roadway a slick overcoat of water reflected the glare of the street lamps. I carefully brought the car to a stop. The light turned green and as I was about to pull away a wheelchair rolled up beside my door. In the chair sat a drenched beggar. The light changed, and with guilt I punched the accelerator. I kept watch on the hunched figure through the rear windshield. She almost got hit by the flow of traffic behind me.

As I was about to enter the tunnel to Jersey, I thought, that was Rena back there in that wheelchair. I tried to shake the idea, but the certainty held me like a leg trap. She's a drug addict. She's returned to drugs. She's broke. She's sick. That was her back there, sick, needing me, finding me. I made a U turn and sped back to the spot where the beggar had rolled up to the car. The shiny streets were empty. I could feel her presence as surely as I could feel my own.

I pulled over. After months of hollow numbness, I was drowning in emotion. I had done something so wrong. I had abandoned her. I had thrown her back into her private hell of loneliness and addiction.

She hadn't conveniently disappeared. She had been swallowed into the rancid gut of the city. She was out there now, in the night, anonymous and dying. It was a one in a million chance that that had been Rena back there. But it didn't matter, did it? If I didn't know where she was, then she could be anywhere, suffering, dying.

My sorrow became surreal. Whether that was her on the highway or not, she was out there somewhere. This was the truth and I had to deal with it. She wasn't gone. She would never be gone. That would have been so convenient for me and for my conscience. How tidy it all would have been, if she simply had shown up in my life and then vanished just as abruptly. She would have been for all intents and purposes locked into my soul where I could mourn her secretly forever the same way I mourned every lost opportunity in my life.

I swung like a pendulum arcing from deep, self-pitying feelings of loss to gratitude for dodging a chaotic divorce. With the self-pity came reverie. I would lie on the couch dreaming about her skin. With the gratitude came remorse. I contemplated suicide. I watched Laura carefully as she went about her business, trying to detect any suspicion. Whether she was aware of it or not, I had damaged our marriage. How could I ever make it up to her? I reasoned to myself that had I been caught and wanted to come back to Laura I would have made a hundred promises. I would have dropped to my knees and begged her to forgive me. And so in my mind I did this, and in my mind I committed myself to renewing our weakened marriage. Laura didn't have to know, it was simply a private penance I had to carry out.

I didn't commit suicide, of course, but something in me did die. Was dying. I had known when I chased Rena away that this would happen. Because to embrace Rena was to embrace life as I had always known it. To embrace lunacy and fear. To stay with

Laura and the children was to accept sanity in my life, to not be afraid and take what I really wanted. For this I would receive a kind of grace, but I would also kill the devil in me. And the devil doesn't die easy.

I returned to therapy with Edith. I carefully retraced every moment of the affair. I was honest and Edith seemed very interested in the minutiae. She recommended Prozac. I tried it. Things still didn't make sense, but now I didn't mind. I assumed a reflective posture regarding the whole thing.

One afternoon I told Edith that I had finally figured it all out. It hadn't been love. I had been obsessed. It was obvious to me now that Rena and I could never have made it as a couple. I told Edith that I was happier now, the dust had settled. I was even happier than I had been before. Things had improved between Laura and myself, perhaps simply because the kids weren't getting up as much in the middle of the night. Laura and I had begun to discuss what we would do when the kids were all grown up and we retired. We planned a trip to Australia. I told Edith that everything was OK again.

Edith said, "I don't believe you." After that I couldn't go see Edith anymore.

TWO YEARS HAD PASSED SINCE I HAD LAST SEEN RENA and there was one place I hadn't looked for her. The town wasn't that hard to find. The family name was still in the old phone books, so was the address. It took an afternoon, but I found the place on a country road with no name, only a three-digit route number. As I rolled up I remembered that Rena had mentioned a gravel drive. A "For Sale" sign was tacked to a post.

The house wasn't what I'd expected. I guess I had some image of an 1840s farmhouse with a rust red barn and silo. This was a plain, two-story frame house sitting on a short bluff off the two-lane. A dry lawn stretched out around it, and a dilapidated chicken coop stood off to one side. Everything seemed trimmed up and in order but without life.

The house was locked so I took a walk into the field that lay behind it. In five minutes I had found the orchard. The trees were much larger than I had imagined. Kind of monstrous. And there were apples all over the place, small, wormy, but lots of them. I picked one and bit into it and the flavor was unlike any apple I'd ever tasted. As if every apple I'd ever known were in there some-where.

Swallows swooped overhead, wasps buzzed, something rus-tled in the scrub nearby. The landscape all around me was inhab-ited, as if by spirits.

I heard someone shouting, in distress, then I realized I was being called. A man was walking toward me from the house. I dropped the apple and turned toward him.

"Hey, hey there."

"Afternoon." I tried to assume my best country-folk tone of voice.

He shielded his eyes as he spoke, "Driving past, saw the car."

"There's a FOR SALE sign out on the road," I said.

"Uh-huh." He came closer, avoiding the brambles.

"You the owner?"

"Hell no, owners are dead."

"Dead?"

"Yup."

"And you have something to do with them?"

"I'm their banker."

So this was Frank standing right in front of me. Not a big guy, maybe five foot ten, shorter than me by a couple of inches. Dark, neither good-looking nor plain. The sort of man you don't notice. In his mid to late thirties, probably. Anonymous in every way, except for his eyes. Dark, angry. A fissure between his eye-brows, permanent. He was sizing me up.

"Do you think I could take a look? You have a key?"

We went inside and walked around. If I thought I was going to find any more evidence of Rena or Billy, I was mistaken. The place had been cleaned out and repainted, only one piece of furniture remained, the table in the center of the kitchen. I thought, Billy sat right there.

"What happened to the owners?"

"You don't want to know."

"I'm curious."

"Cancer got 'em both, left behind two grown-up orphan children. Boy lost his mind, shot himself in the head."

"God."

"Tragic."

"You said there were two children?"

"Girl moved to the city. Got herself in trouble down there."

"She died, too?"

"Oh hell no. She lives down South now. The girls at the bank keep in touch with her. She's the one I'm selling the house for. Actually . . ." Frank rummaged around in his suit jacket and did a miraculous thing. He pulled out a crumpled envelope. In it were some receipts, folded bits of paper, and a snapshot. He tossed the snapshot onto the kitchen table.

"That's her. They say she did some modeling for a while. Pretty girl. Kinda full of herself, though."

I picked up the photo.

Wherever the picture had been taken, it was very sunny. A palm tree in the background, a very blue sky and a thin young woman crouched on a freshly clipped lawn, squinting into the bright sunshine, smiling a weak smile. Before her she held, barely upright, a toddler. Sun on both their faces, deepening the pockets of shadow. It's hard to see them clearly. But of course, I know Rena when I see her. Rena and a child.

Frank's cell phone rang. He stepped out onto the porch to gain some privacy. While he was talking, I took a last look around and strolled out. I passed him on the porch and from my car I waved and said, "Thanks a lot." And I drove off.

That night, after Laura went to bed, I pulled out the stolen photograph. No way was I going to leave that behind with him. I studied it for half an hour. Would I be able to find her? I could go back to the bank and talk to "the girls." I could go down to Florida or wherever she was and meet up with her. And what would we talk about?

I locked the door of my study and snapped on the computer. I began to write.

Dear Rena,
   I can't tell you how happy I am that you're alive. I'm also going to assume the child in the picture is yours. And beyond that, I'm not going to make any assumptions.
   Rena, I want you to know one thing.

I stopped. No words. What was there to say? I had made my choice, she was right. She had inhabited me now for almost three years, and yet I still didn't know how I felt about her. All that mattered was that she was out there somewhere.

I looked at the snapshot again. Two people, a woman and a child. Somewhere. What did they have to do with me? The world is filled with billions of women and children. All strangers. Like these two. They only mean something if I want them to mean something.

Of course, I'd love to be in her arms again. To return to that drugged place. The place of no time, of forgetting. To smell her, to run my hand along her smooth, warm ribs. To trace the insides of her knees, her perfect ear. She was the embodiment of beauty, of grace. Like an absolute of a philosopher.

But if love is what we do when we live together, live on this earth, put one day after another, raise children, eat our meals, nurse one another, lumber through our days—then I did not, and do not love her. I could die with her, but I could not live with her. It's true she was a flower. But a flower that thrives in the wrong place is a weed. She was a weed with roots wrapped round my heart, strangling it.

Time insists on momentum, of all the things, small and great. No one can change that, no matter how hard he tries. My life with Laura and my children is not a bottled elixir, a dreamy warm bath, but a living thing made of love and event and passion and fear. Especially fear. Without fear of the greatest loss, there can be no joy. Death chases life forward.

In Florida or wherever she is (does it make a difference?), with her child, with her moment-to-moment life, she is also a mere mortal now, no longer a spirit defying gravity. She was someone who was created by the pictures taken of her. But in the last picture I have, she's lost the numinous gaze of passion and love and healing and all the rest of it that I thought she possessed. No more angel. Human. That's the way it works, you either become mortal or you die.

She had stepped over a threshold, the old Rena died and became reborn. And so had I. I got to visit a world where everything was as I had dreamed it, the magnetic north pole of passion. The thing about a pole is, once you're there, you can't go any farther. You either head south, or freeze to death.

I placed the photograph in my secret desk drawer and locked it. Then I returned to the calm, still bedroom where my beautiful wife lay dreaming. My love. My soul mate. I crawled in beside her, drew her close to me and fell asleep.

About the Author

Eric Bogosian is the author of *Mall*, the plays *Talk Radio*, *subUrbia* and *Griller*, and the Obie Award–winning solo performances *Drinking in America*, *Pounding Nails in the Floor with My Forehead* and *Sex, Drugs, Rock & Roll*. He is the recipient of the Berlin Film Festival Silver Bear Award, a Drama Desk Award, and two NEA fellowships. An actor who has appeared in more than a dozen feature films and television shows, Bogosian lives in New York City.